FALLEN ANGEL

by Stephen Wheeler

By the same author

THE SILENT AND THE DEAD

Brother Walter Mysteries:
UNHOLY INNOCENCE
ABBOT'S PASSION
WALTER'S GHOST
MONK'S CURSE
BLOOD MOON
KNIGHT'S HONOUR
NINE NUNS
DEVIL'S ACRE

Prologue

Tuesday 25th March 1225. The first day of a new year and the first page of yet another volume of this my chronicle of the abbey of Saint Edmundsbury.

I can hardly believe it. It seems only yesterday we were celebrating the twelfth centenary after the birth of Our Lord, Jesus Christ, and yet here we are already a quarter way through the thirteenth. I was a young man of thirty-five when the century began and I am now an old one of sixty. Where have the years gone? They seem to have melted away with the snows of winter. Brrr!

Many things have happened during those twenty-five years and most of them bad. England has suffered rebellion, interdict, famine, plague, civil war, foreign invasion and the loss of empire - not so very different, I imagine, from the Anarchy of a hundred years ago when the rule of law completely broke down and it was said Christ and his saints slept. Order is slowly being restored but the process is not yet complete. For the past nine years since the death of King John the country has been ruled by a regency council there being no adult heir of the blood royal to succeed him. Of course we are still a kingdom but Prince Harry was a mere boy of nine when he was crowned *Henricus Tertius* in 1216 and at seventeen he is still too young to govern in his own right. But the country is at peace at last which is something I suppose, although how long it will remain so is anybody's guess. To borrow a concept from Saint Augustine of Hippo, we are *in limbo* being neither in heaven nor in hell but somewhere in between. Not a comfortable place to be.

Life here at the abbey hasn't exactly been a bed of roses either. The long summer of Samson of Tottington's abbacy is now seen as a golden age, certainly when contrasted with the more wintry winds that have been blowing since his death fourteen years ago. For four of those years we had no abbot at all and the abbey was run by the late and much unlamented Prior Herbert whose sudden and unexpected death five years ago can only be described as a gift from heaven (God forgive me, but as prior the man was a complete disaster).

Since then we have acquired a new abbot and a new prior although neither can be said to be giants of their kind. Prior Henry Rushbroke is a kindly man but far too accommodating in my opinion trying to be all things to all men, while Abbot Hugh Northwold is never here long enough to make much impact being more concerned with national events rather than those of Bury. What we need is strong and permanent leadership and at the moment we have neither. Thus does the Wheel of Fortune turn. Where it will stop next heaven alone will know.

Samson's and Herbert's weren't the only departures in recent years. Many of the chief players of the last quarter century have gone with it. There was King John of course (lamented by some, though not by all), also Pope Innocent (ditto). William Marshal, England's greatest knight and saviour, was next to go followed by King Philip of France, England's Nemesis. And not forgetting my own mother who died in 1219 at the ripe old age of seventy-six, God rest her soul (and God help those who receive it!)

But the saddest loss of all for me personally has been that of my good friend and brother in Christ, Jocelin of Brackland, who finally gave up the ghost last year aged sixty-nine. In truth it was a mercy. Towards the end he was blind, crippled and longing to join his belovèd Samson in paradise. (I'm not sure Samson will be quite as enthusiastic to meet him again if he continues to fawn over him in heaven the way he did here on earth - but no matter).

Other changes too have taken place recently one of the biggest being the appearance in England of a new breed of preacher, the so-called *friars*. Preaching is not something we monks do terribly well - that isn't our purpose. Ours is a contemplative life cut off from the world so that we can devote ourselves to prayer and meditation for the benefit of all mankind. Preaching we leave to the parish priests who, it has to be said, are not always up to the job. This is hardly their fault since by and large they are no better than the common folk from among whom most are drawn. Many do not even know the catechism and their interpretation of scripture is at times frankly laughable. None of this has gone unnoticed by the church fathers and least of all by his holiness the pope. Much has been made in recent years of correcting past deficiencies and along with the wind of reform that is now blowing through the Church have come the friars who by and large are better educated than the priests.

The first half-dozen arrived from Rome three years ago and made such a positive impression that they have been encouraged to remain. These are known as *black* friars after the colour of their robes. They were soon followed by another group, the *grey* friars after the colour of their robes. The popularity of both these groups has quickly spread especially among ordinary folk. It's not difficult to see why. By way of disseminating the Christian message they tell stories and jokes which are at once both entertaining and instructive while any donations they receive they give away to the poor. In return they ask for nothing for themselves save their dinner and a place to lay their heads for the night. Small wonder they are liked.

Their arrival in Bury has not, however, been welcomed by everybody least of all at the abbey where there has been much debate about them. Some of my brother monks argue that since the newcomers ask for no financial reward they can do no harm. Others insist that the abbey should have the sole monopoly of spirituality within the banleuca and friars have no place here.

My own attitude towards the new men is somewhat ambiguous. Anyone who has followed these jottings of mine will know I have had dealings with one of these groups already: the black friars, or to give them their proper name, *Dominicans* after their founder, Dominic of Guzman. It was one of their number who followed the ill-fated ship, the *Gretchen*, down the coast of France intending to have my friend Lucatz arrested for being a member of the Cathari, that group of heretical Christians based in Toulouse in southern France. The south of France is also where the Dominicans originated and where their reputation has been much as they would like to see themselves as "*Domini canes*" meaning "Hounds of God". This is a deliberate play on the name "Dominican" - appropriately since they have taken it upon themselves to hound Catharism from Christendom. However, so far as I am aware there are no Cathari in England so maybe their role here will be a little different. For the moment, therefore, I am inclined to give the newcomers the benefit of the doubt.

So that is how matters stand at the beginning of this new year which I very much hope will be better than the last. As well as being New Year's Day, the twenty-fifth of March is also the Feast of the Annunciation, of course, when we commemorate the visitation of the Archangel Gabriel to the Virgin Mother announcing her immaculate conception of Our Lord. I believe in some parts of Europe it is also known as the Feast of the Swallows since it coincides with the return of those magical birds thus heralding the end of winter and the beginning of spring. Fields are ploughed and crops sown in the confident assurance that from now on things can only get better. I would like to think they are right. But there is another saying about swallows that one on its own does not make a summer. And summer is still some way off.

Part One

Chapter One
THE TALENTED
BROTHER ESTIENNE

My first encounter with the friars in Bury came one morning in early spring as I was crossing the marketplace on my way to visit a patient in the northern part of the town. A young man dressed in raggedy grey robes had just taken possession of the market cross with the intention, it seemed, of addressing stallholders and their customers.

This in itself is not unusual. The market cross is a common venue for the airing of news and views. These can be official announcements from the government or anything else delivered by anyone who has something they want to get off their chest. As long as the content is not seditious, defamatory or treasonable the practice is usually tolerated by the bailiffs. They can be a source of great entertainment if the speaker has wit (or even more so if there are hecklers in the crowd who are often wittier). Often the message is of a religious nature: a hermit warning of dire consequences if people do not change their sinful ways: "Beware the Wrath of God for the Day of Judgement is at hand!" - that sort of thing. Usually such doom-sayers are ignored as people get on with the more immediate business of buying and selling, and anyway their voices are usually drowned out by traders hawking their wares. If the speakers wish to get their message across it is up to them to attract attention and keep it best way they can.

Doubtless this is what the raggedy young man had in mind when he shinned up the market cross the better to get himself noticed. And noticed he was - by the market reeve who was rapidly making his way over to order the man down. Preaching from the steps of the cross was one thing; damaging municipal property was quite another. The reeve didn't get that far. Having made it to the top of the monument the man lost his grip and fell the twenty feet onto the stone steps below.

A cry of woe immediately went up from the crowd many of whom went rushing to help – myself included. But before I had a chance to remove my medical satchel from my shoulder the man had bounced back up onto his feet again and was grinning all over his insolent face. It was all a ruse, you see? to get himself noticed and to draw a crowd. And it worked. A sizeable group had indeed gathered about him – mostly concerned for his welfare. However, concern quickly turned to irritation as the crowd realised they had been duped and they started to berate the young man for his knavery. But that simply encouraged him the more. In the banter that followed he gave as good as he got and pretty soon he had a lively exchange going with the crowd – which presumably was his intention. I couldn't help smiling at his audacity and should have liked to stay to listen but I had my patient to attend to, so I carried on my way.

Fortunately the visit didn't take very long (the daughter of a local draper was having a fit of the vapours. Love-sick probably, although I gave her a dose of spirit of hartshorn just so her father didn't think he wasn't getting his money's worth out of me). Once I'd finished there I decided to return through the market to see how the raggedy young man was faring half expecting him to have been lynched by the mob. Not a bit of it. He was still there on the steps of the cross, still lecturing and still arguing. By now the crowd had doubled in size and from their laughter they seemed to be enjoying themselves. I stood listening for a while impressed by his antics and by his skilful command of his audience. As anyone who has ever done any public speaking will know, the key to success is being able to read your audience and to know when it is growing bored and that it is time for you to stop. And indeed the crowd was beginning to thin. It was then that the young man got out his begging bowl. He even had the cheek to shake it at me.

'If you enjoyed hearing the word of the Lord, brother, then a small demonstration of appreciation would be gratefully received. Just a crust to keep the wolf from the door.'

'There aren't any wolves in Bury anymore,' I told him. 'Although there do seem to be one or two sly foxes.'

'Whatever gets Christ's message across, brother, is good doing,' he said grinning all over his cheeky face.

'Indeed. But just be careful not to cry "wolf" too often. Next time you pull that acrobatic trick you may find folk less ready to run to your aid when you may need it for real.'

11

'Fear not. I have a few more tricks up my sleeve, brother.'

'Of that I have no doubt,' I said dropping my farthing into his bowl. 'What's your name?'

'Frère Estienne de Saverne, *à votre service*.' He gave a low elegant bow.

'Saverne.' I shook my head. 'Never heard of it.'

'It's near the River Rhine not far from Strasbourg. You know where that is?'

Cheeky young rascal. 'I've a vague idea. Your English is very good for a Burgundian.'

'There would be little point coming to England to preach in French or German, brother.'

'True enough. A preaching brother then. But not a black friar I think. You don't wear the garb of the followers of Dominic Guzman.'

'You know of our sister order?' he asked, impressed.

'Let's just say our paths have crossed.'

'Then I will have to be careful what I say. But you are right, we're not Dominicans. Ours is the Order of Friars Minor. We follow the teachings of Giovanni di Bernardone, though you may know him better as Francis of Assisi.'

'And what does Signor Bernardone teach - apart from trickery and acrobatics?'

'Poverty, brother. Poverty is our watchword. We live by begging and own nothing but the robes we stand up in.'

'Well that's clearly not the case, is it?' I said nodding to the thing that was slung over his shoulder. 'You can't tell me you found that in your begging bowl.'

The object in question was obviously a musical instrument of some kind, but not like any I'd seen before: a long cylindrical pipe with a curious mouthpiece at one end and a flared bell at the other.

'Ah, you've discovered my guilty secret,' he smiled shyly. 'Yes, I admit it, it's mine. But it's not so much a possession as an *aide au travail* – a tool as essential to my work as your vademecum is to yours.' He pointed to the set of charts that I keep hanging from my belt. 'You are a medic, I take it?'

I nodded. 'Brother Walter de Ixworth, physician to the abbey and folk of Bury. And that's not quite the same thing. Without my instrument I can't do my job properly.'

'Nor I without mine,' he grinned.

That was debatable, but I didn't argue the point.

'What is it anyway? Some kind of flute?'

'Not a flute. It's called a shawm - an Arabic invention. Here, I'll show you.'

He took the thing from his back, carefully placed his fingers over the holes and moistened the mouthpiece with his lips. Then he began to play. And what playing it was! He was right, it didn't sound anything like a flute. It had a more doleful sound, animalistic almost, filling the air with all the promise of the mysterious east. I was instantly transported to the souks of Damascus which my father used to tell me about from his time in the wars there. He told me men can charm snakes with instruments such as this although I'd never believed it before. But hearing Estienne play, I might. And I wasn't the only one hypnotized. Other people stopped and turned their heads to listen.

'Very impressive,' I said once he'd finished. 'But that still doesn't look much like poverty to me. And neither does that.' I was pointing to his begging bowl that was filled with silver pennies. 'Goodness, you must have half a marks' worth there. Not bad for an hour's work.'

'It's not for me, brother. I take just enough for my dinner, the rest I give to the poor. That is our purpose and our joy. And now if you'll forgive me, I must away to do just that while there is still daylight to see by.'

'Are you staying in Bury?' I called on impulse.

'That depends,' he called back. 'I haven't decided yet.'

'Then I wish you well.'

'And you, brother.'

So saying he gave another low bow before disappearing into the crowd.

I couldn't help liking the lad despite, or maybe because of, his impudence. He could certainly hold an audience. He'd even had the market reeve chuckling at some of his antics.

One person who wasn't laughing, though, was our sacrist, Brother Arnold. I'd already noticed him watching from the sidelines. He didn't look at all happy. It's not difficult to work out why. The sacrist is one of the most senior officers of an abbey. He is responsible for looking after the abbey's most valuable possessions – the silver and gold plate, the vestments and holy vessels and so on. But that's not his only function. He is also responsible for collecting the fees from the market traders which presumably was the reason Arnold was in the marketplace now.

I've always got on with Arnold but it's not been easy. He's a difficult man. Competent at his job no doubt, but also obstinate and opinionated. I suppose when dealing with money matters that is the sort of person you need. But what he gains in efficiency he lacks in imagination. If the world doesn't fit Arnold's notion of how things ought to be it is the world that has to change, not Arnold. To give you an idea: once he practically caused a riot in the marketplace by interrogating some Hungarian traders who through no fault of their own hadn't paid their proper market dues. Unfortunately Arnold challenged them with the words "Who the Devil do you think you are?" Not understanding the idiom, the Hungarians thought he was calling Satan down upon them and as a result they upturned half the market stalls. It took a lot of persuading to get Arnold to admit his error and apologize – not something he ever did lightly. All in all, I wasn't entirely surprised he'd taken a jaundiced view of our brash newcomer.

Once Estienne had gone he came over. 'You shouldn't encourage these people, brother.'

'What people would that be, brother?' I smiled.

'Beggars. I saw you putting money in that man's bowl just then.'

'Only one beggar, Arnold. In any case, I thought he'd earned it. He was good value for money.'

'Money that should be going to the abbey not into the purses of vagrants.'

'Oh, he won't keep it. He'll give it to the poor. He told me so himself.'

'And you believed him?'

'I've no reason not to. He certainly isn't spending it on himself - you only have to look at his robe to see that. It's more patches than robe.'

'It is the abbey's job to offer succour to the poor.'

'I doubt the poor will quibble over whose hand is doing the offering. Besides, if Frère Estienne is giving money to the poor it's less for our almoner to have to find. I'm sure you'd agree.'

I wasn't sure he would. He tried another tack:

'That's not all. He also claims to be able to cure the sick. As abbey physician that's your job isn't it?'

'I am flattered by your confidence in my abilities Arnold, but even I cannot be everywhere at once. If this young man is willing to share some of my load I am grateful for that too.'

'But he's not qualified.'

'How do you know?'

'You've only got to look at him.'

'Looks can be deceptive. Besides, I'm sure he's as qualified as most of the old crones I see handing out fake remedies in the marketplace. If he doesn't actually do good I'm sure he does no harm. His cheerful countenance will make anyone feel better – and that in my experience is half the battle.'

Arnold frowned his frustration. 'You're too easy with these people, Walter. That's always been your trouble. This one's a fake, even you must see that.'

'What I see is a talented young man with much to offer. So far he has entertained, instructed and collected alms, all at little or no profit to himself. I'm sorry but I see no harm in the lad. God has endowed him with many gifts. It would be a sin for him not to use them.'

Arnold shook his head. 'You may regret your generosity of spirit, brother.'

'That is a cross I am willing to bear.'

Seeing he was getting nowhere, Arnold turned and stalked off. I sighed with regret. That is how many of our conversations end, I'm sorry to say. And in truth I did sympathize with him a little. His is one of the most demanding of all the abbey offices. Men have been known to become ill, physically and mentally, from the stresses of the sacrist job. There is never enough money to do all the things required of them and they are for ever chasing debtors who are doing their best to avoid paying. But while I could understand Arnold's problems none of them was Estienne's fault. For the time being at least I was on Estienne's side.

I have to say, though, that I didn't realise Estienne was offering medical cures. That was a little worrying. I didn't particularly mind for myself - he couldn't compete for the patronage of the draper's daughter and her ilk or expect the same fee. But if he was giving cures for free I could see he might get into trouble with others who have to earn a living doing the same thing.

*

From the marketplace I returned to my laboratorium in the Great Court of the abbey. This, I have to admit, I was somewhat reluctant to do on account of who was there: my new assistant, Rufus. As abbey physician I have to have an assistant in order to do my job properly, especially these days. I'm not getting any younger and there are occasions when stronger limbs than mine are needed to handle difficult patients or awkward procedures. I also have a duty to train someone else to take over from me in times when I am incapacitated for any reason or against the day when I am no longer around. My problem was that I wasn't sure I'd got the right man this time.

I have to admit I have not always been successful in my choice of assistants. I just never seem to find the right combination of ability and enthusiasm. And when I do find someone suitable I never seem able to keep them for very long. A year, two at the most and they are off to do other things. One went off to study the dark arts of the Moors of Spain. Another decided blood and gore were not for him after all and he left the abbey to join the priory of St Peter in Eye. Others still left to join other departments in the abbey. They never seemed to want to stick around long enough to learn the profession properly. I have reluctantly come to the conclusion that either I am not a very good judge of character or there is something about me that puts them off, although I cannot think what. I'm one of the most easy-going department heads I know. Maybe that's my mistake. Maybe I should be a little more like Arnold.

At any rate now I have Rufus. What can I say about him? As his name suggests he is a red-head which is a bad sign to begin with. Red-headedness implies a fiery temperament which comes from having too much yellow bile in their system. It makes a person short-tempered, ambitious and irascible. Also on occasion violent and vengeful. Not that I've seen any sign of this in Rufus but it's early days yet. He's only been with me a month although he's been around the abbey for a number of years as a novice. In fact he was still a novice, his novice master seemingly reluctant to release him. Maybe like me he saw him as a difficult case. Nevertheless he was certainly bright enough to do the job, easily the brightest of the available candidates. (Actually he was only candidate. No-one else seemed interested in grinding up seeds all day in a mortar, boiling solutions for hours on end and scrubbing out pots afterwards, I can't think why). It's just that he's a bit - well, *odd*.

For a start he's no sense of humour which you need in a profession that deals with illness every day. You can't go around all day tearing your heart out and weeping at every tragedy as though it's your own, that way lies madness. Not that Rufus does that either. In fact he seems to have no emotional response whatsoever which again is a bit peculiar.

Also our relationship lacks the camaraderie I am used to in my co-workers. We are meant to be a team, albeit a team of two with me as the senior and him the junior. Even then with Rufus sometimes I feel it is the other way around. To be honest I'm a little in awe of him. I'm never quite sure what he's thinking. He doesn't even acknowledge me as I enter the room.

Today was typical. He was scouring out some pots when I returned from my encounters with Estienne and Arnold and didn't stop or even bother to turn round when I came in.

'I met someone today you could learn a lot from,' I said to the back of his head. 'A young man by the name of Estienne de Saverne. He's one of the new friars. A young man with a great many talents.'

'What can I learn from him?'

'Politeness for one thing. I'm sure he would at least pay me the compliment of facing me while I'm talking to him.'

Rufus stopped what he was doing and turned to face me.

Now I felt like an ogre although I didn't see why I should. Annoyed with myself as much as with him, I persisted:

'And why can't you call me "master" when you address me? All my other assistants called me "master".'

'You wish me to be your slave?'

'No of course I don't wish you to be my slave!' I frowned. 'It's just that – well, you could show me a little deference now and again, especially in front of others.'

'You worry about how people see you?'

'No, but I am a senior officer of the abbey. As such I have a certain standing to maintain.'

'And my calling you "master" will achieve this?'

'Not in itself, no.'

'Then what is the advantage?'

I sighed and shook my head. 'I don't know really.'

I poured myself a cup of ale and was going to offer him one but I could see he already had a drink although it didn't look like ale.

'What is that you're drinking?' I frowned peering into his cup. 'It looks disgusting.'

'Medicine.'

'Really?' I said slightly peeved. 'You should come to me for medicaments. Are you ailing?'

'No.'

'Then what is it?'

'It's something I've drunk since I was a child. It's supposed to be good for me.'

'Prrff!' I snorted looking at the mess. 'Who told you that?'

'My father.'

'And you believed him?'

'Of course. He's my father.' He held the cup up inviting me to try.

I looked at the slimy green liquid again and pulled a face. It smelt revolting. But having just insulted his father I supposed I'd better sample it. And medicine is supposed to be revolting, isn't it? Otherwise it's not doing you any good.

'What's in it?' I said taking a mouthful.

'Mashed-up lug-worm and boiled caterpillars mostly.'

I instantly spewed the stuff out. 'Good God boy, are you trying to poison me?'

He actually paused and gave the question serious thought before replying:

'No, I'm not trying to poison you.'

He then went calmly back to what he was doing before I came in while I continued to gag and gasp and rinse my mouth out with good English ale.

You see what I mean? Odd. I had reluctantly come to the conclusion that Rufus wasn't like other people. I didn't know whether that meant I should treat him better or worse than anyone else. But having taken him on I was stuck with him. Mentally I compared him and Estienne. Both were young men about the same age but a world apart in character. I know I shouldn't but I couldn't help wishing I had Estienne as my assistant rather than Rufus. But that was being uncharitable. Rufus had his good points too. It's just that sometimes they were hard to see.

Chapter Two
DESCENT INTO DISSENT

I thought no more about Estienne de Saverne after that first encounter. We get lots of speakers like that in Bury trying to live by their wits, they never stay long. Once the public tire of them they quickly move on to pastures new. I had every expectation that the same would happen to our young friend. But then the subject of friars came up again a few days later in Chapter.

Chapter, as I'm sure you know, is the daily meeting of all the monks of the abbey when we deal with matters concerning the convent as a whole rather than individual departmental affairs. The meetings take place each morning in the chapterhouse and are normally conducted by the abbot, or in his absence by the prior as indeed was the case this day.

We begin with a prayer in honour of whichever saint's feast happens to fall on that day followed by a reading of one of the chapters from the Rule of our founder, Saint Benedict of Nursia – hence the name. There are seventy-three of these each dealing with a different aspect of a monk's life and cover everything from what boots we put on our feet to how we should go about choosing a new abbot – something that caused a great deal of soul-searching a decade earlier. A different chapter is read each day so you can see that we get through the whole lot several times in a year - not a bad way to keep the brethren on their toes (whatever their choice of footwear). Having done that we then ask any guests who happen to be present to leave, the doors of the chapterhouse are shut and we go on to discuss our private affairs in private.

On this particular day we were mostly concerned with the movements of Abbot Hugh who, as baron of the realm in addition to being our abbot, was at that moment in conference with the king and his council in Winchester. This was largely to do with the machinations of the French who were up to their usual mischief-making. They have long had their eye on English lands across the Channel and were trying once again to cause difficulties for us with the native population hoping to sow dissent. Not that there was much we could do in Bury to thwart their designs other than pray to God to guide our leaders in our actions - and to frustrate the French in theirs, as I'm sure, knowing the rightness of our cause, he would. Having done that we assumed Chapter was over for the day and were just getting up to recite the *Verba mea,* the prayer that ends every session of Chapter, when Prior Henry put up his hand to detain us:

'If I could crave your indulgence for just a short while longer brothers, there is one more item I need to bring to your attention.'

What now? I had a recipe for a new poultice for boils from a friend and colleague of mine, the physician at Ixworth Priory, that I was keen to try and didn't want to be delayed. I dare say others had similar priorities of their own. But Prior Henry was the second most senior member of the abbey so if he wished to speak to us we owed it to him to listen. We sat down again.

'I have just received a letter from the head of the Order of Friars Minor in London, Fratello Agnellus di Pisa.' He held up the document for all to see.

'The grey preachers? What do they want?'

This from Arnold. No surprises there. Like a red rag to a bull, the mere mention of the word "friar" had him pawing the ground.

'I was about to tell you if you will give me the chance, brother,' said Prior Henry equably. 'The fratello is requesting a house for the repose and comfort of his brethren here in Bury.'

Arnold snorted. 'I hope you gave him his answer.'

'I haven't said anything yet. I want to hear the opinion of my brother monks first before making my reply.'

'Then you have it. The answer's no.'

'Is that the wish of you all?'

From the muttering it clearly was not. Some agreed with Arnold, others did not. Oh dear. I could see we were in for a lengthy debate. My new poultice recipe was going to have to wait. I sank down further on my bench, pulled my hood up around my ears and half-closed my eyes.

'We've discussed this many times before in Chapter, Brother Prior,' Arnold continued. 'We all agreed that while we cannot prevent the friars from preaching in the town we should not encourage them. We should certainly not let them establish a permanent presence here.'

Some more mutterings of agreement from among Arnold's allies.

'True enough, brother,' said Henry. 'But that was before Fratello Agnellus's letter. It is less a fraternal

24

greeting than an official request from the head of one brotherhood to another and one that as acting head of the abbey I cannot ignore.'

Arnold folded his arms. 'I don't see why not.'

'Of course you do, Arnold,' said Henry tetchily. 'Fratello Agnellus is a respected leader in the Church, albeit a minor branch of the Church. Besides, a copy of the letter has already been sent to the archbishop. He is very supportive of the friars.'

'Langton?' scoffed Arnold. 'What does he know? This is *Edmunds*-bury not *Canter*-bury.'

A few more nods and appreciative titters at this.

'You insult the lord archbishop with your words, Brother Sacristan,' Henry admonished him.

Arnold inclined his head humbly. 'I do not mean to, Brother Prior. I merely ask where it will end? First a house – then what? A church? A congregation? Here? In Edmund's town?'

To this there was a lot more muttering of agreement.

'The fratello explained all that in his letter,' said Henry. 'The Franciscans are a peripatetic order. They preach in the open air. They have no need for churches. They wish merely a roof under which to shelter from the elements, that is all. Can we deny them that? I urge you not to forget our sacred duty of hospitality as written in the Rule of our founder: "All should be received as Christ because he will say, I was a stranger and you took me in".'

How could we forget it? It was the very chapter chosen by the prior that morning - fortuitously. Other brothers now were nodding their agreement.

Arnold, however, was not to be put off so easily. 'What do they need a house for anyway? There is only one of them.'

'At the moment,' Henry agreed. 'But Fratello Agnellus has been much encouraged by good reports from here and elsewhere, it seems, and he intends to send us more of his people.'

'*More* preachers?' gasped Arnold in astonishment. 'I should have thought one was enough.'

'I'm sure we can accommodate more than that,' said Henry.

'Who is to pay for this house?' asked another monk – one of Arnold's cronies.

'Aye,' agreed a third. 'On their own admission they have no money. They spurn possessions – or so they say.'

More chortles of disbelief and nodding at this.

'Where is the house to be?' asked another.

'Nowhere close,' replied Henry. 'In the south of the vill next to the Linnet. A very poor part of town. It would cost very little.'

Ah yes, the Linnet. A meandering, cesspool of a river if ever there was one. The land on either side is mosquito-ridden marshland where the most unpleasant and dangerous industries of Bury like leather-tanning are located. I ought to know. It is where my old friend Onethumb and his wife Rosabel, the daughter of one of those tanners, live. Property there is cheap indeed.

'Poor or not,' said Arnold, 'it is still within the banleuca - land given to the abbey by King Knut, that most Christian of monarchs, for the exclusive worship of the belovèd Edmund.'

At this I couldn't help muttering under my breath: 'Most Christian of monarchs indeed - ha!'

I'd said it to myself. I truly hadn't intended anyone else to hear me. But I was suddenly aware that all had gone quiet and when I opened my eyes fully I could see that several heads were turned in my direction.

'You wished to say something, Brother Walter?' said the prior.

I gave a sickly smile and half rose from my place. "Twas nothing, Brother Prior. I spoke out of turn. Please, ignore me.' I sat down again.

'No no,' Henry insisted. 'If you have something to say we wish to hear it. We are all entitled to an opinion.'

I didn't really have or want an opinion. But others had different ideas.

'Yes, come along Walter,' said Arnold. 'Let's hear what you think. We all know you are a great supporter of this friar.'

If I was it was news to me. It seemed the gossip-mongers had been on the jungle drums. Still, someone needed to speak up for the lad since he wasn't here to do it for himself and it looked as though the honour had fallen to me. Reluctantly, I rose to my feet again.

'I merely meant that far from being a most Christian monarch, King Nut was a heathen until his father Sweyn Forkbeard was struck down whilst trying to prise open the lid of Edmund's coffin. Only then did he see the error of his ways and acknowledge the truth of the Cross.'

Some nodding of agreement to that. I thought I'd neatly side-stepped the problem. Unfortunately I wasn't to get off so lightly.

'The point Brother Walter is missing,' said Arnold somewhat sourly, 'as I've tried to explain to him before, is that this abbey and the shrine it contains are the true - the *only* – legitimate route to spirituality within the town. King Knut, whatever his private beliefs, gave the banleuca to Saint Edmund in perpetuity which has subsequently been reaffirmed by every successor to the throne even to our present Lord Henry. No-one has the right to take that away from him – or from us his guardians.'

Lots more nodding at that.

I have to admit Arnold's tone was beginning to annoy me. I know it shouldn't. I know I should have merely shrugged and gone back to sleep again. But now I was being attacked along with Estienne. I stood up once more:

'No-one is trying to take anything away, brother. We permit the Jews to worship within the banleuca, do we not? They have their synagogue at the highest, the most prominent position in the town, not secreted away in some hidden backwater out of sight. No-one has ever objected to the Jews.'

No, and we all knew the reason for that: because they could afford to pay the exorbitant rent demanded by the abbey for the privilege – a rent that Arnold as sacristan was happy to accept. Not that all Bury's Jews took advantage of it - my godless brother Joseph for one. But that's another matter.

'I'm talking about *Christian* worship,' said Arnold. 'It's never been permitted before.'

'That's because there's never been another Christian community before,' I replied quickly. 'The Franciscan Brotherhood is a completely new element in England. Nothing like them has ever been seen before.'

'All the more reason to be wary of them.'

Louder voices rose in agreement to this while others opposed. Differences were becoming more entrenched. This wasn't good, monk arguing with brother monk.

'I think we should take a vote on it,' said the prior hoping to settle the argument by a show of hands – never a good idea in my opinion. Nor in Arnold's, it seemed:

'It is a spiritual matter,' he insisted. 'It should be for Abbot Hugh to decide.'

'Abbot Hugh isn't here,' replied Henry. 'And if he were I'm sure he'd approve of a vote. After all that is how he himself was chosen as abbot – unless you fear losing, Brother Sacrist?'

'I fear nothing,' insisted Arnold.

'In that case the house will divide. Those in favour of allowing the Franciscans their house move to the right, those opposed to the left.'

We all moved to our preferred side. It took a few minutes to sort ourselves out but once we had and heads had been counted there was a clear, if small, majority in favour of allowing the Franciscans their house.

'I therefore declare the motion carried,' said Henry with evident relief. 'Fratello Agnellus will get his house. I shall inform him in writing forthwith. Let us now recite the *Verba mea.*'

'Not so fast.' Arnold wasn't quite ready to give up yet. 'Which property did you have in mind, Brother Prior? We should at least know that before we leave.'

'Oh, nothing very big. As you rightly say, Arnold, there is at present only one man to worry about. I'm sure you will be able to find something suitably modest – though not too modest. We don't want the abbey to appear miserly.'

Arnold's jaw dropped in astonishment. 'You expect *me* to find this house?'

Henry contrived to look artless: 'Who else? As sacristan you are responsible for our properties in the town, are you not? No-one knows their value better than you. I'm sure you'll find something suitable.'

If it had been possible to record Adam's face when he first gazed upon the nakedness of Eve after the Fall I am sure it couldn't have looked more shocked and appalled than Arnold's did at that moment. It went rapidly from ashen to red to purple to white. Speechless at last, he stormed out of the chapterhouse without even waiting for the *Verba mea*.

Chapter three
PRIOR HENRY HATCHES A PLAN

Once the brouhaha in the chapterhouse had died down a little and the brothers began leaving, Henry called me over:

'Might I have a word, brother?'

I grimaced. 'What, right now, brother?'

'Yes, right now - if you would be so kind.'

I inwardly groaned. At this rate my poultice recipe was never going to get made today.

I followed him over to the prior's house which is just a few yards behind the chapterhouse. Once inside and with the door closed Henry visibly relaxed. He poured two cups of wine and handed me one.

'First of all I want to thank you for supporting me in Chapter just now.'

'I didn't realise I had,' I said accepting mine.

'Oh I think you do. Between the two of us we managed to swing the vote in Frère Estienne's favour – although I must say it was touch and go there for a while.' He tittered. 'Did you see Arnold's face when I asked him to choose the friar's house? He looked like he was catching flies – teehee!' He slapped his knee and his eyes disappeared behind their lids.

'I'm glad to have been of help,' I said. 'But why was it so important?'

'In a word Walter, Reform. Things are changing. Powerful forces are afoot, forces we cannot afford to ignore. We don't want to make ourselves pariahs in the eyes of those who could do us harm.'

'Who exactly are we talking about?'

'The pope. Archbishop Langton. Justiciar de Burgh. They're all keen on these new friars. They see them as the Church's new front-line troops.'

'Troops against what? Who are we fighting?'

'Not "who" Walter, "what": Corruption. Immorality. Heresy. I'm sure I don't need to tell you that the Church is in deep crisis.'

'It's in need of a little tweaking here and there, I grant you - but crisis? It's not as bad as all that, is it?'

'It's every bit as bad as that. The cancer needs to be cut out root and branch. You're a doctor, you should understand these things. Pope Honorius is keen to continue the good work of his predecessor.'

'You mean like the persecution of the Cathari?'

'*Prosecution*, Walter, not *persecution*. I know you had a friend among these people but they are heretics and it is the duty of everyone in the Church to weed them out.'

'There are ways of doing that without resorting to butchery.'

He waved that aside. 'It isn't just heretics. The entire fabric of the Church needs reform. Over the past few years there has been a marked decline in the Church's authority - not least in England.'

'And you think the friars are the answer?'

'What I think is beside the point. Others think so. Personally I'd rather this friar wasn't here - it would certainly make my life a lot quieter. You saw just now how the subject divides opinion.'

'Then why don't you simply ask him to leave?'

'As I say – friends in high places. Besides, if he went others would only follow - Franciscans, Dominicans, Carmelites. There's a tide washing over Christendom, Walter, and if we are not careful we will be swamped by it.'

'A slight exaggeration surely, Henry.'

He shook his head. 'These people are here to stay. We have to find ways to accommodate them.'

'With respect, Henry, it's not me you should be trying to convince.'

He nodded. 'Arnold's a good man but he sometimes can't see the wood for the trees. Which is why I was particularly pleased that you should have mentioned that business about the shrine.'

I shrugged. 'I was merely correcting an error. King Nut was indeed a pagan until his father Sweyn tried to open Edmund's tomb and was struck down. That was the only point I was making.'

'Nevertheless it was was a timely one.'

'In what way?'

'There has been a suggestion we might do it again - open the shrine I mean.' He looked at me coyly. 'Oh all right, it's my idea, but an apposite one I think you'll agree. It is nearly thirty years since the tomb was last opened. High time we had another inspection.'

'Are you sure that's such a good idea?' I cautioned. 'Edmund died over three hundred years ago. There may not be much left to inspect.'

Henry gave me a stern look. 'Edmund is England's greatest saint, greater some think even than Becket. As such his mortal remains are bound to be incorrupt

- all the theological works on the subject are agreed on that. It follows that there will be plenty to inspect - unless of course you know otherwise?'

He clearly knew that I was one of the witnesses the last time the shrine was opened – as he said, nearly thirty years ago. No doubt he'd also heard about afterwards when Abbot Samson reprimanded me for referring to the saint's body as a "sack of dried bones" - a choice of phrase I now deeply regret. In mitigation I was a young man at the time and given to such ill-considered outbursts – foolishly as it turned out for as I later discovered it was another detractor, Abbot Leofstan, who on an earlier inspection had tugged on the saint's head to make sure it was intact only to have his hands paralysed by the saint for his impertinence. Happily nothing like that has happened to me – yet.

'It might also answer some of Brother Arnold's concerns,' Henry was saying. 'Opening the tomb might restore Edmund to his position as … what was Arnold's phrase again?'

'The only legitimate route to spirituality.'

Henry nodded. 'Quite so. And to that extent he's right. You remember what it was like during the interdict? No masses said, no bells rung, no church services of any kind. Even burial in consecrated ground was prohibited. Yet life went on as normal. Ordinary folk began to question the relevance of the abbey, of the Church - even of religion itself.' He shook his head sadly. 'Opening the tomb will remind people we are here. A clear demonstration of our purpose and authority.'

I didn't think anyone could doubt we were here. The abbey owned the town and half the county surrounding it; countless manors and farms, mills, forests, churches, entire villages. And the edifice of the abbey church was clear for all to see for miles about. But I could see his point. Our authority rested on the presence of the saint in the town that bore his name. If nothing else opening the tomb would prove that the martyr's body was still here – a fact coincidentally that had been called into question only recently.

During the recent civil war a rumour had been circulating that troops of our erstwhile invader Prince - now *King* - Louis of France ransacked the abbey and carried off the saint's body as a trophy and had given it to the Abbey of Saint-Sernin in Toulouse. Having been here at the time I can confirm that did not happen. Oh Louis's troops marched up and down outside the town for a bit and did indeed *threaten* to invade the abbey. But they desisted - out of respect for the saint's sanctity, so they claimed, although I suspect it had more to do with fear of the consequences had they tried; they too had heard the story of Sweyn Forkbeard. In the end they went off to ravage nearby Redbourn Priory instead. So if they have anybody's bones in their basilica in Toulouse it will be those of Saint Amphibalus, the priest who converted Saint Alban to Christianity, not Edmund.

Still, the suspicion remains. After all, there is only our word for it that Edmund's body, or indeed any body, is still in the shrine. It would be good to prove it to all the doubting Thomases.

But there was a problem with this strategy. The last time the tomb was opened in 1198 Edmund's body was certainly there - I saw it, or what remained of it, with my own eyes. But no-one had seen the body since then and it would be devastating to find the tomb had been empty all this time. If indeed it was empty then it would de-legitimize the abbey utterly. Was it worth taking that risk?

'Brother Prior, may I make a suggestion? Could we not take out a little insurance?'

Henry frowned. 'I don't follow.'

'I take it you intend to do this thing in public?'

'Of course. I want as many people as possible to witness the tomb being opened. Let the whole world see how vital the abbey is.'

'Indeed. But it would be embarrassing, would it not, to find as you lifted the lid that the coffin was, shall we say, less occupied than we had hoped?'

'What? Empty you mean? That's impossible!'

But then as he thought about it more his facial expression went from indignation that anyone could suggest such a thing, through apprehension that it might be true, to resignation that it possibly was true.

'What are you suggesting?' he said at last.

'That we make sure of our facts first.'

'You mean check the contents?' He looked appalled. 'It's a coffin, Walter, not a box of sweetmeats. We are talking about the sacred resting place of one of England's greatest – and, I might add, most potent – saints. How could you even think such a thing?'

I put up a compliant hand. 'Quite right Henry. Forget I mentioned it.'

'I should think so too.' He looked at me shyly. 'You seriously think it might not be there?'

'I don't doubt *a* body is in the coffin. Whether it's Edmund's or not is the question. After all, King Edmund died some three-hundred-odd years ago. Since then he's been back and forth to London, moved from one tomb to another, set on fire, dug up, re-interred. He's been in and out of that coffin so many times who knows where he ended up. It could be a dead sheep in there for all we know.'

'Then how do you explain the miracles? Dead sheep are not famous for them.'

'In my experience it is people's belief in miracles that is important rather than their actuality.'

Henry shook his head at me slowly. 'Abbot Samson warned me about you. Well for your information I've already inspected the coffin – from the outside. And I can assure you those sixteen nails holding down the lid that Jocelin mentions in his Chronicle have not been touched this century. Yes, you're not the only one who's read it. They're so rusted in it'd take a modern-day Hephaestus to remove them. Take it from me, if Edmund was there in 1198 he's still there now.'

'Then why do you need me to confirm it?'

'Because you were present the last time the tomb was opened.'

'Me and a dozen others.'

'Yes, but you were specially invited by Abbot Samson to witness the unveiling close up, were you not? One of only three.'

That was true enough. Only Samson, Hugh of Diss the then sacristan and I actually viewed the body at close quarters.

He raised his eyebrows questioningly. 'So? Did you see the body or didn't you?'

'We did. That is to say, we didn't see the actual flesh - it was too well-wrapped for that. But I can confirm there was a body inside all those miles of bandaging. But there was no way of knowing for certain it was Edmund. And there's no knowing it's still there now.'

Henry waved a dismissive hand. 'What about the odour? Didn't that tell you?'

I frowned. 'Odour, Brother Prior?'

Henry tapped his desk impatiently. 'The bodies of dead saints are supposed to smell of lilies - as a sign of their holiness. It's very well documented. The odour of sanctity,' he added with awe.

'I don't remember smelling lilies.'

Henry looked disappointed.

'But no smell of corruption either,' I added quickly. 'If it smelt of anything it was of myrrh and aloes, which as everyone knows is a traditional embalming mixture. It was used on Christ's body by Joseph of Arimathea and Nicodemus the Pharisee when they laid him in the tomb, if you recall.'

I knew the smell of myrrh oil well enough. It has a pleasantly spicy aroma reminiscent of lemons and rosemary. As well as being useful as an embalming fluid for the dead, myrrh also has great healing properties. I use it for treating everything from haemorrhoids to chapped lips - though not necessarily at the same time. Oil of aloe, on the other hand, stinks.

Henry nodded. 'Go on.'

I tried to conjure the scene for him: 'Samson stood at the head as I remember, Hugh at the saint's feet and I was to one side. As he bent over the body Samson muttered something to the saint -'

'Muttered something?' Henry interrupted.

'An apology. Something to the effect that what he was doing was out of necessity and that he was sure the blessèd Edmund would forgive the intrusion.'

'As I'm sure he will for us, for we too have a justifiable purpose which I am sure the holy martyr will understand,' nodded Henry brightly. 'Carry on.'

I shrugged. 'Not much more to add really. Having satisfied ourselves that everything was in good order we re-wrapped the body, put the lid of the coffin back on, nailed it down - with those sixteen nails you mentioned - and placed the coffin in the new shrine which is where it has been ever since.'

'And that's all? Nothing else happened? Nothing … untoward?'

'You mean like being struck dead or rendered dumb? No, Brother Prior. Nothing like that.'

Henry gave a huge sigh of relief. 'Let us hope for the same outcome this time.'

'I'm sure it will.'

'So am I. Which is why I want you close at hand this time also.'

I guessed that was coming, but still I asked:

'Why? I've told you all I know.'

'As you said yourself, only you, Abbot Samson and Sacrist Hugh actually saw the body up close. Samson and Hugh are both dead. You are the only living person who can attest to the authenticity of the remains. If nothing else it will quash your own doubts – which, by the way, I would be grateful if you kept to yourself.'

'I told you Henry, I didn't see the flesh. Even if I did I wouldn't be able say it was Edmund's. I never met the man. I have no idea what he looked like.'

'But you'd recognize his corpse if you saw it again.'

'Possibly.'

He nodded. 'That's good enough. I want you to be present when it's opened. And as I say, this time it will be done in daylight in full view of the world. No skulking around in the early hours of darkness. All right.' He flapped a dismissive hand. 'That's all.'

39

I started to leave.

'Oh - there's just one more thing.'

I sighed and came back. 'Brother Prior?'

'I almost forgot. This business with the Franciscan. I know it's Arnold's job to find him a house but I'd like you to check on its suitability.'

'I have no expertise where property is concerned.'

He looked at me sternly. 'You know a hovel when you see one. Arnold has no love for this boy, he's made that quite clear. I'm sure he'll find him a house of sorts. Just make sure it isn't a rabbit hutch.'

'How will I do that?'

'Visit the lad once he's settled in. Make sure he is comfortable and has all he needs. I don't want any complaints getting back to Fratello Agnellus in London.'

'Why me?'

'You know him.'

'I've spoken to him once.'

'Once more than anyone else. And I'm told you get on well with him.'

Who could have told him that? I wondered. Rufus. It had to be. He was the only other person I'd talked to about my meeting with Estienne. I'd have a word with him later.

Having settled matters more or less to his satisfaction Henry relaxed again. He was evidently still feeling chipper over his victory over Arnold.

'What did you make of him?'

'Estienne you mean?' I shrugged. 'Intelligent. Capable. Talented.'

'I hear he plays the flute.'

'He calls it a shawm.'

Henry nodded. 'I like a good tune myself. In my younger days the ladies used to swoon over my *estampie.*' He did a quick toe-to-heel. 'That was before I took the cowl, of course. I tell you what, bring the lad over. It's about time I met him. See exactly who we're dealing with.'

'I will gladly deliver your invitation when I check on his comfort, Brother Prior. Now, may I go? I have pressing matters to attend to.'

'Yes, your poultice.' He gave another flip of his hand – but then he became serious once again: 'Walter, these Franciscans are a new species. We must tread carefully. The last thing we want is for the abbey to be accused of inhospitality – or worse, be blamed for pushing them out. Just keep a fatherly eye on him, that's all I ask.'

'On who? Estienne or Arnold?'

'Both. Think of it as being a shepherd as Christ was for his disciples. You can't have a better example than that can you?'

No. But Christ didn't have Arnold to deal with.

Chapter Four
HOME IS WHERE THE SHAWM IS

I have often been accused of talking myself into these situations; that I can't help sticking my nose in where it isn't wanted. But on this occasion I swear it was entirely circumstantial. I *happened* to have been in the marketplace when Estienne gave his début performance on the market cross just as I *happened* to have been one of the three unwise men summoned to the tomb of the saint twenty-seven years earlier. Coincidence? Perhaps. But that is to ignore the power of Kismet, that capricious mistress of fortune so beloved of the Ancients who plays with men's lives as a child does with a toy. We have less control over these things than we would like to think.

I suppose I could appreciate Henry's dilemma. He had a delicate balancing act to perform not knowing which way the dice would fall. The friars had powerful friends both here and in Rome, but that could quickly change. Popes and archbishops come and go and the fortunes of the friars may go up and down with them. This might be just a brief moment in the sun in which case the prior wouldn't want to over-indulge them. On the other hand they may be the future in which case it could only benefit the abbey to be seen to be supportive. Having such annoyingly vocal opposition in the guise of Arnold didn't help. Still, it was early days yet. There was only one of their number in the town - although that too could change if Estienne's superiors in London get their way. We would have to wait and see.

In truth there wasn't much I could do about either of my assignments for the present, either Estienne's accommodation or the opening of Edmund's tomb. The latter was scheduled for Saint Edmund's feast day, but that wasn't until the end of November, and it would take a while for Arnold to find a house suitable for Estienne. I didn't want to press him too hard on that score. We had always had a good working relationship in the past and would have to go on living together in the future. But I knew I couldn't let things drift for too long. I decided, therefore, to let matters rest for the present but that if I hadn't heard from Arnold by Lammas Day, the first of August – which, by the way, happened also to be my sixty-first birthday - then I would approach him.

In the meantime I wanted to have a word with Rufus. He was the only person apart from Arnold who had known of my conversation with Estienne so it must have been him who told the prior about it. That was a betrayal of trust that I couldn't let slide. I therefore decided to have a stern word with him about it when I got back from my meeting with Henry:

'Rufus, have you been discussing my affairs?'

He looked at me blank. 'Your affairs?'

'Don't be coy, you know what I'm talking about. My conversation with Frère Estienne. You spoke to Prior Henry about it – yes?'

'He spoke to me.'

I frowned. 'What's the difference?'

'If I spoke to him it would imply I initiated the conversation. He spoke to me meaning he initiated it.'

'What? Oh yes, I suppose so. But you spoke to him – yes?'

'Yes.'

'Well you shouldn't have done.'

'Should I have ignored him?'

I frowned. 'No, of course you shouldn't ignore him. Brother Henry is the prior. You should always treat him with the utmost respect and deference. But what I told you I said in confidence, not something to be broadcast to all and sundry. Our private conversations should remain just that - private.'

'It was a secret what you told me?'

'Not a secret as such, no.'

I kneaded my brow. This wasn't going very well.

'How can I explain this? Sometimes in life, Rufus, we have to be a little circumspect in our dealings with others.'

'Circumspect?'

'Careful about what we say and to whom we say it. A wrong word in the wrong place can do a lot of damage. For instance, if I were to say to you that Brother Terence had smelly feet, you wouldn't go and tell him would you? It would hurt his feelings.'

'Does Brother Terence have smelly feet?'

I snorted. 'My word yes! Sometimes sitting next to him in choir it's like the fumes of Hades coming up from the floor,' I said flapping a hand in front of my nose. 'Have you never noticed?'

'I have no sense of smell.'

Why didn't that surprise me?

Rufus continued to regard me passively, his face completely devoid of expression. Dear Lord, I thought, I had an automaton for an assistant.

'Look, in future just try to use a little discretion, that's all I ask. Don't repeat everything you hear. Do you understand?'

'I understand.'

I'm not sure he did. I could see that training Rufus was going to involve more than just lancing boils and mixing tinctures. But give the lad his due, he took criticism without rancour. I've had assistants in floods of tears for far less than that. Or maybe he was just impervious to feeling. I've met people like that before as well though usually they were soldiers or merchants. Their arm could be hanging off or their warehouse burning down around their ears yet they hardly bat an eyelid. They just carry on as though nothing had happened. I suppose such people have to be admired, but they are hard work sometimes.

But to return to Estienne. As part of my remit to keep a fatherly eye on him, I decided to follow him – discreetly and at a distance. Not a difficult task in itself and quite a pleasant one. The sound of his shawm was very distinctive and could be heard all over the town. He played it to announce his presence at the beginning of one of his perorations. These turned out to be highly popular events. As soon as they heard his call children in particular would flock to him. He would then lead them in a little dance around the arena while continuing to play his instrument before settling them down for that all-important day's lesson.

I say "lesson" but these were as entertaining as they were educational and certainly more engaging than the dour classes at the abbey school where teachers have to whip their charges just to keep them awake. I am sure the children went away remembering far more of what Estienne had taught them as a result. Later he would distribute any alms he had collected to the needy.

I was never quite sure if he was aware of my presence during these sessions and therefore how much of a show he was putting on for my benefit. But he never acknowledged me and simply got on with what he was doing. Not that I was hiding either. He kept up this pace for several days quite wearing me out in the process – I'm not as young as I was and subterfuge is a young man's game. At night he slept in the porches of churches or under the trees and next morning washed himself in the river. This was all very well in the summer but I worried how he would get on as the weather cooled.

Weeks passed. Mid-summer came and went and the days started to grow shorter. The first of August duly arrived and I still hadn't heard from Arnold about Estienne's house. I decided it was time to force the issue.

As well as being Lammas Day when the bread made from the first wheat grain to be harvested is brought into church, the feast of Saint Peter in Chains when Saint Peter was miraculously freed from prison by an angel, and my birthday, the first of August is also one of the so-called *dies mali* or "evil days" of which there are twenty-four in any year. By tradition these are days when it is thought best not to begin any enterprise worth undertaking. Maybe I should have thought of that before I waylaid Arnold outside the refectory. It might have saved a lot of anguish later.

'Arnold!' I beamed with my customary *joie de vivre.* 'How are you, my old friend? May I join you?'

He sniffed back a suspicious greeting.

'Oh come! You're not still angry with me over this grey friars thing are you?' I chuckled giving him a friendly punch on the arm.

'Not at all. You are entitled to your opinion.'

'Good,' I beamed. 'I'd hate us to fall out over something so trivial.'

'You mean we should only fall out over the important matters?'

'What? Oh yes, quite.' We walked a little way in silence. 'Oh, by the way,' I said as though the thought had just occurred to me, 'I've been meaning to ask: have you managed to find a lodging for our young preacher yet?'

'Why do you want to know?'

I shrugged. 'No particular reason. Idle curiosity. So have you? Found him a house yet?'

'As a matter of fact I found one a month ago.'

I stopped dead in my tracks. 'What? Well why didn't you tell me?'

His lip curled. 'Why Walter, I didn't know you'd be interested.'

Of course he knew I'd be interested. He'd have known about my conversation with the prior even if Henry hadn't told him himself, you can bet your life.

'Well now you do know. So can I have the address please? I'd like to pay my respects.'

'Check up on me, you mean. I'm surprised the boy hasn't told you himself. He's been a regular in the marketplace - taking my money as usual.'

I wasn't going to get into all that again.

'I haven't been out of the abbey much lately,' I lied.

'Really? So it wasn't you I've been seeing following him around the town for the past month?'

'Clearly not. If I'd been following him around I'd already know his address, wouldn't I?'

'Then clearly you've not been doing your job properly, have you?'

I sighed. 'Arnold, are you going to give me the address or not?'

He did, with much ill-grace. I knew roughly where he meant. I decided I'd go and pay Estienne a visit that evening.

As I say, I know this part of town well. As a *lieu de résidence* it leaves much to be desired. There aren't any real streets here as such just paths between properties that are more industrial than residential. What passed for habitations were little more than flimsy shacks so I wasn't expecting Estienne's to be a palace. But what I found shocked even me. "Hovel" would be too grand a description. It was semi-derelict. Only three walls standing, half a roof and no door. Somewhere modest, the prior had said. It was certainly that. The Lord only knew what Estienne's masters in London would think if they saw it. Gingerly I inched my way across the threshold fearful of touching anything lest it fell off onto the floor – or worse, onto me.

'Hello?' I called. 'Is anybody alive in here?'

A noise from behind startled me and I turned to see Estienne's grinning face.

'*Monsieur le médecin!* Welcome to my humble dwelling!' He bowed to the floor. 'To what do I owe the pleasure?'

Humble was right. I looked around the ruin with a shaking head.

'You live - here?' I said grimacing round.

'What's wrong with it?' Estienne asked in all innocence.

My jaw dropped. 'What's *wrong* with it? What's *right* with it? I wouldn't let a dog live here. It's a death trap.' To make the point I kicked the wall and a large lump of daub fell off.

'It could do with a bit of a spring clean, I grant you,' he said picking up the piece. 'But give me a chance. I've only just moved in.'

'And you'll soon be moving out again too if I have anything to do with it.'

I was furious. This was Arnold's doing. I might have guessed. If this was his way of persuading Estienne not to stay he'll be greatly disappointed.

Then the boy burst into delighted laughter. 'I'm sorry brother I cannot deceive you longer. No, I don't live in here.'

'Then where?'

'Come. I'll show you.'

He led me into the yard outside and with a flourish indicated to a low hutch. '*Voilà!* Welcome to *Château Estienne.*'

My jaw dropped further. 'You're living in the pigsty? But that's even worse!'

'Not at all. Christ was born in a stable, remember - which he had to share with oxen and sheep. This is luxury by comparison.'

I sniffed. 'It smells.'

'I've slept in smellier places.'

'It's also damp.'

'A fire will soon dry it out.'

'But what about when your brother friars arrive? Where will they sleep?'

'Oh, I'll have done the house up by then.'

'Do it up? It needs demolishing – that's if it doesn't fall down of its own accord.'

'In which case I'll rebuild,' he said with infuriating *sang froid*.

'Don't be ridiculous! You can't build a house by yourself.'

'I can turn my hand to most things. Besides, I may not have to,' he smiled. 'I have plans. But please. Don't spoil it. You're my first visitor. Allow me to play host.' With a flourish he invited me in.

We crouched to get under the lintel leaving the door open to let what little light there was come in. At least it was going to be weather-proof. Pigs are very fussy about where they will and will not live. They don't like the wind and rain. But for a man, especially in winter, I wasn't so sure. As a monk I am used to simple living – it is one of the prerequisites of our Order. But even by our standards this was depressingly spartan.

I sat on the edge of the board that passed as a bed watching a beetle crawl away under the straw while he poured me a cup of ale and sat cross-legged on the floor in front of me.

'Aren't you having any?' I asked taking a mouthful.

'I've only the one cup. I'll have mine when you've finished.'

'You don't seem to have much of anything,' I said looking round.

'I told you, brother. I need nothing but the robe I stand up in.'

From the smell of it, it could stand up by itself.

'I see you still have your shawm,' I said nodding to the object hanging on the wall.

'My one indulgence. It goes with me everywhere.'

I held out my hand. 'May I? I didn't really get a good look at it the first time.'

'Of course.'

He took it down carefully and handed it to me with reverence. It was a beautiful thing, even more impressive up close. The wood was lovingly polished with a bright ring of brass encircling the base.

'Try it,' he smiled.

'Oh no. I'm no musician,' I said trying to hand it back.

But he insisted. He showed me how to hold the thing and where to place my fingers over the holes. I then put the end in my mouth and blew as hard as I could but got nothing out of it other than a fluttering noise.

'It tickles,' I said patting my nose.

'That's because there are two reeds in the mouthpiece that vibrate against each other to make the sound. You have to hold them tightly between your lips and blow out your cheeks like you want to be sick – like this.' He demonstrated the posture.

It looked most ungainly but I did as he instructed and this time managed to make a noise reminiscent of an egg-bound goose. I was also left feeling a little light-headed after all that blowing.

'It's not as easy as it looks.'

'It does take a little practice,' he conceded. 'Try again.'

'No,' I said handing the thing back to him. 'You play something.'

He took the instrument lovingly into his hands, moistened the end with his lips a few times then closed his eyes and began to play. I was once again soaring above the clouds just as I had been the first time in the marketplace. It was addictive. It sounded like angels singing, quite an alien sound. Apart from the borough waits, that band of amateur minstrels who provide accompaniment to our festivals, we don't hear a lot of music – *good* music, that is. We have only our monk voices singing the psalms all on one note. Beautiful too, but a bit repetitive. The twiddles and flows and leaps of Estienne's playing – I don't know the correct terminology – were to me a revelation. I didn't want him to stop. But stop he eventually did and I came back down to earth again.

'Where did you get such a beautiful instrument?' I asked.

'It was given me by an Arab friend in Marseilles.' He smiled. 'Do I shock you?'

I shook my head. 'Not at all. I have a half-brother who is himself half-Arabic.'

That wasn't strictly accurate. Joseph was more a step-brother than half-brother, but I didn't want to go into detail.

'Marseilles is a long way from Saverne. Why were you there?'

'It is a long story,' he said vaguely. 'I have lived in many strange places. Believe me, this is by no means the worst.'

'That's as may be. But I'm not happy about all this. I will have a word with Sacristan Arnold.'

'I doubt it would make much difference. I don't think he likes me very much. I'd prefer if you didn't make waves.'

'No, I'm sorry, Estienne, but this won't do. You might be prepared to put up with squalor but I have the reputation of the abbey to think of. If it got out that this was how we treated our guests we'd never bear the shame. I must report this to the prior without delay.'

'Really, *mon frère*,' he protested, 'it is not necessary.' But I set my jaw. Estienne shrugged. 'As you wish.'

Outside the sunlight momentarily blinded me. But as my eyes adjusted I caught sight of a figure standing against a fence nearby watching us. He looked furtive. His face was in shadow so that I couldn't quite see it.

'I see you've noticed my other visitor,' said Estienne.

'Has he been there long?'

'Since my arrival more or less.'

'Do you know who he is?'

Estienne shook his head. 'No idea.'

'Let's ask him.'

But as I approached the man he pushed himself off the fence and walked smartly away. He had a pronounced limp so it shouldn't have been difficult to catch him up. But still he managed to disappear into the maze of little alleyways that entangle this part of Bury. I could spend all evening looking and not find him. In any case I had a good idea who he was.

I left Estienne and marched back to the abbey still feeling angry with Arnold over the way he had treated the boy and determined to put it right. It was too late to see the prior tonight - I could hear the vespers bell ringing and needed to get into church. Besides, I had a better idea. I would challenge

53

Arnold next day in Chapter before the whole convent. That way I might be able to shame him into putting an end to his nonsense once and for all.

Chapter Five
LOOK BEFORE I LEAP

I'm not normally a vindictive sort of person but I did permit myself a slight smile of satisfaction as I went in to Chapter the next morning. My intention was to expose Arnold's disgraceful treatment of Estienne and to show him up. With sympathy then firmly with Estienne I'd be able to get the brothers to agree to better accommodation for him. I was quite looking forward to it.

The chapterhouse was full this particular morning with all but a handful of monks present. Good. The more the merrier. When I made my presentation no-one would be able to say they didn't hear it or be in any doubt about how badly Arnold had been misbehaving. I couldn't resist giving Arnold a smirk as I passed him. I wondered if he could guess what was coming.

Prior Henry presided as usual, Abbot Hugh being still with the king in Winchester discussing the latest political crisis. Apparently the new French king, Louis, taking advantage of England's temporary difficulties, had made a land-grab for some of our possessions in Gascony. He then, craftily, announced that he was "taking the cross" - vowing to go to fight in the Holy Land - which meant no-one could attack him under threat of excommunication even to recover stolen lands. Of course Louis had no intention of going to the Holy Land, everyone knew that, it was just a ruse. In the meantime he would be free to consolidate his hold on our territories thus making it even more difficult for us to recover them later. Was there no end to French perfidy? And this was the man who wanted to be king of England. Ha!

Having delivered this piece of depressing news Prior Henry then asked if there were any other matters. Many hands shot up hoping to attract Henry's attention. Languidly, I raised mine.

'Yes, Brother Physician. You have something you wish to say?'

'Thank you Brother Prior,' I said. 'I do.'

I rose grandly like a senator of ancient Rome, taking my time and waiting until I had everyone's attention – I didn't want anyone to miss this. I then launched into my peroration describing Estienne's house in graphic detail – not exaggerating but making clear the appalling conditions in which the boy had to live. I had no need to embellish. The truth was bad enough. I told them about the state of the house, about the missing roof and walls and that Estienne was reduced to sleeping in a pig-pen. All of this was received with pleasing gasps of shock and disgust from my brother monks. I then delivered my *coup de grâce*:

'In conclusion may I remind the house of Prior Henry's words about our duty of hospitality to strangers and lament the fact that the sacristan had ignored it and had chosen instead to condemn our guest to such a miserable hovel.'

A good many of my brothers were by now frowning, muttering and shaking their heads in disbelief. At last Arnold's plaintive voice was heard above the clamour:

'But I didn't choose such a place!'

I immediately shot back: 'Brother, you cannot deny it. I've been there. I saw it for myself. The house is as I described it. A shack of the basest degree unfit for human habitation.'

'That maybe so,' said Arnold standing up. 'But I repeat: *I* didn't choose it.'

'Then who did?'

'The boy himself.'

Now, you know that feeling you get in the pit of your stomach when you know you've blundered but you're not quite sure how? I was getting it then. I'd missed something, but what? Jolted out of my reverie, I tried to brazen it out:

'And why, pray, would he do that?'

'Because that's what he wanted. I've told you before, Walter, these people court misery and deprivation. I tried to dissuade him. I offered him several other houses but he insisted that was the one for him. Did he not tell you that while you were quaffing his ale and being entertained *en soirée*?'

By now I could feel my face growing hot. Was it possible? Yes of course it was. From what I knew of Estienne it was entirely possible he would have deliberately chosen the most run-down wreck of a hutch he could find to inhabit. But why couldn't he have told me before I made a complete fool of myself before the entire convent? Prior Henry was frowning and shaking his head. Arnold on the other hand couldn't have looked more pleased with himself if he'd just been told he was to be made pope. His smirk easily out-smirked mine. In reply all I could manage was a weak:

'Well you couldn't have tried very hard.'

Flustered, I sat down amid a great deal more shaking of disapproving heads – this time at me. I'd bungled it in the most public way. I wanted to crawl away and die. If the ground could have opened up and swallowed me at that moment it would have been a mercy.

After Chapter Prior Henry called me to his office:

'I apologize Brother Prior,' I blustered in before he had a chance to say anything. 'I was too hasty. I know, I'm sorry. I should have been certain of my facts before opening my mouth. I was wrong to accuse the Brother Sacristan of dereliction and will accept whatever penance you deem appropriate.'

True to his forgiving nature Henry merely smiled kindly - unlike his predecessor, Prior Herbert, who would have relished the opportunity to punish me with a whipping before my brother monks in Chapter. And in truth, I'm not sure which would have been more painful: Herbert's lashes or Henry's sad look of disappointment.

'Do not distress yourself, Walter. At least you drew attention to the boy's plight.'

'It was his plight I was trying to ease.'

'I doubt if you could have succeeded. These friars relish discomfort, Arnold is right about that. It's impossible to know how to deal with them. You think you are helping when in fact you are doing the opposite. I fear it has been the martyr's lot since time immemorial.'

He poured two cups of wine.

'You have to understand what these friars are about,' he said handing me mine. 'They want to get back to the simple life. Originally their founder,

Francis of Assisi, wanted them to be known as the "Wandering Poor" - did you know that? But Pope Innocent was fearful that this might prompt some to make comparison with the wealth of the Church – quite unjustly of course.'

'Oh – quite unjustly,' I agreed enthusiastically.

'Well, maybe not that unjustly,' smiled Henry. 'Anyway, they settled instead on "Friars Minor" the term deriving from the Italian *fraticelli* meaning "little brothers". That's also where the word "friar" comes from, by the way.'

'You seem to know a lot about them, Brother Prior,' I said sipping my wine.

He gave a modest shrug of his shoulders. 'I happened to be in Rome when Francis first approached the pope asking to be allowed to preach. At first the Holy Father was sceptical. It all sounded to His Holiness a bit like the Waldensians - you will remember, they were declared heretical by Lateran IV. But eventually Innocent was persuaded – mostly because of Francis's devotion to the pope as head of the church, unlike Peter Waldo who wanted the pope defrocked, priests pensioned off and Church property handed to the poor. In a moment of divine revelation Innocent saw the shabby preachers as ideal warriors in his fight against the forces of corruption and heresy – those front-line troops we were talking about before - as long as they continue to acknowledge the supreme authority of the Holy Father, naturally.'

'Naturally,' I echoed.

Henry sat down. 'It is interesting, by the way, that Estienne has chosen to live in a pigsty. According to one account Innocent's first response was to send Francis off to keep swine,' he chuckled. 'One of those amusing little ironies. No doubt Arnold would agree.'

'So you believed him when he said Estienne chose the hovel himself?'

'Bearing in mind what I've just told you about them, yes, I'm afraid I do.'

'In that case you don't think there's more to Arnold's antipathy towards Estienne than he's saying?'

Henry shook his head. 'You have to understand Arnold. He's from the old school, suspicious of anything new. He won't be satisfied until Estienne and his ilk are gone from these shores altogether. He won't succeed, of course. As I said before, the preaching friars are here to stay. That means, alas, we may be in for rather more of the same.' He shook his head sadly. 'I still haven't met our one, by the way. You were meant to bring him over.'

'Yes, I'm sorry Brother Prior. I was somewhat distracted by the condition of his house, it slipped my mind. I'll make a point of asking him as soon as we're finished.'

He nodded. 'As for your penance, I think perhaps you should apologize to Arnold. I can think of nothing more painful than that - can you?'

'No, brother,' I said through gritted teeth. 'Nothing.'

I would apologize to Arnold - but not just yet. First I wanted to make sure he was telling me the truth. I only had his word that Estienne had chosen the hovel himself. I decided therefore to pay Estienne another visit - and deliver Henry's invitation at the same time.

Unaware of the ructions that had been taking place in his name, Estienne merely confirmed what Arnold had told us, that he had indeed been offered other houses owned by the abbey. Better-appointed houses. Houses that at least had a roof and four walls.

'Then why on earth did you choose this one?' I asked him looking around the place. It hadn't improved in twenty-four hours. 'And why didn't you tell me before I made a complete ass of myself before the entire convent?'

'I didn't know you were going to announce it in Chapter, brother. And I didn't ask you to fight my battles for me.'

Such ingratitude. Henry was right, he was impossible to help.

'You have to understand we are exhorted by our founder to lives of extreme poverty in emulation of Christ's life and ministry.'

'So everybody keeps telling me.'

'Then you will see why I had to turn down Brother Arnold's other offers.'

'I'm sure he didn't need much persuading. How much is he charging you for the privilege of living here? Whatever it is it's too much.'

'The rent is reasonable. And the folk of Bury are generous. Some are even helping me to rebuild. I did get the impression, though, that Brother Arnold doesn't much approve of what I am doing.'

'I'm sure it's nothing personal,' I tried to reassure him. 'And let's drop the subject. I don't want to defend him any more than I have to. Have you seen any more of the limping man?'

'I have seen him about. But I haven't managed to speak to him yet. I want to embrace him and bring

61

him into the fold with love. But whenever I approach him he quickly hobbles away.'

'Good Lord! You surely don't think he's hanging about hoping to join the Friars Minor?'

'Why not? It happens. Everyone is susceptible to the love of God, brother. He seems a troubled soul to me.'

I snorted. 'The only thing troubling him is the fear of getting caught.'

'You know who he is?'

'I have a fair idea. By the way, before I forget, the prior wishes to meet you.'

He bowed. 'It would be an honour.'

'Expect an official invitation, then.' I got up to leave. 'You know, you should be careful who you take into your confidence my friend.'

'Do you think I am in danger?'

'All I'm saying is not everyone understands or approves of what you are doing. And stuck out here in the middle of nowhere on your own – you are vulnerable.'

'Oh, I won't be on my own for long.'

'You mean more of your order are coming?'

'I mean I expect to recruit here in Bury. If not the limping man then others.'

'Then I'd better let you get on and make the house ready for all these new recruits. And when you've finished I hope Arnold is appreciative of the improvements you've made and reduce your rent accordingly. If you ask me he should be paying you to live here not the other way round.'

Chapter Six
ESTIENNE GETS A NEW ADMIRER – AND A NEW ENEMY

For the next few days I kept myself busy in the laboratorium trying to avoid too much contact with my brother monks - I was still feeling embarrassed about my *faux pas* in the chapterhouse. This is easier for me than most of my brothers since I don't have to sit around in the scriptorium for hours endlessly copying texts or in the cloister reading as they do. Fortunately Rufus hadn't been in Chapter that morning so missed the spectacle of his master making a fool of himself. If he'd heard what had transpired he gave no indication. But then Rufus wouldn't – one of the advantages of having a machine for an assistant I suppose.

However, it was not to be. It was while I was in the laboratorium one morning that a now familiar sound caught my ear: the distinctive whining of Estienne's shawm, and it appeared to be coming from the direction of the prior's office. It looked as though Henry had made good his promise to invite Estienne over and by the sounds of things was being treated to an impromptu display of his musical talents. It really was a hypnotic sound and impossible to ignore. I went outside to listen. Aristotle said that music imitates anger and gentleness. It can certainly soothe and excite the emotions – even in Rufus, it seemed, who joined me outside.

'Before you ask, it's called a shawm,' I told him.

'Yes I know.'

'Do you, indeed?'

There were a few more of my brother monks standing around listening to the music, among them Brother Kevin, our flamboyant novice master. His job was the care of the young novices and oblates as well as running the choir school. Never one to use one hyperbole where two would do, Kevin was effusive in his praise:

'What simply *marvellous* music!' he gushed coming over. 'I've never heard a flute played so *beautifully*.'

'It's a shawm,' I corrected him.

'Delightful, quite delightful! Who is it playing, do you know?'

When I told him his mouth fell open in amazement.

'You mean the friar? The young person we were asked to vote about in Chapter? I voted *against*. Oh,' he frowned, 'I wish now I'd voted *for*. I wonder if he could be persuaded to play for my boys?'

'I'm sure he'd be open to suggestions.'

Another brother came over. 'What's that noise?'

'It's called a shawm,' I sighed.

'No, I mean the other noise. Like someone banging on a floor.'

I listened. There was indeed a thumping sound also coming from the prior's office.

'I fear it's Prior Henry,' I grimaced. 'Dancing.'

'*Dancing!*' Kevin choked back a snort of glee. 'How divine! I *must* meet this young man. He sounds *exquisite!*'

He didn't have long to wait. The door to the prior's office opened and amid much laughter Estienne and Henry emerged together like a couple of old pals. I gathered the interview had been a success.

'Walter!' beamed Henry practically skipping down the stairs. 'Frère Estienne here has been giving me a demonstration of his instrument.'

'So we heard.'

'A wonderful invention! And from Arabia, he tells me! Who'd have thought the infidels could have made such a thing? It's a pity we can't find some way to use it in our services.'

'Brother Kevin has one or two ideas on that score,' I said. I introduced him to Estienne.

'*Enchanté*,' bowed Estienne.

'Likewise, I'm sure,' gushed Kevin going red in the face. 'I was wondering – if you have time - to play to the children? J-just a small demonstration,' he stammered. 'The novices don't get a chance to hear much music other than those dreary chants in chapel.'

'It would give me the greatest of pleasure, *cher* Brother Novice Master,' Estienne bowed again.

'Oh, Kevin please,' blushed Kevin. 'C-call me Kevin.'

This budding love affair was brought to an abrupt halt by the arrival of two more uninvited guests: Arnold and an elderly woman who strode purposefully towards us looking extremely angry.

'That's him!' she said pointing a craggy finger at Estienne. 'That's the one!'

Prior Henry scowled annoyance. 'What's the meaning of this invasion? Brother Arnold – who is this woman?'

'She claims Frère Estienne has been stealing her business,' said Arnold casually.

'That he did!' said the woman.

Henry frowned. 'Stealing her business? What's she talking about? What business? I don't understand.'

Henry may not have understood but I did. I recognized the woman as the widow Mab, a local wise-woman who plied her trade in the area around Estienne's house - there's one in every neighbourhood. It's to people like her that folk go when they fall ill - ordinary folk, that is, those who can't afford the fees of qualified physicians like me, which is just about everybody. They rely on women like Mab with her home-spun remedies and quasi-magical cures to ease their suffering. Sometimes they work. Mostly they don't. But if you are poor and sick where else do you go?

These quasi-medicine women do have some of the trappings of the profession which they've picked up mostly by observing us real physicians. They know how to take a pulse, mumble a bit of dog-Latin, intone an incantation or two, but it's mostly for show to create the illusion of expertise. Their great asset, of course, is their cheapness – certainly cheaper than me. Still, they manage to scrape a living from it. But if Estienne had been treating some of this woman's patients, which I suspected was Mab's complaint, he would have been doing so for free which would have meant a loss of income for her. Not that Prior Henry was in any mood to sympathize:

66

'Madam, you have no business bringing your temper and your accusations here. This is a house of God not a bear-pit. Kindly leave at once.'

'I'll leave once he gives me what he owes me.'

'Which is what?'

'Five of my patients he's stole. That's five pence.'

I stifled a scoff at that. From five patients she'd be lucky to get one penny, the cheeky old crone.

Henry turned to Estienne. 'Can you pay her?'

Estienne shook his head. 'I take no fee for what I do. I have no money.'

'There's your answer, madam,' said Henry. 'Frère Estienne has no money. He cannot give you what he doesn't have.'

'In that case I'll take this.'

So saying, the woman made a grab for Estienne's shawm. Naturally Estienne refused to relinquish it and in the ensuing tussle both of them lost hold of the instrument which fell to the ground with a heart-wrenching crack.

'Oh now you've *broken* it!' cried Kevin.

'Serves him right,' said Mab. 'Teach him not to thieve my patients.'

Estienne gasped and fell to his knees. He picked up the two broken pieces and let out a sob. It was the first time I'd seen him anything but cheerful.

Taking advantage of the moment, Mab made another grab at Estienne but this time Rufus, to my amazement, stepped between them. She tried to reach around him to get at Estienne but Rufus blocked her each time. I must say I was impressed by his quick reaction. In frustration all Mab could do was point a threatening finger at Estienne:

'In future stay away from what's mine if you don't want worse!' So saying she glared round at the rest of us before turning and stomping away.

'What a perfectly foul woman,' said Kevin watching her go.

Foul or not she did have a point. It was her livelihood Estienne had taken albeit for good reason. To forestall any further trouble I ran after her and caught her up at the gate.

'You want some too?' she said clenching her fists.

I held up my hands. 'No, nothing like that, mother. I merely wanted to say it won't happen again. You have my word.'

As proof of my sincerity I gave her five silver pennies from my own purse. It was a month's earnings for her and at last she seemed placated.

'Just make sure he does.'

With one final defiant snort of contempt, she pulled up her skirts and went on her way.

I returned to the others. Poor Estienne. He was still on his knees and beside himself with grief. Tears were flowing down his cheeks as he held the two broken halves of his belovèd shawm in his hands.

'Do not worry, my son,' Henry was trying to console him. 'We have some fine wood craftsmen in the abbey. I'm sure we'll be able to find someone to repair it.'

'It's not a piece of furniture,' Estienne snapped. 'You can't just stick it back together again.'

'No, quite,' said Henry, backing down. 'It's irreplaceable. I understand.' He pulled a face at me.

I admit I was nearly as heart-broken as Estienne. I'd grown quite fond of hearing the sound around town and would miss it if it wasn't there. Others too I was sure – though possibly not Arnold. Did he know

68

what Mab was going to do? Seeing his smug face now did make me wonder how he knew where to bring her. That question was quickly answered. Standing in the shadows quietly watching was the same limping-man I'd seen outside Estienne's house. He must have told Arnold where to find him. Seeing him now I was reminded again of that last comment of Arnold's in Chapter about "quaffing ale" with Estienne and being entertained *"en soirée"*. How would he have known that if this man hadn't told him? There was one way to find out.

'Rufus,' I said quietly. 'Do you have any of your medicament left?'

'I made a fresh batch this morning.'

'Go and fetch it.'

By the time he returned the man had gone, but this time I'd noted which way he went. We caught sight of him crossing the Mustowe, the wide open area in front of the abbey, before disappearing up Cooks Row. I was determined he wasn't going to get away again.

He was obviously aware that we were behind him and was making for the network of little roads and alleyways off to the south hoping to give us the slip as he had last time. But this was where my brother Joseph had his shop and I knew the area well. As Rufus and I rounded the end of Heathenmans Street I saw him disappear down a side alley.

'Got you my beauty,' I muttered.

Sure enough the man had ventured into a street that had no other way out. Rufus and I walked slowly towards him looking, I thought, impressively intimidating.

"Ere, what's going on?' said the man backing away from us.

'That's what I was going to ask you,' I said in my most masterly voice.

'I don't know nothing.'

'You don't know nothing about what?'

'Whatever it is,' he frowned looking confused.

'Well, we'll soon find out won't we?' I nodded to Rufus who produced a leather bottle. He held it up for the man to see.

'What's that?' asked the man suspiciously.

'It's a truth drug.'

At first his eyes widened, but then he snorted. 'Truth drug! There ain't no such thing.'

'Then you won't mind trying it.'

Rufus removed the leather bung from the bottle neck and held it up for the man to see. Immediately the warm aroma of newly mashed-up lug-worm and boiled caterpillar juice rose to his nostrils.

'Urrgh!' he grimaced. 'That's disgusting.'

'That's in the nature of a truth drug I'm afraid my friend,' I sighed.

But the man wasn't quite as stupid as he appeared – or at least he thought he wasn't. Slowly an idea dawned on him and spread across his face. It was easy to guess what he was going to say next:

'I don't believe it's a truth drug. I could tell you anything – you wouldn't know.'

'Oh, we'd know all right,' I assured him pouring some of the revolting green slime into a cup. 'It's never been known to fail – has it Rufus?'

Rufus slowly shook his head from side to side without taking his eyes off the man.

Still uncertain, the man scowled at the foul-smelling stuff again. 'How does it work?'

'It's very simple. If you don't tell me the truth,' I said and thrust the cup under his nose. 'Rufus here will make you drink it.'

It was as I'd thought. The man was working for Arnold. His remit was to check on all Estienne's goings-on in the hope of finding something to condemn him. Since none of us is perfect I'm sure if he'd have found something, (even the archangel Gabriel will have forgotten to wax his wings once in his thousand-year life). But I thought it despicable of Arnold to try anything so underhand. This man and the widow Mab. He'd use anybody to undermine the boy. Very well. If Arnold wanted to play rough I could do the same. From now on I would be watching him watching Estienne. And as for receiving an apology from me – he could sing for it.

Chapter Seven
MURDER MOST FOUL

Much as I was annoyed with Arnold I did have other things to think about - the shrine-opening being the most pressing. We were still some weeks away from the ceremony but there was much to do. And now, thanks to the prior, it was up to me to make sure everything was ready on time and the ceremony went smoothly.

Before I did anything, however, I wanted to go over to Estienne's house to see how he was. I'd never seen him so distraught as he was outside the prior's office – understandably: I knew how important his shawm was to him. I was also conscious of the fact that he was very much on his own in a strange town and I wanted him to know that he had friends in Bury. Above all I didn't want him to give up and leave. That would have meant Arnold had won, and that would have annoyed me even more.

'I shan't be doing that, brother,' he smiled. 'Thank you for your concern, but my mission here has only just begun.'

'Does that include curing the sick? If so I would advise you to proceed carefully. You don't want any more episodes like the one with the widow Mab.'

'I have had a little training in the mysteries of physic. None as wide as yours, of course,' he smiled.

'It's just a shame about your shawm,' I said picking up the two halves and tentatively bringing them together. 'I shall miss hearing it.'

'You will again. I'm sure I'll be able to find someone able to repair it. In fact, I know I will.'

'Of course you will,' I smiled laying the thing gently back down again. 'I have every confidence.'

I didn't like to say so but I doubted if there was anybody in Bury who could mend such a delicate instrument. The sort of wood it was made from certainly didn't grow in England. I suppose he might find a back-street joiner who could possibly cobble the two halves together somehow but it would never sound the same again.

'Oh, and by the way, you needn't worry about the limping man. I'm pretty sure you won't be bothered by him again.'

'You've spoken to him?'

'Let's just say we've come to an understanding.'

'Thank you for that too.'

'Not at all. Well, if you're sure there's nothing more I can do, I'll leave you alone. Don't forget though, if you need someone to talk to my door is always open.'

'I won't forget.'

I left him to return to the abbey. He seemed all right. Most importantly he was confident about getting his shawm repaired. I just hoped it wasn't confidence misplaced. It was fortunate the thing had only been broken in two pieces. Left to the widow Mab I'm sure it would have been smashed to pieces. I suppose we had Rufus to thank for that. I have to admit I was impressed with how he had handled himself during the incident and again later with the limping man. Maybe I'd underestimated him. Maybe he could be more useful than I'd given him credit for. It would certainly help if he could keep an eye on Arnold for me. I tentatively mentioned the possibility when I got back to the laboratorium:

'You wish that I should do for you what you were condemning in the limping man?'

'Not exactly. I'm not asking you to follow him about. I'm simply saying that if you happen to see Brother Arnold in the course of your normal duties to tell me about it that's all. What he's doing, who he's talking to, that sort of thing.'

'Like who?'

'Like that little man with the limp, for a start.'

'I see. You do want me to spy for you.'

I grimaced. 'Spying is such an emotive word. I prefer the term "keeping watch". Not that there's anything wrong with spies. Everybody uses spies. How else are we supposed to know what's going on?'

'I don't like spies.'

'No, of course you don't – and you're quite right. It's deceitful and demeaning and it would be wrong of me to ask you. Just keep your eyes and ears open and tell me what you see or hear - all right?'

He nodded.

'And Rufus – mum's the word. Understand?'

'Mum,' he repeated mechanically.

I'm not sure he did understand but I wasn't going to get into another verbal tangle trying to explain it.

'By the way, thank you for protecting Estienne from the widow Mab's fist. That was quick thinking of you.'

'He was on his knees. She was bigger than him.'

'Quite so. But thank you anyway.'

He shrugged and went back to what he was doing.

74

Good. I felt happier now that I had an extra pair of eyes to help me even if they were only Rufus's eyes. It meant I could concentrate on the shrine-opening without worrying about what Arnold was getting up to. And there were things that needed my attention - one complication in particular that I'd forgotten about and I wasn't sure Prior Henry was even aware of. I sent Rufus off to collect some stock from my brother Joseph's apothecary while I went over to the church to try to sort it out.

It's not always appreciated but abbeys are more or less permanent building sites. This is certainly true of Saint Edmund's. There is always some project or other on the go – altering this, restoring that, improving something else. The biggest undertaking at this time was the work being carried out on the west end of the church. This was Abbot Samson's pet project and had been going on for as long as anybody could remember: the erection of his belovèd twin towers on either side of the west doors.

Since his death in 1211 the steam – and the money - had run out and work had largely ground to a halt. When the towers would be finally finished was anybody's guess. Meanwhile there was another legacy left over from Samson going on at the opposite end of the church, work commemorating the great man himself. For this there was money - Samson had specifically made provision for it in his will. But with all the trouble in recent years it had only now become possible to do anything about it. Not that the project was a particularly onerous one. It was simply the removal of one set of carvings and replacing them with a row of rebuses to commemorate Samson's life – as befitted a servant of the servants of God.

A rebus, as everyone knows, is a sort of visual puzzle carved in stone and represents the subject in some way, usually a play on his name. It's an honour that is only reserved for the most revered among the church hierarchy – or the most wealthy. A sort of permanent memorial to their memory. Not everybody's name lends itself to this sort of treatment. It would be hard, for instance, to think of something to represent Abbot Northwold: a carving of Boreas the north wind, perhaps, puffing out his cheeks to blow icy winds across a wooded upland, a "wold". Not an easy image to depict in stone. My own name on the other hand would be simplicity itself. Some wavy lines to represent water: Water/Walter – get it? Not that anybody would wish to. Commemorate me, I mean. I'm not nearly important enough. Or wealthy.

In Samson's case the sculptor had thought of something rather ingenious: a depiction of that other Samson – the one who pulled down the Philistine temple of Dagon. Everyone knows the story of Samson and Delilah, it must be one of the best known in the Bible. Samson was a man given great strength by God but lost it when he was betrayed by the arch-harlot Delilah who cut off his hair while he slept (it was his hair, you see, wherein his strength lay). Later when his hair grew back again he regained his strength and was able to tear down the temple pillars with his bare hands. The clever part of Samson's rebus are the pillars that the Biblical Samson is seen to be bestriding. They are quite obviously Samson's twin octagonal towers. A sort of commixture of the two Samsons while at the same time suggesting physical strength and moral rectitude – two qualities for which Abbot Samson would doubtless like to be remembered I'm sure. Anyone who knew the Biblical story and saw the rebuses would understand the connection immediately.

Fourteen identical copies of the Samson rebus had to be carved one to sit above each of the fourteen pillars of the chancel. From ground level they didn't look particularly big but up close they were half the size of a man. The carver was an Italian called Udo, a particularly fine sculptor and former pupil of Master Hugo, the genius who had built the great west doors of the abbey church and carved the fine ivory cross that now stands on the altar in the choir.

It had taken Udo a year to carve the rebuses and he was now in the process of mounting them. My problem was that if the work didn't get finished soon the scaffolding erected around the apse to facilitate the task would still be in place while the shrine-opening ceremony was in progress. There wasn't a lot of space in the apse as it was, the shrine taking up most of it. With the scaffolding there too there would be even less, which meant less room for the many visitors that Prior Henry hoped to invite. In short, we really needed the scaffolding to be down well before the ceremony which meant inducing Udo to get a move on.

I found him up on the said scaffolding high above the chancel apse overseeing the work in progress. After much exaggerated clearing of my throat I eventually managed to catch his eye:

'Master Udo - might I have a word?'

He stopped what he was doing and descended the ladder still with his chisel and hammer in hand and muttering in Italian as he came.

'What-a is it brother? I am-a rather busy.'

I gave him my most charming of smiles. 'So sorry to disturb you master, but have you any idea when you might be finished?'

Udo's eyes narrowed. 'Finished, brother?'

'The work on the rebuses.' I pointed to the rafters.

His eyes followed mine upwards. 'The "work", as you call it, will-a be finished when it is finished and not a moment sooner. You cannot rush great art, *fratello*. Of course if all-a you wanted was something slipshod...?'

'No no,' I protested quickly. 'The erm ... must progress at its own pace. But it would be helpful if you could be done by, say, the middle of next month to give us time to prepare for the ceremony.'

'Ceremony?'

'The opening of the shrine. Surely you've heard? On the saint's feast day – the twentieth of November?'

Udo glanced dispassionately at Edmund's edifice towering a few feet away.

'It *might* be finished by then - *if* I am-a permitted to get on with it.'

'Of course,' I beamed. 'I quite understand. Great art cannot be rushed. Don't let me stop you. The, er, sculptures are beautiful by the way. Simply stunning. But if you could bear the twentieth in mind?'

'Hmph!' He started to climb the ladder again.

These artists. They're so prickly about their art.

When I got back to the laboratorium Rufus still hadn't returned from his errand.

Where was the boy? I'd only sent him off to collect a few herbs from Joseph's shop not pick them himself.

Eventually he turned up. Having taken off his cloak he began unloading his parcel without a word of explanation.

'You've been a while,' I said, slightly peeved. 'Any particular reason?'

'There's been a murder.'

I tutted and shook my head.

That may sound callous but it's a sad fact that there were so many violent deaths in those lawless times one had become inured to them. The countryside around the town were full of bands of brigands, mostly mercenaries left over from the various armies that had been fighting in the recent wars but with peace were no longer required – or paid. No-one on the open road was safe and anyone travelling alone was asking for trouble. The body would be brought in to Bury, usually naked having been stripped of everything of value including clothes so we rarely knew the identity of the victim much less that of the perpetrator. Happily murders inside the town were usually more easily solved.

'Anyone we know?' I asked vaguely.

'The old wise-woman.'

I stopped what I was doing. 'Which old wise-woman? You don't mean the one who was ranting at Estienne? The widow Mab?'

'Yes, that one.'

'Then why didn't you say?'

'You said to tell you about anything to do with Arnold.'

I rolled my eyes in exasperation. 'The widow Mab *is* to do with Arnold. Do they know who did it?'

'No. But they've arrested the friar.'

'*What?*' I closed my eyes and counted to ten. 'Where did this purported murder take place?'

'In the old cattle market.'

I handed him his cloak again. 'Come on.'

'Where are we going?'

'Where do you think?'

The new cattle market lies just beyond the town wall. It replaced the old cattle market which the town had long since outgrown but which is within the town boundary. By this time it was more or less deserted waste ground covered in weeds and detritus of all kinds - mostly refuse that had been dumped there by market traders and residents too lazy to take it to the town ditch. Children use it as a playground by day, adults for a different kind of sport by night. Many of the town's orphans and urchins actually live there. It's not a place I would venture onto alone at night if I valued my neck. Even the town bailiffs refuse to patrol there after dark. In the pitch black of a moonless night no-one would see an assailant. Fortunately it was still daylight when Rufus and I arrived.

'Show me where the body was found,' I said to him. '*Exactly* where it was found.'

He led me to a corner just inside the wall and hidden from the road. The body had gone by now of course, taken away by the sheriff's men. There was a lot of rubble thereabouts, the remains of a demolished wall by the look of it. I bent over to study the ground carefully.

'How did she die, has anyone said?'

'No.'

'Oh come on Rufus. If you knew about the murder you know what the gossip is.'

'I never repeat gossip.'

'Make an exception this time.'

He shrugged. 'It is said she was hit over the head.'

'Hit with what? A hammer? A piece of timber?'

'A lump of rock.'

I frowned. 'Rock? What do you mean, rock? Suffolk doesn't have any rock. We are famous for our lack of rock. We have flint. That's why our churches have round towers because we build with flint. We have no rock. What rock?'

'Maybe it was flint they meant.'

'They? Who is "they"?'

'I cannot remember.'

He was beginning to annoy me again.

I did some more searching of my own. I lifted a sheet and found the body of a dead dog. Lots of flies and maggots, the scurry of mice and rats. I clambered over a pile of what looked like some merchant's entire delivery of rotting fish holding my nose. At last I found what I was looking for.

'Here, hold this.' I handed Rufus a large piece of flint-and-mortar rubble.

He took it in both arms and nearly dropped it. 'It's heavy.'

'That's why you're holding it and I'm not. Where is the body now?'

'It was moved to the sheriff's office.'

'And Estienne?'

'The same.'

'Right. Then that's where we're going next.'

Chapter Eight
FALSE ALARM

The sheriff's office in Bury stands right at the top of the town just inside the town wall. It's a good vantage point. From up here he can oversee the entire vill laid out before him all the way down to the abbey in the valley bottom below. Next to it is a barrack of armed guards ready to spring into action should the need arise. Well, not "spring" perhaps; more "lurch".

What is a sheriff? The word itself is a corruption of *shire-reeve* - the officer, or *reeve*, in charge of a county, or *shire*. He is the king's man-on-the-spot tasked with everything from keeping the peace to raising the militia. As such he is the most powerful man in the county. His word is – literally - law.

A sheriff can be in charge of more than one county at once which in our case is exactly how things are. Because so much of Suffolk lies within the purlieu of the abbot we don't really need a sheriff of our own and we share ours with our neighbouring county of Norfolk which is where the current incumbent preferred to spend most of his time – the magnificence of Norwich Castle rather than a poky little office in Bury. His day-to-day duties in Bury were in consequence carried out by his sergeant - an able and honest man who'd been doing the job for the previous ten years. It was an audience with this man that Rufus and I sought when we knocked at the door of the sheriff's office…

'How long am I to hold on to this?'

Rufus was still carrying the lump of flint and mortar that I'd removed it from the cattle market.

'Just keep it until we've seen the sergeant.'

'It's very heavy.'

'Then put it down, boy,' I said with exasperation. 'Good God, Rufus, do I have to tell you everything? I swear, talking to you sometimes is like dealing with a trained ape.'

That was mean of me I know but I was in no mood for niceties. Fortunately Rufus was too thick-skinned to be hurt by my words. To be honest I wasn't sure who'd be more insulted by the comparison. Apes were God's first attempt at creating human beings, of course - he hadn't quite got the formula right yet. With Rufus I wasn't sure he'd arrived at the final version even now.

Eventually a servant appeared. 'The sergeant will see you now, brother.'

We were ushered into a small office that was a hive of activity. The walls were stacked floor-to-ceiling with scrolls of parchment and a bevy of clerks were scratching away at one end of the room. Seated behind the desk at the other end was a harassed-looking man in his early forties. This was the sergeant. Nobody knew his real name, or if they did they never used it. (I had an idea it was Robbie, but I wasn't certain). He was always referred to simply as "the sergeant". With him, and not altogether to my surprise, was Arnold.

'Good day, sergeant,' I said pointedly ignoring Arnold. 'It's good of you to see us at short notice. This is my assistant, Brother Rufus.'

'Good day to you, brother,' the sergeant replied. 'You two know each other, of course.' He waved a desultory hand towards Arnold.

'Indeed we do. How are you, Arnold?'

'You're here about the murder,' said Arnold without preamble.

'You too. No doubt keen to have Estienne blamed.'

'As you are to have him excused.' He shook his head. 'You're wasting your time, Walter. He did it. It's been proved.'

'You have witnesses?'

'A dozen at least. We all saw the widow Mab attack the friar outside the prior's office. This was his retaliation.'

I smiled sweetly. 'I meant a witness to the murder.'

'I don't need one. The victim herself has identified him.'

'Oh really? And how exactly did she manage to do that given that she's dead?'

Behind me I heard a giggle and the scratching stopped as the clerks put down their quills to listen.

'Brothers please,' said the sergeant wearily. 'I know you two don't see eye to eye over the friar, but can we conduct this in a civilized manner? So far all that has happened is a body has been found and a suspect arrested. There's no proof of anything yet.'

'If you'll forgive my saying sergeant,' Arnold butted in, 'that isn't quite so. The friar was taken into the presence of the body and it bled – you saw it yourself. A clear indication that he was the murderer.

It's a well-known fact that murder victims bleed in the presence of their killers.'

I snorted loudly. 'Good Lord, you don't still believe in that old wives' tale, do you?' I looked incredulously at the sergeant.

'It's true what the sacristan is saying,' said the sergeant. 'The body did indeed bleed when the preacher approached it.'

'Approached - or touched?'

Arnold frowned. 'What's the difference?'

'Quite a lot. I'm sure I could make a corpse bleed if I prodded it hard enough.'

'The friar didn't prod it,' said Arnold. 'He didn't even touch it. He merely walked around the body and it bled spontaneously. She all but pointed her finger at him and shouted *j'accuse!*'

'The brother's right. There was blood in her ears and her nose,' the sergeant confirmed. 'I saw it for myself.'

'So *you* touched her?' I asked him.

'Only to turn her head. I didn't prod her either.'

I thought for a moment. 'How exactly did she die?'

'She was struck on the head.'

'Having first been brutally raped,' Arnold added with relish.

I looked up. 'Rape? This is news to me. Nobody mentioned rape before.'

'From the position of the body it certainly looks that way,' said the sergeant. 'I've seen enough rape victims. This one had all the markings.'

'She was lying on her back with her skirts pulled up and her nether parts exposed,' explained Arnold with a slight curl of his lip. 'What more do you want?'

'And you think Estienne did that?' I scoffed. 'Good Lord, the woman was old enough to be his grandmother.'

Arnold shrugged a negligent shoulder. 'What difference does that make?'

'Well if you don't know Arnold, you've been in the cloisters too long.'

Behind me I heard the clerks snigger.

'Who found the body?'

'I did,' pouted Arnold.

'I see. You just happened to be passing by the old cattle market at the time. How convenient.'

'No Walter, not convenient. I was having the boy watched. I've told you before, I don't trust him. And it seems I was right not to.'

'So we only have your word that she was found in that condition.'

'Are you saying I'm lying?'

'Not lying, Arnold – mistaken. You say she was bludgeoned to death. What was the weapon used – do we know?'

'A lump of rock,' said the sergeant. 'There were fragments found in the wound.'

'A lump of rock - like this?'

I signalled to Rufus to bring his flint boulder over. He placed it carefully on the sergeant's desk and stepped back.

'That could be any old piece of masonry you found lying about,' scoffed Arnold.

'This one has blood and hair on it. Grey hair - like the widow Mab's.'

The sergeant made a cursory examination of the boulder. 'Where did you get it?' he asked.

'From the cattle market right next to where the body was found. I'm surprised you didn't see it,

Arnold. But then, you probably weren't looking very hard. You'd already made up your mind who the murderer was. Well?' I said to the sergeant. 'Could this be the murder weapon?'

'It could.'

'Arnold? Look closely, now. I wouldn't want you to be in any doubt.'

He did so then frowned. 'So what if it is? All you've done is confirm what we've been saying.'

'But you're happy this probably is the murder weapon?'

'I just said so, didn't I?'

I nodded. 'Pick it up.'

'Why?' he asked suspiciously.

'Just pick it up.'

Arnold shook his head. 'I'm not playing your games, Walter.'

'Oh do as he asks please brother,' sighed the sergeant. 'Or we'll be here all day.'

Reluctantly, Arnold tried to lift the stone, first with one hand and then two. He was finding it as heavy and as unwieldy as Rufus had.

'Well?' I said. 'Could you hit someone over the head with it - bearing in mind this is a struggling woman who is presumably trying not to be raped?'

'Mab was a frail old woman. As you pointed out, old enough to be the friar's grandmother.'

'Old yes, but frail? You saw widow Mab attack Estienne outside the prior's office. In a straight fight, who would you put your money on?'

'He could have come at her from behind. In fact that's probably what he did do judging from where the wound was – on the back of her head.'

'And then raped her whilst holding her down with his other hand? Oh really Arnold!'

'A man is capable of much when gripped with lust and hate.'

'There speaks the voice of experience.'

This brought more sniggering from the clerks. Arnold angrily dropped the boulder back onto the desk. It landed with with a pleasingly heavy crunch.

'Your trouble, Walter, is you simply don't want to see what is plainly before your eyes. The friar was the only person to have a grudge against the widow Mab.'

'How do you know that? This is all assumption on your part born of prejudice.'

'Oh, and you're not prejudiced of course?'

'Since you ask, yes I am. I don't believe Estienne murdered the widow Mab. In fact I don't believe it was murder at all – or rape come to that.'

'Really?' said Arnold. 'Then what, pray, was it?'

I shrugged. 'A call of nature.'

That took the wind out of his sail I'm pleased to say. For a moment he couldn't reply. All he could do was stare at me.

'Rubbish!' he eventually exploded.

'Why not? It fits all the facts. She's an old woman – I think we've established that much. She goes onto the cattle market to relieve herself as old women do, squats down, loses her balance and hits her head on the boulder.'

'That wouldn't have been enough to kill her,' objected the sergeant.

'I didn't say it did. You said there was blood in her ear and in her nostril, sergeant. I've seen that before. It's cause is an apoplectic contusion of the brain brought on by straining the bowels.'

Arnold practically choked incredulity. 'You're making this up.'

I shook my head. 'Not at all. It's a very common occurrence. I wish I had a penny for every patient I found squatting on the privy for all the world looking as alive as you and me yet dead as a brush. They nearly all emit a small drop of blood from an ear or a nostril just like the sergeant described. It's a sign of internal haemorrhaging from their apoplexy.'

'We've only your word for any of this,' protested Arnold.

'And we've only yours that Estienne was anywhere near the body.'

He smiled. 'Well that's where you're wrong. You asked for a witness, Walter. I have one.' He turned to the sergeant. 'May I?'

The sergeant shrugged. 'Be my guest.'

Arnold then signalled to the sergeant's servant who opened the door and in walked – or rather hobbled – the limping-man.

I turned immediately to the sergeant. 'I protest, sergeant. This man is a rogue. You can't believe a word he says.'

'You believed me before,' sneered the man. 'Give me some more of your truth drug. You'll believe me then.'

'This man works for me,' Arnold explained grandly to the sergeant. 'He will testify as to what really happened last night. William, tell the sergeant what you told me.'

The man drew himself up. 'I followed the friar as per my instructions from you, Master Arnold...'

Master Arnold! Now there was a revealing detail if ever there was one.

'...and I saw him follow the old woman onto the cattle market.'

'There – you see?' said Arnold. 'He saw the friar follow the widow Mab onto the cattle market.'

'No he didn't.'

So far Rufus hadn't said anything. I'd almost forgotten he was there. We all looked at him now in amazement.

'What do you know about it?' the sergeant asked him.

What indeed? I dearly wanted to know the answer to that, too.

'Yes, come along Rufus,' I brazened. 'Answer the sergeant. Tell him what you know.'

Rufus pursed his lips. 'Mum,' he said.

I frowned. 'What?'

'Mum,' he repeated.

It took me a moment to realise what he meant. I grinned stupidly at the sergeant.

'Rufus, you're embarrassing me.'

'You told me to use my discretion. Not repeat everything I hear.'

'Not now, you idiot. That was before. Now is the time to speak. If you saw something for heaven's sake say so.'

'You want me to tell?'

'Yes, I want you to tell.'

'Very well.' He faced the sergeant. 'I was following the limping man as I was instructed to do by Brother Walter.'

'Were you, indeed?' interrupted Arnold. 'Why were you doing that?'

'Because we didn't trust him,' I said. 'Just as you don't trust Estienne. We knew he was your spy.'

'Spy!' snorted Arnold.

'Go on,' said the sergeant.

'I was following the limping man,' Rufus said again. 'He was following Estienne. Estienne was following the wise-woman.'

'You see?' said Arnold. 'The friar was following the widow Mab. Even your own assistant confirms it.'

'Only because he didn't want her to see him,' said Rufus. 'He held back. He never got closer than I am to you. He stopped each time she staggered.'

'Staggered?' said the sergeant. 'Just a moment. Why was she staggering?'

Rufus looked at me. 'Do I have to say?'

I nodded.

He faced the sergeant again. 'She was drunk.'

'Aha!' I said triumphantly. 'The last piece of the puzzle. It's obvious now what really happened. Having drunk too much ale – probably paid for by money I gave her, I'm sorry to say - the widow Mab went on to the deserted cattle market to relieve herself – as I said. She strained and fell backwards – as I said. She was probably already dead before she hit the ground. If not the cold night would have done the rest.'

'She went onto the cattle market alone,' Rufus repeated again. 'Estienne went home. He didn't enter the cattle market.'

'Is it true?' the sergeant asked the limping man. 'Think carefully before you reply. If later I find you've been lying I will have you tongue removed.'

'Answer the sergeant,' said Arnold. 'Did the widow Mab go on to the market alone or not?'

'It's his word against mine,' the man mumbled.

'Is it *true?*'

The man's face crumpled. 'I thought it was what you wanted me to say, master.'

Arnold drew himself erect and slapped the man hard across the face. Then he turned to the sergeant. 'I disown any connection with this man.'

'But master -' the man started, holding his face.

'True or not,' said the sergeant, 'Brother Walter's explanation makes more sense to me. That business about blood in the ears - I've seen it before as well. And I can confirm there was ale on her breath. I therefore conclude the widow Mab died from misadventure. The friar will be released forthwith.'

He nodded to the servant who bowed and withdrew.

'As for you,' he said pointing at the limping man. 'If I ever see your face in Bury again I will have your tongue cut out as I promised so that you can tell no more lies. Clear?'

The man barely had time to nod before scuttling out of the room.

'And now brothers, if there's nothing more…?'

Outside I confronted Arnold. 'Well, that didn't work. What will your next trick be, I wonder?'

Arnold frowned at me. 'It was no trick, Walter. I genuinely believed the friar was the culprit.'

'Well now you know he wasn't. Perhaps from now on you can leave him alone.'

Before he could reply an iron gate opened next to the guard barrack and Estienne emerged blinking into the daylight. He looked pale and disorientated. Arnold gave him the merest glance before stalking off without another word.

'Do you think he's right?' asked Rufus watching him go.

'Do you?'

'He lost the argument.'

'For now. With his kind of conviction argument is never enough. If Arnold believes black is white then that is how it is.'

'Black is never white.'

I smiled at his open face. 'If only everyone saw things as simply as you do, my young friend.'

A disorientated Estienne was still staggering around, squinting in the sunlight and trying to get his bearings.

'Come on,' I said to Rufus. 'Let's get him home.'

Estienne looked dreadful, even more bedraggled than usual. I sent Rufus off to buy a meat pie and a flagon of ale as there seemed to be no food in the house.

'Are you going to be all right?' I asked him as he gorged on the pie.

He put on a brave face: 'Oh yes. Fine now that that's out of the way.'

'You were innocent. You were never going to be convicted for something you didn't do.'

'I wish I had your confidence.'

'Well, what now?'

He shrugged. 'I carry on.'

'Is that wise? Estienne, you've seen how things are. Not everybody is as appreciative of your efforts as we are.'

'My work here isn't finished. I have much to do still.'

'Like what?'

He pointed to the roof and smiled. 'I haven't finished the house yet. And I still have my shawm to repair.'

I shook my head. 'Have you found anybody capable of doing it yet?'

'I think I may have done.'

'Well when it is you might think about moving on. We don't wish to lose you but we mustn't be greedy by having you all to ourselves. Others could benefit as we have. Cambridge is a nice town. I hear the university there is making great strides. Or there's Ely. They may be more -'

'Welcoming?'

'I was going to say accommodating.'

'And what will my brother friars say when they arrive and I am not here to greet them?' He smiled and shook his head. 'No, brother. I will stay.'

I was disappointed but not surprised by his reaction. He didn't strike me as the sort to give in to intimidation.

'Then can I give you some advice – as a friend? Carry on if you must, but try not to be quite so conspicuous.'

'You mean don't rock the boat?'

'Just trim your sail a little, that's all.'

'I'm not sure I can do that, brother.'

'In that case you may be in for some rough seas ahead of you.'

When we got back to the abbey Prior Henry called both Arnold and me into his office. He wasn't nearly so understanding as the sergeant. In fact he was the nearest I've ever seen him to actually being angry:

'Look at the pair of you! Bringing the entire abbey into disrepute by your behaviour, squabbling in public like a couple of fish-wives.'

'Hardly in public, Henry,' I protested. 'We were in the sheriff's office.'

'And you think it will stay there?' He shook his head. 'I won't have it. You, Brother Physician, in

94

particular had your assistant with you I believe. What kind of example is that to set to a young man?'

I doubt whether Rufus would have taken much notice. But Henry was the prior and it was my duty to obey him.

'You are quite right, Brother Prior. I apologize most sincerely and humbly.'

'Have you apologized to Arnold as I asked you to?'

'Not yet.'

'Then do so now.'

I reluctantly faced Arnold. 'I apologize for any hurt I may have caused you, Brother Sacristan.'

Henry grunted acceptance. 'And you, Arnold. I can't imagine what you were thinking of accusing a brother cleric of murder. And before you say it, I know you don't accept him as a brother.'

'Er, rape *and* murder brother,' I pointed out.

'Yes, thank you Walter. Apart from anything else you make it very awkward for me. I don't need to tell you about the difficulty we have with the civic authorities over jurisdiction. I am responsible for clergy and the sheriff is responsible for everyone else. These preaching friars are neither one nor the other. Awkward for the sheriff's sergeant too I would imagine. It wouldn't surprise me if that wasn't the real reason he decided to drop the matter.'

'He dropped it because Frère Estienne was innocent.'

'So you say,' said Arnold.

'Don't start again,' warned Henry tapping his desk top. 'How is the boy?'

'Shaken but resilient. I'm sure he'll bounce back.'

'He was only incarcerated for a day,' said Arnold. 'Hardly a lifetime.'

'Have you ever been locked in a gaol?' I asked him. 'I have and I can tell you it is no picnic.'

'Well he's out now,' said Henry, 'so let's say no more about it. And no more arguing please. Let's try to remember who we are. Now Arnold, Walter has apologized to you. What have you to say to him?'

Arnold thought long and hard. Finally he said: 'This time I may have been a little hasty, I admit. But I haven't changed my opinion about these people. I will continue to press my case against them because I believe that is what God wishes me to do.'

'That doesn't sound much like an apology to me,' said Henry. 'But I suppose it will have to do. Let that be an end to the matter.'

But it wasn't the end. It was barely the beginning.

Part Two

Chapter Nine
ANNIE SPIKETONGUE

At this point in my tale I need to deviate for a moment - you'll understand why shortly. But first, a geography lesson:

I won't need to point out to anyone who has visited the shrine of Saint Edmund, as I'm sure practically all of you have, that the abbey that contains his bones lies on the banks of a river. Indeed, it is precisely because of that river that the abbey is located where it is. The Lark is no Nile or Euphrates, or even a Thames or an Orwell, but a gently flowing stream that meanders its way across the shallow Suffolk valley that is our home. Even so, it is powerful enough to drive a water-mill and provides us monks with a constant supply of fish. Once in a while it floods sending its waters to lap against the walls of the abbot's garden and testing our engineers' skills of plumbing in the process, but not very often. Most of the time it is simply there, as constant as the northern star and largely taken for granted.

So why do I mention it now? Because there is one other role that the Lark is occasionally called upon to perform, though not one of which I am particularly proud or even necessarily approve...

'You swine! You pack of dung-eating dogs! You filthy blood-sucking lice! You scabs on the arse of the Devil! I'll make you pay for this, you see if I don't!'

That, and a good deal worse, emitted from the mouth of one Annie, wife of Rafe, otherwise known as Annie Spiketongue for obvious reasons, as she hung suspended ten feet above the river. It wasn't the first time she'd uttered such words. Those of us who had gathered to witness her punishment this day had heard them all before. The fact is Annie was a notorious scold not only to her long-suffering husband but to anyone who from time to time fell foul of her temper, which was just about everybody. This wasn't the first time she'd been strapped on the cucking-stool either and few thought it would be her last.

It's called a *cucking*-stool, by the way, from an old Saxon word meaning "defecation" which referred to what came out of the top end of the digestive tract rather than the bottom. Some also call it a "ducking stool" but I prefer "cucking" as being more pertinent, certainly in Annie's case. Either way it is little more than a harness attached to a beam jutting out over the water. The victim is strapped in the harness which is suspended from one end of the beam while three sturdy men counter-balance it on the riverbank and lever her in and out of the water several times, the number depending on the degree of punishment decreed her by the town fathers.

I say "her" because it is mostly women who are so branded, although the occasional man has been known to be similarly dealt with. This time it was Annie's turn to occupy the scold's throne. She didn't do so willingly but had to be forcibly strapped in the chair with her hands and ankles manacled to the sides. After each dunking she would dangle above the river with water pouring off her head and abuse pouring out her mouth. A priest would then ask her to repent her sins and cease her wicked ways. He had to be careful not to stand too close while doing this since, although shackled, Annie was not entirely without ammunition. In addition to spewing obscenities she could also spit with remarkable accuracy. Many an unwary priest has found as he opened his mouth to speak that he was instead choking on one of Annie's well-aimed eructations.

In Annie's case repentance never came. Nor did anyone expect it to. So she was dunked again and again all to little effect. In fact, the more times she was submerged the angrier and more abusive she became as she twisted round and round screaming insults to the jeers and applause of onlookers. But what else can you do with someone like Annie? Only bring her back to the riverside every time her husband had had enough of her abuse.

To be fair Annie had not always been such a virago. She came from a well-respected family of weavers, the youngest of five daughters. A mother herself, it was after the birth of her last child that she started to get a reputation as a shrew. All the usual reasons were given: a husband who had lost interest in her; the change of life; the loss of her looks and figure as the result of a lifetime of domestic drudgery. But Annie was only in her early forties and, if I'm any judge, still an attractive woman once she stopped scowling. Her neighbours had a more fundamental explanation: she was the Devil's child. From her language she certainly seemed conversant with that gentleman invoking his wrath on all who crossed her.

I was always in two minds about these humiliating episodes. On the one hand I sympathized with the victim: it can't be pleasant being strapped in a halter stripped down to just a smock and then dunked repeatedly in the freezing waters of the river in front of your neighbours and friends. On the other hand something had to be done to curb that foul mouth of hers. The town fathers were at their wits' end to know what else to do. And so she was brought back here to the Lark's edge once or twice a year. It had become something of an annual ritual.

The townsfolk, needless to say, loved it. Once word had got out that Annie was to be punished again half the town would take a holiday and come to enjoy the spectacle. It was quite an entertainment with families bringing picnics and making a day of it. True to her name, the sharp-tongued Annie kept up a constant barrage of abuse kicking and biting anybody unwise enough to come within striking distance. Even trussed up she was dangerous. One young man who was trying to secure her ankles wasn't quite quick enough and received a well-aimed kick in the groin. With a cry of "Oof!" the poor lad sank to his knees before rolling onto his side in obvious agony much to Annie's satisfaction and the delight of the crowd who whooped and applauded. You could see a dozen men draw their knees together in vicarious sympathy – myself included. Annie certainly had spirit, you had to give her that.

But now I come to the point of my narrative. First, visualize the scene: a dull overcast September afternoon by the river bank with a group of us monks from the abbey standing hands clasped together in solemn attitudes of prayer. Beside us is a group of officials from the sheriff's office looking bored but resolute and another group of town worthies looking grim and determined. Elsewhere parties of townsfolk are disporting themselves on either bank of the river in various degrees of relaxation – and various stages of inebriation. At the centre of it all suspended above the water was the star attraction: the half-drowned, dripping-wet Annie Spiketongue living up to her name by shouting abuse at all who came into view as she twisted this way and that on the end of a rope ready to be lowered for the umpteenth time that afternoon into the brackish river.

Now into the midst of all this walks a lone figure. He strolls purposefully up to the men holding the rope and says something to them. He also speaks to the aldermen who consult amongst themselves and with the sheriff's men who shrug, nod their heads and walk away. Meanwhile the crowd is becoming restless. What's going on? Has Annie been reprieved? Is the afternoon's sport over before it's even begun? Or is perhaps an even greater punishment being devised this time?

What did happen next amazed us all. First Annie was lowered onto the bank and her fetters removed. Once freed, we half expected her to lash out with her fists and feet which is the usual culmination of these occasions. But she didn't. Instead she waited meekly while the stranger placed a blanket around her shoulders and calmly led her away up the riverbank, through the crowd that parted for them and on up into the town. We all watched this with a mixture of wonder and disappointment at having our afternoon's entertainment abruptly curtailed.

The stranger was, of course, Estienne. I don't know what it was he said to Annie or to the men holding her but somehow he had them all behaving like children. No-one interfered or attempted to stop him, not even the sheriff's sergeant. Confused and bewildered, Annie's husband, Rafe, looked about for explanation. Receiving none he set off after the pair while the rest of us shook our heads in bafflement.

'Well,' muttered Prior Henry. 'What did you make of that?'

A good question. Like everyone else I was unsure as to what had just taken place. Never had there been so dramatic a change in a person in such a short space of time as there was in Annie. In an instant she had gone from foul-mouthed termagant to compliant slave. It was as though Estienne had cast some kind of spell on her - and on the rest of us for we did nothing to interfere.

Eventually, though, I managed to shake myself into action.

'Will you excuse me brother?'

Before Henry could stop me I took off after the little party fearful of what Rafe might do and curious to find out what had occurred. There was only one place they could have gone: to Estienne's hovel by the side of the River Linnet, so that's where I went.

By now the house was at least liveable – that is to say it had all four walls and, miraculously, a roof. Despite this Estienne had taken Annie into the former pig-pen which he appeared to have converted into some kind of chapel.

I found Rafe hovering outside uncertain what to do. Apart from anything else there wasn't room for a third person inside the pen. He looked utterly distraught and confused. He was clearly concerned about his wife but hesitant to do anything about it. Annie appeared to have gone along willingly and with the apparent consent of the town fathers.

'They're in there brother,' he said to me as I approached. 'Together. I saw them go in. But I can't hear nothin'. What's he want with her?'

'Don't do anything hasty,' I cautioned. 'I'm sure it's all perfectly innocent.'

Like Rafe, I too wanted to know what was happening inside the pen but it was impossible to see in. Other than the door there was only one opening: a window with sacking pinned against the weather. There was a gap but it was dark in there and it took a few moments for my eyes to adjust. But then I did see and I gasped.

'What is it?' asked Rafe urgently. 'What's he doing to her?'

I put up my hand for patience and continued to watch.

What I saw was Annie kneeling on the floor before Estienne. He had removed the blanket from around her shoulders and now she was taking off her smock. Underneath she was completely naked except for her undergarments.

I pulled back with a gasp and closed my eyes, not wishing to see.

'What is it? What's happening?' Rafe repeated. 'If he's violating her, by Christ I won't be answerable!'

He hovered a moment more but could wait no longer.

'I'm going in,' he said and started towards the door.

But before he got to it the door opened and Annie appeared framed in the doorway. She was hardly

104

recognizable. Dressed now in a grey smock and wimple with a veil covering her head, she emerged from the sty with her hands together in an attitude of prayer. In place of her usual scowl she wore an expression of serene tranquillity and calm. What's more, the years had dropped off her. She looked like a young girl again.

Seeing her, Rafe hesitated then stepped back, shocked by the change. His wife smiled at – or rather, *through* - him.

Recovering himself, Rafe stepped towards her, but she held up her hand to stop him:

'I am the way, the truth and the life sayeth the Lord. Go now, and give thanks to Almighty God for I who had dwelled in the shadow of ignorance, upon me hath the light shined.'

Rafe was stunned into immobility. Behind Annie Estienne now appeared.

'What have you done to her?' Rafe snarled at him.

'I have relieved her pain.'

'Pain? I'll show you pain.' And Rafe drew back his fist to hit him.

But I caught his fist before it could descend.

'There's no need for that,' I said pulling him away. 'You can see she's unharmed.'

'I don't know what I see. But I've had enough of this.' Rafe turned to his wife. 'Woman, get you home!'

But Annie just smiled benignly at him - which of course angered him all the more:

'Did you hear me, wife?'

'I heard you, brother. But I have another lord now.'

'Brother? I'm not your brother. I'm your husband. And as your husband I am ordering you, come away!'

Yes, well that was never going to work, was it? If Annie didn't obey him before she certainly wouldn't now. She simply smiled again first at Rafe then at me.

'Go in peace my brothers,' she said, then turned and went back inside the pig-pen-cum-chapel leaving Rafe spitting obscenities outside.

They were a matching pair, these two. It's a good thing no-one other than I was about to hear him or he'd be next in line for the cucking-stool.

Chapter Ten
A MIRACULOUS TRANSFORMATION

What had happened? Something momentous, clearly, but what do you say to a woman that can change her from being a foul-mouthed harridan one moment to a saintly milksop the next? Mind you there are precedents: Paul's conversion on the road to Damascus being the obvious one. But Annie? Call me a cynic but I was more than a little sceptical. I'd known Annie Spiketongue for more years than I care to remember. She was no pushover. Once again, Prior Henry had the answer:

'Poor Clares.'

'Poor who?'

'Poor Clares,' he repeated. 'That's what the female equivalent of Estienne's brand of friars call themselves. They were founded shortly after the men's group by an admirer of Giovanni di Bernardone, a young woman called Clare of Assisi - hence the name. Like their male counterparts they are devoted to a life of extreme poverty owning nothing and living by begging.'

'And you think that's what Annie is about to do? Give up her home, her husband and her children to follow Estienne? I don't believe it.'

'Not just her. Many of her neighbours have joined them. She seems to have started something of a craze.' He smiled wryly. 'Clever of Estienne to have chosen Annie Spiketongue as his first convert. If he can persuade someone like her then surely he can attract anyone. As a strategy it seems to be working. Estienne's pig-pen has become something of a sanctuary for malcontented wives.'

'How many wives?' I asked nervously.

'A dozen at least. Their husbands are none too pleased, mind. They've been left holding the baby – literally,' he chuckled.

Is this what Estienne meant when he said his work in Bury wasn't finished? If so he was embarking on a dangerous course indeed. Ministering to the sick and poor was one thing. Coming between a husband and wife was something else. Was this his idea of being less conspicuous?

I have an observation of my own to add here. I've noticed before with religious converts that the female is often more passionate than the male. I well remember a visit Samson and I once made to the convent of Saint George's in Thetford. The nuns there couldn't do enough for him, going down on their knees in the freezing mud before him and practically kissing the hem of his robe. One was even willing to perjure herself for him. And if the man is young and presentable as Estienne was it was even more so.

Needless to say, none of this was lost on Arnold who brought the matter up at the next Chapter meeting:

'You see now my brothers that I was right in my warnings. This new religion is spreading like a cancer. Soon it will have infected the whole town.'

'I think Brother Arnold is exaggerating just a little,' I said. 'It's only one neighbourhood.'

'There you go again, Walter, defending this man. It may be one neighbourhood now but soon it will be everywhere. And then what? These people live by begging. What happens when all are beggars? Who then will be the providers?'

There were a few nods from other monks to that.

'You've already tried to defame Estienne once, Arnold, and failed. Is this another attempt?'

Arnold shook his head sadly. 'What is it going to take to open your eyes, brother? The friar is dividing families while we stand back and do nothing. And there is a darker side to his purpose not yet mentioned.'

'What do you mean?' I asked.

'Women, brother. I see no men among his converts.'

One or two shouts of agreement to that. He seemed to be winning the argument and I was beginning to feel rather isolated. Was no-one else willing to defend the lad? One was: Kevin the novice master.

'I have to agree with Brother Walter,' he said rising to his feet. 'I've met Estienne. He seems a perfectly nice young man to me.'

'We can't trust Brother Kevin's opinion,' said Arnold with barely-concealed contempt. 'With old age the novice master has grown a little, shall we say, *incautious* in his affections – especially when the person in question is young, pretty - and male.'

This brought a few sniggers from some of the brothers and shaking of heads from others.

I'm sorry to say there was a small group of my brother monks, Arnold being prominent among them, who found Kevin's flamboyant mannerisms distasteful. They particularly didn't like the fact that he was in charge of the choir school. They considered his influence with the young novices malign, although there had never been any hint of impropriety. Personally I'd always found Kevin rather refreshing. He was a talented musician and the novices seemed to like him. He added a touch of colour to an otherwise bland assemblage of dour masculinity. But much as I appreciated Kevin's support, on this occasion it was no help. It would only add to their bias against Estienne.

'What do you mean by that?' Kevin asked going red in the face.

'He doesn't mean anything by it,' intervened Prior Henry. 'And we are getting away from the point. Clearly this young man is having an effect on our town. The question is do we think it is a good effect or a bad one? My own opinion, should anybody wish to know it, is that we should not rush to judgement. We may well find later that his effect has been a good one. Only time will tell. But please don't be influenced by me. I will abide by the decision of Chapter.'

He waited. There was a lot of mumbling and grumbling but the consensus seemed to be that it we should give the lad a little longer to prove himself. It was close - closer than the vote had been about the friar's house. In the light of what happened later, of course, it might have been better if he had been asked to go then. But that's with the benefit of hindsight.

Henry concluded the session: 'For now I propose we do nothing and review the matter again at a later date.'

'So long as we don't forget,' said Arnold.

'If I do, Brother Sacristan, I'm sure you won't.'

As we filed out Prior Henry called me over.

'Walter, I'm worried. You see what's happening. Arnold is slowly turning opinion against the lad, and if it's happening here you can be sure it's even more so in the town.' He frowned. 'What is the lad up to? Can't he see? Turning the vill into a recruitment centre for the Poor Clares is a mistake. It will simply make him more enemies.'

'What do you propose?'

'Go and see him. See if you can persuade him to slow down a bit.'

'I've already tried that.'

'Then try again. Also find out how many of his colleagues he expects to join him and when.'

'Won't your contacts in London be better able to tell you that?'

'I'd rather not bother Frère Agnellus unless I have to. He may start to suspect all is not well here. It would be better if it came from you. Two friends having a quiet chat over a cup of wine – what could be more natural? Take a bottle from my private cellar with you. Use some of that famous Walter charm. Or would you rather I sent Arnold?'

On my way back to my laboratorium I found Rafe, Annie Spiketongue's husband, hovering outside. As though I didn't have enough problems.

'Brother, can I have a word?'

'Certainly my son,' I said cheerfully. 'How can I help?'

'It's a bit delicate.'

'Then you'd better come inside.'

Rufus was absent again but this time it was probably to the good. With just the two of us Rafe might be more forthcoming. I sat Rafe down on a stool.

'So my son, what's this about? Your wife presumably.'

Rafe snorted. 'If you can still call her that.'

'What do you mean?' I said, alarmed. 'You're still married aren't you?'

'Yes, we're still married - only God can change that. But since she met that friar she's become a different woman.'

I didn't like the sound of that. 'Different in what way?'

'Well for a start she no longer shares my bed.'

'You mean ...?'

He shook his head. 'No, nothing like that. She still comes home to me at night. But now she sleeps on the floor. If I insist on my rights as her husband she does her duty - but on sufferance. She just lies there stiff as a board. It's very ... off-putting.'

I was beginning to understand. I'd come across complaints like this before. It's usually some physical dysfunction of the husband. Women are fortunate in that way. Being the passive partner they can fake it. Just lie back and think of ... well, anything they liked really. Any problems they do have they tend to take to other women, *Deo gratias* - I'd hate Annie to come to me for marital advice. I wasn't sure I was the right person for Rafe to speak to, either. But I did have one suggestion to make:

'Have you thought of bathing, my son?'

He frowned. 'Bathing brother?'

'Yes, bathing.' I tried to put it as delicately as I could: 'In the intimate confines of the connubial bed

112

it can get a bit ... close. Women are more sensitive about these things than us men. Tell me, when did you last immerse your body in water?'

'April, during the spring floods.'

'There weren't any floods last April.'

He shrugged. 'Last year then.'

Hm, recent enough I supposed. I'd have to try something else:

'How long have you been married?'

'Nine years come Whitsun.'

'And how many children do you have?'

'Eight. Five still living.'

'Well, there you are then,' I smiled.

He looked confused. 'There I am - where?'

Dear God, did I need to spell it out? It seemed I did:

'Perhaps you are too demanding. It's a well-known fact that women don't have the same appetites as us men. If you were to give Annie some space you might find her a little more … responsive.'

He shook his head. 'It's not that either, brother. That's the one thing that's never been a problem. If anything Annie's keener than I am. Some nights she fair wears me out with her demands. And she knows how to kindle me – if you take my meaning.'

Unfortunately I did, and for once I was glad Rufus wasn't there to hear it. He certainly wouldn't have "taken Rafe's meaning" or understood it which would have meant I'd have had to explain. I could imagine the exhaustive question and answer session we'd have until he did take Rafe's meaning – in every intricate and embarrassing detail.

'If not that then some other aspect of married life. Annie does have a reputation for being, shall we say, not the most enthusiastic home-maker.'

'Huh! She doesn't even do that much anymore. When she's not with the friar she's on her knees, praying.'

'Well, that's all to the good isn't it? At least she isn't throwing your dinner at you or kicking your shins. It's surely better she's devoting herself to quiet prayer?'

'No it isn't. I can't stand it. I want my old Annie back - the noisy, argumentative, foul-mouthed she-devil I married. Not this new one.'

'I see,' I nodded. 'What do your neighbours say? They must be glad for the respite at least.'

'That's just it. Some of their wives and daughters are doing the same. In fact the whole street's turning into a commune of bloody nuns – 'scuse my French, brother. Either that or worse,' he added ominously.

'Now, you've no reason to think that, my friend,' I cautioned sternly. 'This is England not France. I'm sure it's all perfectly innocent.'

'Maybe. And then again, maybe not. That's why I've come to you. We want you to have a word with him. You seem to be friendly with the friar. He'll listen to you.'

Somebody else who thinks I've got special influence with the lad.

'I really don't see how I can help, Rafe. If they went of their own volition we have to assume they were moved by the Holy Spirit and as such they will have the support of the Church.'

'That's as may be. But I meant what I said before, brother. If I find the friar's been using my Annie for his own pleasuring there'll be blood spilt. And my neighbours the same. Fair warning. We won't stand idle for long.'

Perhaps Henry was right. Estienne didn't seem to appreciate the strength of feeling that was growing against him. I had a couple of hours spare before vespers so I took one of Henry's best Burgundies from his cellar and went off immediately to Estienne's house.

When I got there it was worse than I thought. There were a few men standing around by the gate and they didn't look as though they were there for a neighbourly mardle. One of them was practising throwing his knife at a tree while another was oiling his bowstring.

'What are you men doing here?' I demanded sternly.

'Just passing the time o' day, brother.'

'It doesn't look that way to me. You should go home, all of you. It will be curfew in a short while and I know for a fact that the sergeant's men have orders to patrol around here tonight. If they catch you passing the time here you may find you'll be passing it in the town gaol.'

It was a bluff. I had absolutely no idea what the sergeant was planning in the neighbourhood or indeed if he was planning anything. But it might make the men think twice.

'Our women-folk is in there,' said the knife-thrower nodding towards Estienne's compound.

'And I'm about to go and see them, so you've no need to worry, have you? There is no harm here. You have my word.'

'Easy for you to say, brother. You don't have a wife or daughters.'

I looked at the man who had spoken. 'Robin, isn't it? You know me - Brother Walter. I tended your

115

youngest last year when she had the whooping cough. You trusted my word then and you can trust it now. I would be the first to intervene if I thought there was any danger. Believe me, you do no good here. Go home. I promise you, all will be well.'

Still they hesitated.

I clapped my hands to shoo them. 'Go - before the sergeant's men arrive and I have to tell them you've no business here.'

Reluctantly they moved off. They were good men, all of them. I could understand their fears about their wives and daughters but I was sure they were groundless. But as the knife-thrower said, it was easy for me. They only had one chance to be wrong.

Inside the compound there were women about but they were all busy working in the garden or on the house. A hive of worthy activity. I was impressed. The house was really starting to look like a home. A woman's touch makes all the difference. Outside Estienne was sewing some sacking.

'To cover the windows,' he explained. 'It will keep out most of the rain and the wind.'

'You've done wonders,' I told him.

'I couldn't have done it without the sisters. They may be weak and fragile women but they can do the work of a dozen men.'

'Yes, these women,' I frowned. 'I take it now their working day is over they will return home to their menfolk?'

He smiled. 'Do I detect a note of anxiety in your voice brother? Is that why you're here?'

'I came to see how you are - and to share a potation with you.' I held up the leather bottle I'd been carrying. 'See? In celebration of your acquittal – and your new home.'

He took the bottle from me and examined it. 'Burgundy.' He nodded appreciatively. 'Expensive. Prior Henry must have something really special he wants you to say to me. Please thank him for his kindness, but I never drink alcohol.' He handed the bottle back.

I could see the famous Walter charm was not working. He was too spry for my deceits. I decided to come straight to the point:

'Estienne, do you remember what I said the last time we spoke?'

'Something about trimming my sail.'

I nodded. 'You seem to have gone about it in an odd way.'

'I'm not a very good sailor,' he grinned. 'I get seasick easily.'

I shook my head. 'I'm not joking, Estienne. That business by the river. In front of the whole town like that. Hardly subtle was it? You couldn't have been more public if you tried.'

'There's no point hiding your light under a bushel, brother. You have to bring it out into the open where it can be seen.'

'Yes, well you certainly did that. But remember what I said before. Buryites are a conservative lot. They'll accept change but if it happens too quickly it can make life difficult. There will always be an element that resists.'

'Is that what Prior Henry sent you to tell me? Thank him for the advice, but any change that happens will be at God's speed, not mine.'

'It's up to you, of course. I only hope you know what you're doing.'

We were interrupted by a familiar sound coming from inside the house. It sounded like Estienne's shawm. But it couldn't be.

'Is that -?' I started to say.

Estienne beamed. 'I told you I'd find someone who could repair it.'

'But that's marvellous! Who is this genius?'

He smiled. 'Come and see.'

I followed him into the house and was shocked when I saw who was there.

'Rufus!'

He was sitting on a stool with the shawm laid across his knees giving it a final buff with a duster.

'I think it's all right now. Maybe not quite as before. I've had to shorten it a little, raised the tone a mite, but I doubt if anyone will notice.'

Estienne took the thing from him. He looked at it carefully then held it out for me to see. 'What do you think, brother?'

I took the instrument and examined it. It had to be the same one, there surely couldn't be another. Where the break had been was now a thin repair line, barely noticeable. It was little short of miraculous. As for the sound – I've no ear but to me it sounded as good as it ever did. If I hadn't known it was broken I would never have guessed.

I turned to Rufus. 'Was that you I heard playing just now?'

'It's not difficult once you get the hang of it, master.'

'It most certainly is difficult. I've tried. And that's not the point. Is this what you've been doing while you were supposed to be out restocking my shelves?'

'Estienne asked me to help.'

'Well he had no business to. And you'd no business to accept.'

'Master?'

'Don't play the innocent, Rufus. You're a monk. You know full well you're not supposed to leave the abbey without permission – without *my* permission.'

'I didn't think you'd mind.'

'Well you thought wrong.'

He lowered his eyes. 'I'm sorry if I have caused offence.'

'We'll discuss it later when I return.' I went to the door and held it open for him.

He took the hint, laid the shawm gently down on the seat and left without another word.

'Please don't be angry with Rufus,' said Estienne once he'd gone. 'It's entirely my fault. He was only trying to help.'

'He's not a child. And for that matter neither are you. Good God, Estienne how could you be so stupid? Can you imagine what Arnold would make of it if he knew he was here? You're playing right into his hands.'

'Oh dear,' he pouted. 'Now you're angry with me too.'

'Do you wonder? You disregard all the norms of convention and you encourage others to do the same. Arnold is right. Your presence in Bury is disruptive.'

'You want me to leave?'

I frowned. 'No I don't want you to leave. I'm glad you're here and I'm glad you got your shawm repaired. But please, for pity sake, try to be a little more discreet in future.'

He smiled. 'Trim my sail?'

'Exactly. And while we're in the subject what did you say to Annie that made her change so suddenly and so publicly? Her husband would dearly like to know.'

'Nothing much. I merely pointed out that if she followed me she would no longer have to live the life of a drudge.'

'Really? Well I'd like a word with her if that's possible.'

He shrugged. 'Of course.'

Damn the boy! It was as though he was deliberately setting out to stir up trouble. At this rate Arnold won't have to make the case against him, he'll do it all by himself.

I found Annie in the garden - another of Estienne's conquests. Or was she? I watched her for a minute without her being aware I was there. She was struggling with a difficult weed and muttering what sounded like curses. But that couldn't be, could it? Not the new, reformed Annie.

'Good day to you Annie,' I said in a clear voice.

'What?' she started. 'Oh it's you brother.' Her frown instantly evaporated and she adopted an expression of ecstatic sublimity. 'How good to see you.'

'You too, my child. You are well?'

'Very.'

'Happy in your new life?'

'Sublimely,' she fluttered her eyelids at me. 'God's work is good doing.'

'Indeed. I must tell Rate. He'll be pleased to hear you're content.'

At the mention of her husband's name her brow instantly furrowed with concern. 'Have you been to see him?'

'As a matter of fact he came to see me.'

'How is he? Is he eating properly? He'll be worried about me of course. Please tell him there is no need.'

'No need at all – I can see that. He'll be relieved. It'll make him feel less guilty.'

'Tell him he has nothing to feel guilty about,' she smiled.

'Oh, but he does.'

'About what?'

'About taking a new wife of course. He was in two minds, but now that I've seen you I will be able to put his mind at rest.'

Her smile momentarily faltered. Aha! A spark of the old Annie perhaps?

'You mean you hadn't heard?' I asked innocently.

'Not a word.'

'Well, you can't blame him, can you? A man has needs, and Rafe is no monk. All perfectly correct and above board in case you were wondering – and most importantly approved by Holy Mother Church.'

'But surely you're mistaken, brother. A husband cannot take a new wife while his old one still lives. Those whom God hath joined together let no man - or woman - put asunder.'

'No-one's putting anything asunder, Annie. You've taken the veil. In the eyes of the Church you're now married to Christ – which leaves Rafe free to marry again also.'

'But this is not a proper convent. And I'm not a proper nun.'

'It is a religious community recognized as such by none other than the pope himself. As far as the Church is concerned Rafe can marry whomsoever he pleases. Oh, and don't worry about the children, by the way. His new wife has said she'll take good care of them.'

'He has someone in mind? Who?'

'Her name's Millicent. You probably know her. The daughter of one of your neighbours - Thomas the furrier.'

Annie's eyes flashed. 'But she's scarcely fifteen. My eldest is older than her.'

'I know. Lucky old Rafe, heh?' I winked.

She set her jaw again and forced another fixed smile. 'He must do as he sees fit.'

'I'll tell him you said so. Well, I can see you've lots to do. Plenty of weeds to pull up.' I started to leave.

'Will you bless me before you go, brother?'

'Of course, my child. I'm always happy to bless God's creatures. Even the most wayward.'

She knelt before me and I made the sign of the Cross over her head.

'May the Lord enfold you in his tender and everlasting love, and guide you back to the true path - whenever you stray. Amen.'

'A-men,' she echoed.

Chapter Eleven
MY OWN SWEET ROSABEL

I should really have gone straight back to the abbey and reprimanded Rufus for his negligence more fully, but I didn't have the heart. In truth I was feeling a bit foolish over my outburst. I'm not that much of a stickler for rules. As long as he came back in time to sing the offices I didn't really mind him leaving the abbey grounds. I was more irritated by the fact that Estienne seemed to have forged a firmer bond with the lad than I'd been able to do. He certainly seemed to understand him better. Who would have guessed Rufus possessed such skills with a shawm? The sin of envy I suppose. Since I was in the area and still in possession of an as yet unopened bottle of Burgundy's finest, I decided instead to pay a visit to my old friend Onethumb, something that's always good for the soul - my soul at any rate.

For those who have not met Onethumb before I'll briefly explain who he is and how I came to know him. I first met Onethumb a quarter century ago when he was still a child running around the streets of Bury with one of the packs of other orphaned street urchins. There were many such children in

Bury then as, alas, there still are today. They have no home, no family other than each other and live by thievery or other trickery they practise on unwary members of the public. Naturally I deplore such criminality and do my best to dissuade them from it, but since they would probably starve if they didn't do it I find it hard to condemn them outright. They are all tragically young. Most never make it to their fifteenth year of life. If they haven't already been murdered by then or died of some dreadful disease or accident they will probably end up at the end of a rope.

Onethumb started out worse off than most. Indeed, it's astonishing he'd lived as long as he had when I met him. He'd been abandoned as a baby probably because of a birth defect that his mother, whoever she was, would undoubtedly have regarded as a curse from God. You see, Onethumb was born with a mizzened right hand that was little more than a stump with four pea-sized fingers and a normal thumb – hence his name. And if that wasn't enough he is also mute and has to communicate with a sign-language of his own invention.

Despite these handicaps he survived better than many of his fully-appendaged confrères, and mostly by his wits. He was a bright boy, plucky and deserved a chance to live, so in due course I got him work as assistant in my brother Joseph's apothecary shop where he's been ever since. I was also pleased to be able to confound those who said he was a child of the Devil and would amount to nothing. And he more than fulfilled my confidence in him. Joseph hardly knows how he coped before him. Later on he married Rosabel, the fiery daughter of a local tanner, and started a family. They now have two children:

Hal who must be about twelve by now, and Little Rosa a couple of years younger.

Over the years our relationship has had its ups and downs but we have managed to remain firm friends. Indeed, I regard his family as my own and still feel protective towards Onethumb. Not that he needs my help anymore. I sometimes forget he's no longer a child but a grown man quite capable of looking after himself and his family. He was seated in front of the fire when I knocked at his door which is just a few streets away from Estienne's hovel.

'God bless all in this house,' I intoned making the sign of the cross.

Onethumb immediately jumped up beaming all over his cheeky face and greeted me like a long-lost friend. Not that we're strangers. I see him all the time in the course of my abbey duties since he delivers my herbal supplies from Joseph's shop, but visits to his home are a rarity. And that is something I regret for while there are few things about the world beyond the cloister that I miss, having a family and children of my own is one of them. Playing with the children of one's friends is the next best thing – as long as I can leave them behind when I return to the abbey. And beautiful children they are too neither of them showing any signs of their father's impairments thus further confounding the gain-sayers.

As soon as they saw me the children jumped all over me, Hal on my back with his arm around my neck trying to pull me over and Little Rosa tugging at my robe. Choking and struggling I pretended to be overwhelmed and went down first onto my knees and then onto my back with the children pummelling away at me and screaming. And not really pretending either. Children are utterly merciless when it comes to winning. I was doing my best to fight them off but somehow laughter got in the way. This went on for several minutes until, finally exhausted, I lay on my back while the two of them jumped up and down on my chest. When at last they'd had enough of destroying me they found my vademecum, my chart of diseases that I always carry on my belt, and started playing bat-a-ball with that instead. Onethumb did nothing to stop them – as if he could anyway.

'I'm sorry, old friend,' I panted as I struggled to my feet. 'I should have warned you I was coming. It was a spur of the moment decision. Happened to be in the neighbourhood. I hope you don't mind.'

Onethumb shook his head and signed that I was always welcome. I then greeted Rosabel's mother and father who were seated by the fire. It was because of Rosabel's father that the family lived in this neighbourhood. He used to be a tanner until his lungs gave out. Tanning is probably the smelliest job a man can have other than gong-scourer and as such has to be located well away from the town. Retired now, he and his wife still live in the area - in the house right next door in fact.

'How are you Brother Walter?' asked the old woman.

'I'm very well, thank you mother – I think,' I said rubbing my painful shoulder. 'And you are in good health?'

'The usual aches and pains of old age, but otherwise we are both well.'

'As a matter of fact -' began her husband who started patting his chest.

'No Wilf,' interrupted his wife. 'Brother Walter doesn't want bothering with your old lungs. Sit you

126

down, brother,' she said indicating a stool next to the table. 'Tell us all your news.'

I was about to when I heard a noise from behind:

'What do you want?'

I turned to see Onethumb's wife, Rosabel, framed in the doorway and my stomach immediately lurched.

Ah, Rosabel. Just the mention of her name brings a smile to my face. I confess I have long had a yen for this lady. Such beauty – and such spirit! *Bella Rosa*, meaning beautiful rose, of course. Aptly named with sharp barbs to match. But that is part of the attraction. The best dishes are a mixture of sweetness and spice, are they not? I have often thought, in my weaker moments, that if she were not married to my dearest friend and I were a younger man and free… But I have to remember I am a monk avowed to a life of chastity.

But then so was Abelard when he met his Heloise and look what happened to them.

In truth she is the real reason I rarely pay a visit for I believe a man should go where he isn't tempted – and not go where he is. And sometimes, with Rosabel, I am sorely tempted.

I contrived to look hurt by her words. 'Can a man not visit his most cherished friends without having an ulterior motive?'

'Anybody else, yes. You, no.'

'Now now, Rosa,' frowned her father. 'Brother Walter has honoured us with a visit. You should show him the courtesy he deserves.'

'I thought that's what I was doing.'

'Ach, Rosabel!' tutted the old man shaking his head.

You see what I mean? Painful barbs indeed, but delicious pain. And not entirely unexpected or undeserved if I'm honest for Rosabel and I have a history, too. She once helped me out of a tricky situation and nearly got herself killed in the process. She was convinced I'd tricked her then and has never really trusted me since – quite unjustifiably, I might add.

'Look what the good brother has brought,' said her mother. She held up the bottle of Burgundy for Rosabel to see.

'It's a present,' I beamed.

Her eyes narrowed even more. 'Why? You've never brought presents before.'

'I have,' I protested. 'I've brought you lots of presents.'

'Name one.'

I thought for a moment.

'In any case, this one is special - specially for you, dearest Rosabel.' I pushed the bottle towards her.

'It's a good one,' said her father. 'Feel the quality of the leather.'

Rosabel picked up the bottle and turned it over in her hands before grunting and handing it back.

'It's from the prior's cellar,' I continued. 'A special reserve. I thought it would go well with one of your delicious scones.'

She smiled sweetly. 'What a shame I haven't any. The batch I made this week have already been eaten by the children.'

'Not all,' said her mother. 'There are one or two in my larder.'

'It would be a pity to waste a good wine,' I said.

'Go and fetch the scones, girl,' said her father. 'Don't embarrass us any more than you already have.'

128

Rosabel sighed heavily, threw down her pinafore and went off to her mother's house glaring at her as she passed.

As soon as she was out of the room I spoke quickly and quietly to the others. 'Actually I do have an ulterior motive for coming. We only have a moment so I'll make this brief: I want to recruit Rosabel for a mission.'

Onethumb's arms instantly started cartwheeling and Rosabel's parents groaned.

I contrived to look surprised. 'What's the problem?'

What's the problem? signed Onethumb. *Have you forgotten last time?*

I flapped a dismissive hand. 'Oh, that was years ago. This is different. Something only she can do.'

That's what you said last time.

'What is it you want her to do?' asked he father.

'Your new neighbour.'

'The preacher-man?'

I nodded. 'Frère Estienne. He's been recruiting women for his sister order, the Poor Clares, from among the wives of some of your neighbours.'

'Yes, I know,' said the old man. 'Some of them are not happy. There are rumours of dark goings-on.'

'You shouldn't listen to rumour. But that's why I want Rosabel. I want her to confirm that's all it is.'

'Or not,' said Rosabel's mother.

'What exactly do you want her to do?' asked her husband.

'Nothing very much,' I said airily. 'Just become one of the Poor Clares.'

At this Onethumb erupted. I shan't interpret his signing. I couldn't if I wanted to to. He was going too fast for me to keep up. But the gist of it was that he wasn't happy.

'I just need someone to infiltrate Estienne's house, that's all.'

That's all? signed Onethumb and went into another flap.

'That's all. Dispel any of these malicious rumours. Nothing to it really,' I said reasonably. 'But it needs someone with a bit of spirit capable of looking after herself should that become necessary – not that it will, of course,' I added quickly.

'And you think that's Rosa?' frowned her mother.

'Rosabel?' I snorted. 'I should say so. She'd be ideally suited. Someone who'll take no nonsense from anybody. Someone wilful with a vicious tongue in her head. Someone headstrong and obstinate. In short, a bit of a shrew… Why are you all looking at me like that?'

A noise behind made me spin round. Rosabel was standing a few feet behind me holding a tray of scones and tapping a toe on the flag.

'Bad-tempered is it? Shrew am I? I'll show you what a shrew does. This!' She threw the tray of scones over me. 'And this!' She kicked the stool from under me sending me sprawling on the floor. 'And this!' She poured the remainder of my wine over my head. And then she started pummelling my painful shoulder.

Thinking it was another game, the children piled in and started jumping on me all over again. For a few minutes all was pandemonium with Onethumb trying and failing to separate us. But at least the children provided a shield against Rosabel's more potent blows. She stood astride me, a lock of her hair floating adrift from her coif and glaring down at me with her fists clenched.

'Coming here with another of your mad schemes! If you think I'm falling for that again you're crazy. Last time you nearly got me killed.'

'All right, all right,' I laughed rubbing my painful shoulder. 'It was only an idea. To be honest I only just thought of it when I saw you. I see now it was a mistake. You're quite the wrong person. I'll ask Annie Spiketongue instead. She's much more suitable.'

Rosabel stopped. 'Annie Spiketongue? What's she to do with this?'

'She's one of Frère Estienne's new recruits. He's made a lamb of her. I spoke to her not half an hour since. She'd do it in a flash I'm sure.'

I knew Annie and Rosabel had been rivals in the past. There'd even been talk of her setting her cap at Onethumb at one time – mostly to spite Rosabel.

'Annie Spiketongue, a lamb? More suitable than me?' Rosabel pushed the stray curl of hair back under her coif. 'In a duck's arse.'

Chapter Twelve
YE OF LITTLE FAITH

I knew she'd do it. Rosabel never could resist a challenge. It was just a matter of finding the right words. And after all, what actually was I asking her to do? Merely to join most of her women neighbours for a short while to see what really was going on in Estienne's compound. Nothing difficult or dangerous in that. Her testimony might benefit all for Rosabel was well-known in those parts. If she said nothing inappropriate was going on their husbands would have to believe her. (They wouldn't dare do otherwise).

Mind you, it didn't come without cost. I smelt like an old wine-soak and had to go to the lavatorium in the cloister to rinse away the remnants of Henry's Burgundy that Rosabel had tipped over my head. That done, it was time to have that word with Rufus:

'What were you doing at Frère Estienne's house?' I asked him in my sternest voice.

'Repairing his shawm, master. I thought you saw, master.'

'Yes I did see – and don't be clever, you know what I meant. You shouldn't have been there. I am responsible for you. Leaving the abbey without telling me - anything could have happened to you.'

He was looking confused. 'But you wanted me to follow Brother Arnold, master.'

'That was different.'

'How, master?'

'It just was. And don't change the subject. We were talking about Frère Estienne. Since when did you become an expert on shawms?'

'I think I learned as a child, master.'

'You *think?* Don't you know?'

'I can't remember, master.'

'Oh really Rufus, how can you not remember something like that?'

He just shrugged.

I sighed. In all conscience I couldn't rebuke him further. He had done an excellent job on the shawm however he came to know about it. And I didn't think Rufus would deliberately lie. I didn't think he was capable. If he said he couldn't remember I would have to take his word for it. And he was right, I did ask him to follow Arnold so I suppose that was partly my fault.

'Look, in future just ask when you wish to leave the abbey precinct – all right?'

'Yes, master.'

I frowned. 'And for heaven's sake stop calling me "master" all the time. It's very irritating.'

'You told me to, master.'

'Not all the time.'

'When should I call you master, master?'

I was going to explain that the term was a courtesy; that it should be used sparingly to demonstrate the proper relationship between master and pupil. But in the end I just shook my head.

'I tell you what, forget I said anything about it.'

And do you know what? I think he did just that.

For the moment there wasn't much more to be done until I heard from Rosabel. Just as Rafe had predicted the husbands were growing impatient. They wanted their wives back and I was fearful that some might be tempted to take matters into their own hands. Those two men I saw outside the compound wouldn't be the only ones. They even sent a delegation to Prior Hugh to complain. But what could he do? Estienne wasn't a member of his flock. He had no authority over him.

Poor Hugh. He disliked any suggestion of bad feeling between the town and the abbey. The abbey had had the lordship of Bury since its very beginning but there were signs of a growing resentment of our role and a desire to have more freedoms as other towns in the region like Norwich and Ipswich were winning – another change of which Arnold would doubtless disapprove. Situations like this could easily spark trouble between the abbey and town - it wouldn't be the first time if it did. Estienne wasn't a monk but he was more clerical than not and in people's minds he represented the abbey even if he didn't. Henry was pinning his hopes on the shrine-opening ceremony to remind people of the abbey's role as the town's protector – it's *alma mater*. He asked me again how things were progressing. I assured him all would be ready in time for the Edmund's feast-day on the 20th November. He nodded and went away muttering to himself.

Meanwhile I decided to keep a discreet eye on Estienne. He was easy enough to track. The haunting tones of his shawm, now fully restored by Rufus, could be heard all over the town. As ever they were the prelude to one of his orations. More often than not I found him in his favourite *théâtre de performance*: the marketplace.

His audience this day was made up largely of street children who were sitting quietly cross-legged on the ground listening to his preaching. This in itself was a novelty. These kids spend nearly all their time trying to avoid the eye of the market reeve who was for ever trying to prevent them from pestering market traders and their customers. As such they are never still for very long.

The morning's session was coming to an end as I arrived and the Poor Clares were helping with the collection boxes. Whilst this was going on I decided to quiz the children. I was impressed at how docile they all were. Some were even helping the women with their collecting - under the ever-watchful eye of the market reeve. Was this another Pauline conversion? Somehow I didn't think so.

'Well now, aren't you Frère Estienne's good little helpers!' I smiled. 'Have you finally decided to give up your nefarious pursuits and become honest citizens?'

'Oh yes, brother,' said a gangly youth of about fourteen summers. 'Brother Estienne has shown us the error of our ways. For sure – hasn't he?' He nudged the younger boy next to him.

'That's right,' said the younger lad. 'We've given up our, erm ...'

'Nefarious pursuits,' I prompted.

'Yeah, them.'

'I'm glad to hear it. So I can take it from now on the good folk of Bury will be able to go about their business without having to worry about their purses disappearing from their belts or their goods being snatched from their baskets?'

'We don't do nothing like that, brother,' said the first youth with a look of innocence on his face an angel would have wept over.

'Besides, we en't been paid yet,' said his younger friend who yelped as the older one jabbed an elbow in his ribs.

'I like the flute,' whispered one wide-eyed little girl.

'Do you cherub?' I smiled down at her. 'It is an unusual sound isn't it?'

She nodded slowly and stuck a filthy thumb in her mouth.

Now the Clares came over and started distributing some of the coins they had collected to the children. Once they had their prize they ran off with it.

'Good to see the Holy Spirit at work among the young,' I said pointedly to the market reeve and grinned.

A grizzled old warhorse with side-whiskers and bowed legs, the reeve gave me a knowing look and wandered off, beating his wand of office against his thigh.

I'd already noticed Rosabel among the Poor Clares but decided for the moment not to speak to her – I didn't want to raise suspicions. She certainly looked the part dressed like all the other Clares in grey smock and wimple. I was impressed. She seemed to have taken to her role with enthusiasm. If I didn't know better I'd swear she was the genuine article.

Seeing me, Estienne came striding over beaming all over his face. He looked much happier than when I last saw him.

'Brother Walter! This is a pleasant surprise.'

'I heard your playing and thought I'd come and see how you were getting along. We parted under something of a cloud last time. I wanted you to know there are no hard feelings.'

'Certainly none from me, brother. But thank you for taking the trouble.'

'The shawm sounds as good as new.'

'It is. Rufus did an excellent job. I can't tell you how relieved I am. I was lost without it.'

I couldn't help noticing a large bruise on the side of Estienne's head.

'That looks painful.'

His hand went up to his face. 'I … walked into a tree.'

'A tree married to one of your nuns?' I asked wryly.

He just smiled.

By now the women had finished distributing their alms and were waiting patiently for Estienne's next orders, Rosabel included. I wondered how much she had managed to glean of the situation in the Estienne camp and was keen to find out.

'Erm, I know this woman,' I said to Estienne. 'She's married to friend of mine.'

'*Was* married,' corrected Estienne. 'Sister Rosabel is Christ's bride now.'

'What? Oh – quite,' I agreed. 'If you wish I'd be happy to see her home – her *former* home. I'm going that way in any case.'

'That would be very kind.' Estienne caught Rosabel's eye and summoned her over.

'You wished to speak with me, brother?' she asked smiling angelically.

137

Oh, wonderfully done Rosabel! Even more convincing than Annie Spiketongue.

'Brother Walter has offered to escort you home, sister. I have other business to attend to so it might be an idea if you were to take the day's takings with you. The brother will make sure it arrives safely, I'm sure.'

'Yes of course, I'll be happy to,' I nodded vehemently.

Couldn't be better. It would give me the perfect excuse to speak with Rosabel.

'Then I'll bid good day to you, brother.'

'And to you, Frère Estienne.'

He led the remaining Clares away.

'Right,' I said to Rosabel once he was gone. 'Let's get you home. We've much to discuss.'

I set off at a pace in the direction of the Linnet but as I did so I noticed Rosabel stayed a few steps behind me.

'Come along *Sister* Rosabel,' I chuckled. 'Keep up.'

But she remained resolutely behind me.

I went back to her. 'Very good, Rosa,' I said beneath my breath. 'But there's no need to continue the pretence now. Estienne is well out of earshot.'

But Rosabel shook her head and looked at me seriously. 'I know my place, brother.'

'Yes, all right, you can drop the sisterly act.'

But there was no budging her. She would not join me but insisted on walking behind me. The look on her face was serene but determined.

'Very well. Keep up the charade if you must. But only until we get you home.'

We set off again, me in front and Rosabel following. People looked as we passed. I felt a complete idiot weaving our way through the narrow alleys with Rosabel maintaining exactly five paces behind. Each time I stopped she stopped. It was becoming annoying.

It was then that it happened. A figure suddenly leapt out from the shadows and made a grab for the box of takings that Rosabel was still holding. It was the same gangly youth I'd been speaking to earlier. I thought it was too good to be true. He must have been following us and waiting his chance.

'Here! What do you think you're doing?' I yelled stepping smartly back to intercept him. But Rosabel put up her hand to stop me.

'No, brother. It's only money and his need is greater than ours. Here.' She held the money-box out for him. 'Take it.'

I was aghast. 'What? Rosa you can't!' and I grabbed the box. Now all three of us had hold of it tugging in three different directions.

'No brother. If it's God's will that he should have it, then he should have it,' she insisted.

'See?' said the youth. 'The sister says it's mine.'

Dear Lord, could it be true? Rosabel of all people? Well if it could happen to Annie Spiketongue I supposed it could happen to anyone. Heaven alone knew how I was going to explain it to Onethumb, though. But I suppose she was right about the takings. It was only money. And it had been collected specifically for people like this boy, so in a sense it already belonged to him. Reluctantly I let go the box and stepped away as Rosabel pushed it into his hands.

The boy could hardly believe his luck. He'd obviously been expecting a fight. But instead he gave me a smug smile of satisfaction and turned to go with his prize.

He managed two paces before a foot shot out and sent him sprawling in the dirt. A moment later Rosabel was on top of him.

'Steal from me would you, you little bugger?' she snarled. 'I'll teach you to try to steal from me!'

She grabbed hold of his hair and started banging his head on the ground. Then she twisted his arm round his back.

'Ai-ee-yah!' He screamed - more in astonishment than in pain I should think.

Alarmed, I looked about to see if Estienne or the other nuns had seen her but fortunately they were nowhere in sight. The lad continued to squeal like a stuck pig as Rosabel put a knee into his back and twisted an ear. In spite of myself I couldn't help but sympathize with the lad. I remembered being in the self-same position just few days earlier and almost felt sorry for him. But he was much more agile than I was. Somehow he managed to get to his feet though Rosabel kept hold of his shirt and continued screaming abuse at him. But they were rags and easily ripped in her hand allowing him to wriggle out of them.

Suddenly freed of her grasp he saw his chance and didn't hesitate. Without waiting for more he raced off naked down the street leaving the money-box, his clothes and his dignity lying in the dirt behind him. Rosabel would have gone after him and no doubt would have carried on across town till she caught him if I hadn't grabbed her and enveloped her tightly in my arms.

'Get off me!' she said slapping me. 'You're letting the little sod get away!'

Once I thought the boy was far enough away I released her and then burst out laughing:

'I knew it! I *knew* it!' I chortled.

'Huh!' she sneered adjusting her smock. 'Easy to say now. But I had you fooled for a while there, didn't I?'

What a woman! She was magnificent! I fell in love with her all over again.

'Rosa,' I said softly once we'd both regained our breath. 'Since we are … technically … still brother and sister, would you …?'

'What?'

'Give me a kiss. Just to show there are no hard feelings? For the other night, I mean.'

At first she screwed up her face, but then softened it and smiled at me sweetly. 'Of course I will. Just a sisterly-brotherly kiss, mind. And don't tell Onethumb.'

'Oh, I won't say a word. I promise.'

'Come here then.' She held out her arms.

She drew me closer. I fully admit my heart was pounding in my chest as I felt her hot breath on my face. She put her cheek tenderly against mine – and bit my ear, *hard*.

'Aow!' I yelped pulling away. 'What did you do that for?'

'Teach you a lesson – brother.'

'What lesson?' I said trying to scotch the flow of blood.

'If you play with fire, expect to get burnt.'

Chapter Thirteen
THAT BURNING FEELING

'As far as I can tell,' said Rosabel once we were back at her home, 'those women are there because they want to be.'

'But not you?'

'I … might be tempted,' she said giving Onethumb a dismissive look. 'Frère Estienne makes fewer demands on a woman than any husband.'

Poor Onethumb. He was looking utterly despondent. He never liked the idea of Rosabel becoming my spy, but the more he protested the more she'd been determined to go. Like every other husband in the neighbourhood he was highly suspicious of Estienne's motives. Needless to say Rosabel said nothing to dispel his fears. She was enjoying his discomfort.

'But you wouldn't do that, would you?' I said. 'Leave your husband and your children to follow him?'

Rosabel thought about it for a moment then shook her head. 'Nah.'

'Because you recognize what a wonderful family you have here,' I offered nodding encouragingly to Onethumb.

She shook her head. 'Because I hate the sound of flutes.'

My eyes rolled to heaven. How many more times did I have to say it? 'It's not a flute. It's a shawm.'

'Whatever it is, it's just noise to me.'

I gasped. 'How can you say that? It's a beautiful sound! Have you no ear?'

'No – and neither do you anymore,' she smirked.

My hand automatically shot to my earlobe. I was still feeling embarrassed by what had happened earlier. It's not something I'd ever done before – at least, since taking the cowl. I really don't know why I did then. A sort of irresistible urge came over me. That's the effect women have on men and why we monks are right to exclude them from our lives. I paid the penalty of my indiscretion – a sore earlobe. I'd managed to scotch the flow of blood but it was still encrusted. It's not a wound that can be hidden very easily, unfortunately. I just hoped nobody saw how I got it and it gets back to Onethumb. He was already looking at it suspiciously but so far hadn't asked for an explanation. His youngest child, however, was not so reticent:

'What happened to your ear? It looks like someone bit it,' said Little Rosa.

'You shouldn't ask questions like that,' chided her brother. 'It's rude.'

'That's all right,' I laughed jollily. 'I don't mind. It's called hubris, cherub. Like Icarus, I flew too close to the sun and got my fingers burnt.' I gave her mother a quick glance.

'Oh.' Little Rosa nodded and went off to play with a rag doll.

Her mother tore off her wimple and started scratching her head luxuriantly. 'Ooh, I'm glad to be out of that. I don't know how nuns put up with them.'

'What about the other women?' I asked. 'Did they give any reason for their conversion?'

'Love,' said Rosabel.

'Of Estienne's message?'

'Of him. They're all besotted with the dear frère. The thing is they don't even realise it. Pathetic really. They'd do anything for him, he only has to ask.'

'Do you think he would? Take advantage of his position, I mean.'

Rosabel frowned. 'Funny enough, no. I think he's here for the reasons he says: to help the sick and the poor. Mind you, he's not lacking for opportunity. It's that bloody flute.'

'Shawm!' I said rolling my eyes.

'You know when you flew in the sun,' said Little Rosa holding her rag doll top of her head. 'Is that how you got your bald spot?'

'Don't be silly, Rosa,' said her brother. 'That's called a tonsure. All monks have them – isn't that right, brother?'

'I don't want to fly in the sun,' said Little Rosa.

'Why not, cherub?' I smiled.

"Cos I'll look old and shrivelled like you.'

I heard nothing more from Estienne and his Poor Clares for several weeks, my time being taken up with work in my laboratorium and keeping a watch on the progress of the renovation work in the abbey church. It seemed to be taking for ever. But then I was in my laboratorium late one afternoon when I heard the rumbling of a cart coming rapidly in through the abbey gate followed by an urgent banging on my door. I opened it to see Onethumb looking frantic. Before I could open my mouth he'd dragged me outside. To my horror laid out on the

144

cart was Rosabel. She looked dead. Her face was black and her clothes were smoking. Her father was there too, exhausted from running and looking as anxious as his son-in-law.

'What's happened?' I asked him.

'A fire,' panted the old man. 'In the goose hut.'

I put my ear to Rosabel's lips but heard nothing. Was she even breathing?

My initial reaction was to take her inside the laboratorium but changed my mind.

'Quickly! Let's get her to the infirmary.'

Together the three of us trundled the cart across the great court. Onethumb and I lifted her off just as Thomas, the infirmarer, came out and immediately took over. I was too frantic to think straight.

'Lay her on the table,' he ordered.

We did so and he then put his ear to her lips as I had done.

'Well?' I asked.

'She's alive.'

'*Deo gratias*,' I said crossing myself.

He pinched her ear and rubbed his knuckles hard along her breastbone. No response. So he pinched her again, harder and this time. Rosabel gasped and sat up. She couldn't speak for coughing. She started to try to get off the table but Thomas gently pushed her back down again.

'She'll be all right. She just needs to breathe deeply, clear her lungs. I'll get her some water.' He went off to the lobby.

I desperately wanted to hold her in my arms and comfort her, but of course that was out of the question.

'How did this happen?' I asked her father.

145

He shook his head. 'She was cleaning out Griselda
- '

'Who?'

Our prize goose, signed Onethumb impatiently.

'Me and Bella was in the house when Griselda
starts to honk,' said the older man. 'At first I ignored
it – Griselda's always honking about something. But
it went on and on. Then Bella said she could smell
smoke, so we went outside. It was then we saw the
goose hut was on fire but there was no sign of Rosa.
So I tried the door handle but it was too hot to touch
and I couldn't get it open. I sent Bella off to fetch
Onethumb from the shop while I got a pitchfork and
smashed down the door. I found Rosa lying on the
floor. We managed to get her out before the hut
collapsed. There's not much left of it.'

Bugger the goose hut, signed Onethumb. *What
about my wife?*

By now Rosabel was trying to speak but couldn't
stop coughing long enough to make any sense.

'How did the fire start?' I demanded.

No-one seemed to know.

Thomas was soon back with the water. He poured
some into a cup and held it to Rosabel's lips.

'Just take small sips at first,' he cautioned.

But Rosabel snatched the cup from him and
drained it which made her cough all the more. 'Fat
lot … *cough* … of use … *cough* … you lot are,' she
managed to gasp out.

'She's all right,' smiled Thomas. 'No great harm
done. You managed to get her out in time. She'll
have a sore throat for a few days, and a terrific
headache afterwards. But apart from that she should
be fine.'

This is all your fault, signed Onethumb suddenly turning on me. *If you hadn't made her go to the preacher.*

'Oh … *cough* … shut up … *cough* ... Onethumb!' Rosabel managed to choke out.

Her father drew me to one side:

'There's something else you should know, brother,' he said to me quietly. 'The door handle.'

'You said it was too hot to open.'

'It wouldn't have made any difference if it wasn't. There was no way she could have opened it from the inside.'

'Why not?'

He turned from the others and showed me something hidden inside his shirt. It was a small piece of stick.

'Lodged in the handle.'

'Then that means …?'

He nodded. 'It was deliberate.'

The following day Chapter was abuzz with rumour about the fire. Naturally Arnold was quick to identify the culprit:

'It was the preacher,' he said.

A groan went up from parts of the room.

'Isn't this becoming a little tiresome?' I asked wearily. 'Next you'll be blaming Estienne for the Flood.'

'Fires start accidentally all the time,' said Prior Henry. 'That's why we have curfews.'

'This one was deliberate,' Arnold insisted.

'Why would Frère Estienne wish to harm a tanner's daughter?' asked Henry.

'Because he rumbled that she was Walter's fake nun, that's why.'

'And how would you know about that, Arnold?' I asked him. 'Another one of your spies?'

Arnold shook his head dispassionately. 'Yours this time it seems, Walter. Admit it. You don't trust him any more than I do.'

I didn't know what to think. The previous day when we'd gotten Rosabel home her parents had put her to bed while Onethumb and I went to inspect the burnt-out goose hut. The remains of the door lay amongst the debris but the handle was intact. I tried it. There was no way the door could have been accidentally locked from the inside. It had to have been deliberately secured the way Rosabel's father said with a piece of kindling. Onethumb had no doubts about who had done it and wanted to go straight round to Estienne and have it out with him, but I'd managed to dissuade him. I just couldn't believe Estienne would do such a thing. Onethumb then accused me of preferring Estienne to Rosabel, which was ridiculous. He'd stomped off angrily before I could say any more.

Now Kevin, Estienne's only other supporter, stood up:

'There's no proof the boy was responsible. It's as the prior says, fires can occur anywhere at any time. It's simply your prejudice against this young man.'

Arnold snorted. 'We can't take anything Brother Novice Master has to say. As far as he's concerned the friar can do no wrong. And we all know why, don't we?'

A few nods and sniggers at that.

Kevin blushed crimson. He turned to Henry: 'Brother Prior, do I have to suffer these continual insinuations?'

'No you don't,' said Henry. 'Arnold, apologise to Kevin please.'

Arnold sat down and folded his arms across his chest.

'Brother Sacristan, you will apologise to Brother Kevin now or remove yourself from Chapter.'

Still Arnold refused. We waited. The atmosphere was growing very uncomfortable. Finally it was Kevin who left in floods of tears – much to my disappointment. Henry's too, it seemed. He was plainly furious with Arnold. We all continued to sit in silence. At last Arnold stood up and, with a good deal of bad grace, sauntered out.

At least with Arnold gone the tension eased somewhat. But it was only a brief respite.

For several minutes I'd been aware of a curious snuffling sound at the back of the chapterhouse but with all the commotion at the front I hadn't taken much notice. Suddenly from the back of the chapterhouse there came a cry and a dozen brothers jumped to their feet. At first I couldn't make out what the fuss was about but then I saw: a big black rat was snuffling in the corner. And it wasn't on its own. With growing horror I saw there many more crawling around in the corner.

By now something like suppressed panic was breaking out. Some of the younger brothers started to push towards the front of the chapterhouse while others tried to kick the rats away. But that just made the creatures become agitated and run around all the more. And then out of the corner of my eye I saw something else: something was thrown in through one of the window openings. It looked at first like white flour and it began descending through the still air. But I quickly realised it wasn't flour. As soon as it touched my skin I knew what it was: quicklime.

Quicklime is evil stuff. Harmless on dry skin but as soon as it comes into contact with moisture it starts to burn. If it touches the eyes they start to water which makes them burn all the more. Sailors sometimes use it in wartime to blind enemy crews although this can be problematic. Being a powder any sudden change in wind direction can blow the vile stuff back onto your own men and then they become the victims instead. I'd come across the debilitating consequences before when treating men returning from the French wars. The injuries can be horrendous. Some were left permanently blinded and ended up with terrible scars on their eyes and face.

There was no wind inside the chapterhouse of course so the powder remained suspended in the air affecting anyone who came in contact with it. And not just the monks. Rats have eyes, too. As the quicklime drifted to the floor it affected them in the same way and they were soon running about literally in blind panic which made matters worse by them getting under feet and tripping up the fleeing monks.

I was fortunate being near the front. As soon as I realised what was happening I knew I had to get out as fast as I could and away from the all-enveloping cloud. I held my breath, ducked as low as I could and made a dash for the door. Others were doing the same but somehow I managed to get out. Once there I quickly found a rainwater bucket and pushed my head deep into it to wash as much of the powder from my eyes as I could. Even so they were stinging and watering ferociously.

It was then I heard a familiar sound. I was still unable see too clearly but could just make out a figure on the far bank of the river. It was Estienne – and, absurdly, he was playing his shawm.

The image was bizarre: all around me monks were falling about in agony while across the river this lone piper was playing a serenade. Meanwhile in their confusion the rats were running headlong towards the river where in the shallows other monks and abbey servants armed with sticks and anything else they could lay their hands on were clubbing the creatures to death.

I looked around me in bewilderment. Clubs flying, bells ringing, monks wailing and stumbling blindly about, and over all was the sound of the shawm. It was like a scene from the last day of the Apocalypse.

Chapter Fourteen
AFTERMATH

I spent the rest of the morning treating those affected by the quicklime attack helped by Thomas the infirmarer and any of my brother monks who were fortuitous enough not to have been in the chapterhouse at the time. Not that I was much use being a victim myself. I could barely see what I was doing, my eyes were so sore. River water was our main method of treatment – gallons of it to wash out the burning powder from the eyes as quickly as possible, and then bandages, lots and lots of bandages to cover the eyes and face. By the time we'd finished, the cloister garth was looking like the aftermath of a battle.

Those nearest the door were the fortunate ones having managed to exit the building before the dust cloud reached them fully. Included among these was Prior Henry who was rushed out the door by some quick-thinking brothers. Others at the rear of the building were not so lucky taking the full impact of the evil stuff.

One question nagging at me was where had the rats come from? Rats are everywhere of course, you can never get away from them although they usually stay out of sight, at least during daylight hours.

These didn't. They were running about everywhere, a couple of dozen at least. I've seen rats congregate in groups before. They do this whenever they are getting ready to move home - but usually out in the fields not in a building and certainly not in the chapterhouse. And these were big black specimens too which is what was really worrying me. You see, I keep rats myself, purely for experimental purposes you understand, but always safely locked away in cages. When I'd finished bandaging my last patient I went down to the river's edge to inspect the drowned and battered corpses for myself. They looked uncomfortably familiar. And my worst fears were confirmed later when I got back to my laboratorium. All of my cages stood open and empty.

'Dear God, how could this have happened?' I asked Rufus.

'I cannot say, master.'

'But you were here the whole time. Did you see anyone come in?'

'I saw no-one.'

'Well they didn't release themselves. Someone must have let them out. Was it you?'

'Why would I let your rats out?'

'I don't know, but someone did. Did anyone come in while I was in Chapter?'

'Like who?'

I hesitated to ask: 'Like Frère Estienne for instance?'

He shook his head. 'Estienne has not been here today.'

I heaved a sigh of relief. 'And you're positive you didn't go out? Not even to answer a call of nature?'

'I was here the whole time you were in Chapter.'

'Then how was it possible?' I repeated in bafflement.

Rufus shrugged.

What more could I say to him? If he said no-one came in to the laboratorium and he didn't go out I had to believe him. But that just deepened the mystery further.

No mystery to Arnold of course as he was happy to tell Chapter when we met later in emergency session in one of the chapels of the abbey church, the chapterhouse being still contaminated with quicklime:

'It was the friar - and this time, Walter, you cannot deny it. We all saw him.'

Cries of "Hear! Hear!" from some of my brother monks – walking wounded most of them with eyes and heads bandaged to high heaven.

'I don't believe it was Estienne,' I said quietly.

This was greeted by a groan of derision.

Arnold looked at me with exasperation. 'Walter, how can you continue to defend this man? We all saw what he did. He was controlling those rats with that confounded pipe of his.'

'Shawm. And what is he now, an animal trainer on top of everything else?'

'Very possibly. You don't know what he's been getting up to in that compound.'

'Well I do know one thing: those rats weren't his.'

'Oh? How do you know that?'

I cringed. 'Because they were my rats from my laboratorium. Someone let them escape.'

More gasps of incredulity from the brothers.

'Yes,' agreed Arnold. 'The friar let them escape.'

'My assistant says not.'

'Well he would, wouldn't he?'

'Are you saying he's lying?'

'I'm saying you are determined to find excuses for the friar come what may.'

'And you need to be a little more consistent in your accusations, Arnold. Either Estienne trained the rats himself or he let mine escape. He can't have done both.'

Some nods of agreement to this.

'It doesn't matter how he did it,' said Arnold. 'All the evidence points to him being the culprit.'

'Like what?'

'Like him being on the river bank at the appropriate time. Like him playing that *thing*, whatever you want to call it. Why was he playing it if not to control the rats?'

More nods of agreement.

'I don't know. But I'm sure there's a reasonable explanation. Let me go and ask him before you pillory him.'

'So that you can concoct another fabrication between the pair of you?'

More howls - from both sides of the house this time.

'Brothers please,' said Henry, frowning. 'These constant accusations and counter-accusations are getting us nowhere. Walter will go and see the friar. If he thinks he was responsible I am sure he will come back and tell us so. In the meantime can we please try to conduct ourselves like reasonable men of God and not like hounds in a dog-fight.'

He was interrupted by one of the infirmary servants coming into the chapel. He went straight over to the prior and whispered something in his ear. I couldn't hear what was being said but Henry's face grew darker. He said something to the man who nodded and withdrew.

Henry stood up slowly. 'Brothers, I have some sad news. Brother Percival has died.'

A loud groan went up from all the brothers at this.

'Percival?' said Arnold. 'He was right at the back of the chapterhouse. He would have taken the full force of the quicklime attack. Now the boy has murder to add to all his other crimes.'

'Percival was old,' said Henry. 'His time was drawing near.'

'He was as fit as you or I,' insisted Arnold.

More shouts of agreement.

Henry put up his hands for calm. 'He is with God now. Let us therefore devote the rest of our time here to remembering our departed brother. And no more recriminations, please. Percival would not have wanted that.'

We all went down on our knees as Henry led the prayer for the dead:

'Eternal rest grant unto him O Lord, and let perpetual light shine upon him. May he rest in peace - Amen.'

If only we all could do the same.

I needed to find Estienne quickly to hear his side of the story before anyone did anything they'd regret. But first I wanted to have a quick word with Arnold to try to clear the air a little. It had got a bit heated in the chapel. I waited for him outside the west door of the abbey church:

'Arnold, can we speak?'

'So that you can accuse me again?'

'No-one should accuse anyone of anything until we know the facts. That's my point.'

'Well you know my opinion.'

'But you still haven't explained why Estienne would do such a thing.'

'I don't have to give a reason. All I know is that nothing like it happened before he arrived.'

I sighed heavily. This wasn't working out the way I wanted it to at all. I tried once more to smooth his ruffled feathers:

'Arnold, you're a fair man – I know, I've seen it a thousand times. Frère Estienne is a young man alone in a strange town. His only purpose is to help the poor and relieve their suffering – which he has done a thousand-fold. Can you not extend your generosity to him also?'

He shook his head. 'He's too dangerous.'

'One lone friar?'

'One becomes a trickle becomes a flood and before we know it we will be swamped.'

'Don't you think you're being a little alarmist?'

He pointed up at the west tower of the abbey church. 'Walter, I love this place and everything about it. I've lived here since I was first oblated as a ten-year-old child. It's all I know. It's all I want to know and I don't want to see it destroyed. But it will be if we lower our guard just an inch. The world is changing and not for the better. If we don't stand firm all of it - all of *us* - will be history.'

I snorted. 'I doubt that. Saint Edmund's has been here for eight hundred years. I'll wager it will be here for another eight hundred.'

He smiled sadly. 'I wish I had your confidence.'

I left him and went on to Estienne's house hoping to find him there. He'd disappeared after the quicklime attack – probably wisely bearing in mind the mood

157

of the brothers. Fortunately he'd been on the far side of the river at the time where they couldn't get at him - and that got me wondering.

Estienne was with his "nuns" when I got to the house. They'd evidently heard what had been going on and were very defensive of him – Rosabel had been right about that. But once they saw I was alone they backed off a little and let me speak to Estienne alone. I took him to one side to ask him what he knew about the attack.

'I'm as baffled as you are, brother.'

'You were baffled about being in abbey grounds? How? You must have had a reason for being there.'

'It wasn't my idea.'

'Then whose idea was it?'

He shrugged. 'I received a note.'

'From?'

'I don't know. A small child brought it. She said a man gave her a farthing to deliver it.'

'What man?'

'She didn't say. Just a man in a robe.'

'You mean a monk's robe? A monk from the abbey?'

'That's what I assumed.'

I nodded. 'What did the note say?'

'Simply that I was to go down to the abbey and wait there. It didn't say why. I assumed it had something to do with my work.'

'And you've no idea who this monk was?'

He shrugged and shook his head.

'Where is this note now?'

'I threw it away it.'

Of course he did. He wouldn't have kept it - that would have been too easy. Without the note it was impossible to verify what he was saying was true. Then I asked him the question that was troubling me:

'If the note said to go down to the abbey, why did you go to the east bank of the river? The abbey is on the west bank.'

'A simple mistake. I'm new here. I still don't know the town very well.'

'Oh, come along, Estienne. It's almost impossible to end up on the wrong side of the Lark by accident. There are only two bridges. And you've been in Bury long enough to know which side of the river the abbey is on.'

'All right,' he said, 'I admit I went to the other side of the river on purpose. The truth is I was suspicious. The note, the lack of explanation. I thought it might be a trap.'

'Why would anyone wish to trap you?'

'Do I really need to explain? There are some who would like nothing better than to have me driven out of Bury.'

He meant Arnold and his supporters of course.

'Why did you take your shawm with you?'

'It goes everywhere with me. As I say, I thought I was being summoned as part of my work.'

His explanation sounded plausible but I needed more if I was to convince others.

'All right. Talk me through what happened. You were on the river bank. What happened next?'

'Nothing for a while. I expected someone to come and meet me – one of the monks. I waited but no-one came. I was about to leave when suddenly everything erupted. Monks running down the bank towards the river screaming and rubbing their eyes. I didn't know what to think. And then I saw the rats. So I took out my shawm and began playing.'

'Why? That was an extraordinary thing to do.'

'I don't know why. It was instinctive. I could see the monks were in distress and I wanted to help. I couldn't get across the river. It was all I could think to do. And at first it seemed to work – the rats did seem to come to me. But now I'm not sure. I think they were simply making for the river. It just looked as though I was drawing them.'

'Well now my brothers think so too,' I said shaking my head. 'You know they were my rats from my laboratorium?'

'No, I didn't know.'

'So you didn't free them? Some monks think you did. They also think you started the fire in Rosabel's goose-hut.'

'Why would I do that?'

'Because you knew she wasn't a genuine convert but working for me.'

He smiled. 'I killed an old medicine women because she damaged my shawm. I burned one of the sisters because she was spying on me. I tried to blind half the abbey in some sort of revenge attack. I'm quite the villain, aren't I?'

'Either you are or someone is trying to make you appear so.'

'Do you think I am?'

I just frowned. 'Estienne, if you want my advice you should think seriously about leaving Bury now. It's becoming too dangerous for you here.'

'I told you, I can't leave. Not yet. Not until my mission here is complete.'

'And when will that be? When you're dead?'

'If that is God's will.'

There was no point arguing with him. I started to leave.

160

'Was anyone hurt?' he asked. 'By the quicklime I mean.'

'Brother Percival, an old monk, died in the attack.'

Estienne closed his eyes. 'I will pray for him.'

'As I will for you.'

Did I believe him? I wanted to. If what he was saying was true then it sounded as though he was right and a trap had indeed been set for him. But by whom and for what reason? The obvious answer was Arnold in order to force him to leave. He could have sent that note. He was also absent from the chapterhouse when the quicklime was thrown. But he couldn't have known Prior Henry was going to ask him to leave for insulting Kevin – unless, of course, he engineered it. Did I really think Arnold was capable of such deception?

I'd had no luck finding out who opened the rat cages but I might have better luck discovering who got hold of the quicklime. It's not an easy substance to acquire since it has to be made in a kiln, and there weren't very many of those around. I knew of one such kiln about half a mile west of the town. I decided to visit it and see what I could discover.

As I understand the process, lime stone is brought by mule from where it occurs naturally – somewhere in the English Midlands, I believe, there being no deposits in Suffolk. In its natural state lime stone is perfectly harmless. To create quicklime it has to be burned in large pits in the ground using sea coal. Over several days the raw stone is slowly burned to quicklime in the course of which much toxic smoke and ash is produced which is why kilns are located in such out-of-the-way places. The resultant quicklime is then broken up onto smaller lumps or ground into powder and sold mainly to farmers to spread on the land which is thereby enriched in some way. Once again water is the key – in this case rainwater. I'm told if you stand in a field which has been spread with the stuff during a rain-storm you can literally hear the ground fizzing around you.

But it's not just farmers who use quicklime. It is also used to render plaster in buildings. Estienne might have needed some to rebuild his walls. Before I left his house, therefore, I had a quick look inside. As I thought. It did indeed have fresh plaster on the walls. So he could have acquired some quicklime. Maybe the limester would know.

The lime manufactory at Briar Wood is run by one man, Harben by name, and his daughter, Agata. Shovelling cartloads of lime rock and coal is such heavy work, you might not have thought it suitable for a woman. But Agata was a big girl - what my mother would have called "big-boned" - and years of labouring had given her better muscles than I have. She was also a bit slow in the mind and her father was a bit blind - both I suspect the result of working with such toxic agents. Harben's eyes I noticed were permanently watering. Thankfully they had just come to the end of a session of burning and the kiln was cold and waiting to be raked out.

They were quite surprised to see a monk turn up out of the blue but were welcoming, no doubt pleased to see some company in such an isolated place. I wasted little time on pleasantries:

'No,' Harben assured me shaking his head firmly. 'No-one from the abbey bought lime from me. And no-one could have taken any without me knowing.'

'You're sure? Not even a single sack? Just one would have been enough,' I said indicating the several stacked up by the wall waiting to be collected.

'It's all carefully accounted for,' said Harben. 'It has to be. Quicklime's dangerous stuff, see? Can't have none going missing. The rules is very strict. Here, I'll show you.'

We went over to one of the sacks and cut the hessian cord. Then taking a knife he dropped a small piece of the stuff into a bucket of water. After a few moments the water started to fizzle and smoke, and the quicklime began breaking up and dissolving into a sludgy mess. Heat was also produced along with toxic fumes which burnt my eyes and throat so that I had to draw back. It was no wonder the brothers in the chapterhouse were crying out in agony.

'You're sure you can account for every scrap of quicklime you produce?' I asked him.

'Like I say the rules is strict. Nasty stuff, lime, once it's cooked. It's kept under cover and counted. Twelve rows, ten bags in each row. Count them for yourself if you don't believe me.'

'I believe you. But can we try one anyway? Just to be certain.' I pointed to a bag that looked slightly different from the rest. 'How about that one?'

Reluctantly he took out his knife again and slit the bag open. He then repeated the earlier process of dropping a lump of the white stone into water. But this time nothing happened. However long we waited the stuff just sat in the bottom of the bucket unchanging. It certainly didn't fizz.

Harben frowned and crumbled the lump in his hand. 'I can't understand it. I filled them sacks myself.'

As I had suspected, one bag of quicklime – the one that had been used at the abbey – had been substituted for a bag of ordinary lime – this bag. Easily done. The two forms, raw and processed, looked pretty much identical, only the bags were slightly different. Even someone with perfect eyesight wouldn't necessarily notice unless they were looking for it, and Harben's eyesight was less than perfect.

'You saw no-one do this?' I asked him.

The man shrugged helplessly.

'What about Agata?'

Harben turned to his daughter. 'You see'd anything, girl?' he asked her. 'Speak up if you did.'

But Agata blushed and shook her head.

Why would anyone suspect a theft? Quicklime was not something most people would wish to steal – unless, of course, they had a good reason for doing so.

I thanked my host and started to leave.

'You won't be telling anyone will you, brother? If I lose my licence me and the girl would be destitute.'

'No, I won't be telling anyone. But if I were you I'd find a better accounting system.'

'I'll do that brother,' said Harben with relief. 'Oh yes. You've no fear there. I'll do that right away.'

As I left the yard I heard the clump of heavy feet behind me. I slowed and turned. It was Agata. She looked flushed and kept glancing back nervously to where her father had disappeared into the house.

'Is there something you want to tell me, Agata?'

She shrugged.

'You said you saw no-one,' I prompted gently. 'Are you sure about that? No-one perhaps in a robe like mine?'

She blushed crimson. 'Not like your'n,' she said fingering my sleeve. 'Different.'

'How different? A different colour, perhaps?'

She shrugged again.

'Is there anything else you can tell me about him?

She shook her head.

'All right. Thank you Agata.'

She hovered. 'You won't tell father will you?'

'No, I won't tell your father. It'll be our secret.'

She gave a brief smile before running back to the yard.

A man in different coloured robe. Not black like mine. A grey one perhaps. Grey like the friars wear?

Chapter Fifteen
PRIOR HENRY HATCHES (ANOTHER) PLAN

When I got back to the abbey a message was waiting for me to go and see the prior - wanting to hear the result of my visit to Estienne no doubt. For once Rufus passed the message on to me without my having to ask. Wonders will never cease!

In his office Henry was looking tired. Although he'd managed to avoid the worst of the quicklime attack he hadn't escaped entirely and he kept dabbing his eyes with a damp cloth. His voice, too, had been affected. He poured us each a cup of wine, quite a good one I think although it might have been vinegar for all I could taste of it - another effect of the quicklime. From the expression on Henry's face after his first mouthful he was probably thinking the same.

'What did the friar have to say?' he croaked.

'He denied knowing anything about the attack.'

'Do you believe him?'

'He was on the wrong side of the river. He wouldn't have had time to distribute the quicklime and get over to the far bank.'

'That won't convince the likes of Arnold. The mere fact that the boy was in the vicinity is enough to condemn him.' Henry scowled. 'Damn the boy, what was he doing there? He had no business even being inside abbey grounds.'

'He says he was invited.'

'By whom?'

'He doesn't know. Someone sent him a note. A monk.'

'A monk!' Henry shook his head in disbelief. 'Where is this note now?'

'He lost it.'

'Convenient. What did it say?'

'Only that he should be by the river immediately after prime.'

Henry nodded. 'The office before Chapter. Someone knew what they were doing.'

'In other words a trap. Estienne suggested as much himself. It was lucky for him he was on the far bank of the river. If he'd been on the abbey side he might well have ended up the same way as the rats. I suspect that may have been the intention.'

'Do you think it might have been Arnold?'

'I don't know what to think anymore. And I wouldn't like to speculate. No-one saw anything – either who released the rats or who distributed the quicklime. It's hardly credible. Someone must have seen something. It didn't happen by itself.'

'Not by itself, no.' Henry frowned. 'Of course, there is another possibility.'

'What other possibility?'

He took another sip of his wine and pulled a face. 'I hope my tongue recovers soon. This wine tastes like cat's piss.'

'Henry, what other possibility?'

He gave me a sly look. 'You say we don't know who released the rats. I agree. It's because no-one did - no-one *living*, that is.'

'Then who -?'

'Saint Edmund.'

My jaw dropped open. 'You're jesting of course.'

'It's not something I would jest about.'

'You seriously think Saint Edmund released the rats and poisoned the chapterhouse? From his coffin?'

'Not in person - obviously. But he could have induced someone else to do it for him.'

'Assuming it's even possible, why would he?'

Henry opened his hands imploringly. 'Why do saints usually do these things? To punish the abbey, of course.'

'For what?'

'For our perceived moral laxity; for not performing the daily offices correctly; for any number of reasons we have fallen short of what is expected of us. Or simply to remind us that he's there. Edmund's done it before. The fire that nearly destroyed the shrine back in '98. It was widely accepted that Edmund made the guardians of the shrine fall asleep and then he overturned the candle that set fire to the shrine so as to draw attention to its neglect.'

'Not everyone thought that.'

'Abbot Samson did.'

'I'm not sure that's true either. He was trying to drum up business to pay for a new shrine.'

Henry shook his head slowly. 'Ever the cynic, Walter. You shouldn't underestimate the power of the saints.'

'I don't. But don't you think you're the one being a little cynical this time?'

'Not at all. Your assistant, Rufus, was in your laboratorium at the time the rats were released and saw nothing. And again, no-one saw anyone distribute the quicklime. Yet both things happened. Given that we agree supernatural involvement is a possibility, why not Edmund? It's his abbey after all. And if it was Edmund then it couldn't have been the friar. It might even persuade Arnold to ease off on the boy.'

I snorted. 'The only thing that will do that will be when Estienne leaves Bury for good.'

'Well that's not going to happen - at least, not for a while.' Henry lowered his voice. 'I've had another letter from Frère Agnellus in London.'

I groaned. 'He's not sending us another friar, is he?'

'No, not another friar. Another five.'

My jaw dropped further. '*Five?*'

'Ssh! Keep your voice down,' he said glancing nervously at the door. 'We don't need everyone to know. So you see, we need to quash this anti-Estienne feeling as soon as we can. Which is why I've also decided something else.' He looked at me a little sheepishly. 'I intend to invite Estienne to the shrine-opening ceremony.'

'You can't be serious!'

'Why not? I think it will be a Christian gesture, show that we are being ecumenical. He doesn't have to be right at the heart of the ceremony. He has his flute again, doesn't he?'

'Shawm.'

'He can join Brother Kevin in the choir.'

'Oh, Kevin will love that.'

'That's what I thought. The only question now is how to connect Edmund with your rats. It was easier with the fire, it was his shrine that got incinerated. How do we prove Edmund was involved this time? Saying is one thing. Convincing is another.'

We both thought about that for a few minutes. Henry took another sip of his wine, pulled a face, poured the cup away, then poured himself another.

'I suppose you might have had a dream,' I suggested at last.

Henry cocked an interested eyebrow. 'Go on.'

'Saints often speak to the world in dreams, it's a well-known fact. I'm thinking of the Lincoln man who killed his brother and his two nephews with a pitchfork. In a dream Saint Edmund told him to make pilgrimage to Saint William of Norwich to ask for forgiveness.'

Henry nodded. 'I remember the case. Saint William did indeed forgive the man who was never prosecuted as a result. Yes, that might work,' he said drumming his fingers on his chin. 'Edmund appearing in a dream magnanimously bringing the abbey and the friars together in a demonstration of fraternal reconciliation. I like it.'

'And the rats?'

'They could be symbolic of the bad feeling within the abbey being driven out. Like that passage in Mark about the pigs. What was it? Something about the unclean spirits entering the swine that then ran down into the sea where they were all drowned taking the unclean spirits with them. It could almost be an exact copy of what happened to us. Except for the pigs, of course. And the sea. But other than that...'

'Well?' I ventured. 'Did you have a dream?'

170

'I – may have done,' he said stroking the underside of his chin.

'You'd surely remember if you did.'

Henry pouted. 'Not necessarily. Dreams are notoriously nebulous. Do you remember all your dreams? I'm sure I don't remember all mine. We can't all be as clear somnambulists as Pharaoh or as succinct in interpretation as Joseph.'

'Henry, if you can't remember your own dream, how do you know you even had one?'

He flapped a dismissive hand. 'Don't split hairs, Walter. Let's just say I had a vision and leave it at that. It's just that…'

'What?'

'It's a pity they were rats. It would have been better if they'd been pigs.' He looked at me shyly. 'I don't suppose they could have been pigs, could they?'

'Hardly.'

'No, I suppose not. But I wouldn't want the saint to think I was maligning his name by associating it with vermin. His wrath can be terrible.'

'Now you really are being cynical.'

'Not if it achieves a good purpose – which it will. I'll pray to the blessèd king-martyr, explain what we are doing and why we are doing it. He'll understand.'

'I hope you're right.'

'If I'm not struck dead by this time next week we'll know his answer.'

'Or if you are.'

He grimaced. 'Or if I am.'

I wanted to go to see Rosabel to see how she was recovering after the fire. The last time I'd seen her was in the abbey infirmary when she was barely able to speak. I wanted to know if she had anything to add to what her father had told me. By now he must have told her about the piece of stick lodged in the door handle preventing it from being opened from the inside and that therefore the fire was probably caused deliberately.

As I was crossing Exchequer Square I heard a group of street urchins singing a ditty. I recognized the tune: it was a well-known nursery rhyme that my own nurse used to sing to Joseph and me when we were children. The words, however, were not quite the ones we were taught:

Three blind mice, three blind mice,
See them scurry, see them run,
In the house, out the house,
Make the brothers spin.

Three blind mice, three blind mice,
See them tarry, see them turn,
Down by the riverside,
Make the brothers burn.

Nearby Arnold was leaning against a post with a grin on his face.

'I suppose you taught them that?' I said to him.

He shook his head. 'Not me. They came up with it all by themselves. It's like I said to you before Walter, respect and deference is gradually being eroded.'

'It's just children's song, nothing more.'

'It's not just that. I've been looking at the accounts.' He nodded towards the abbey's counting house on the opposite side of the square. 'Have you any idea how much money we've lost in the time the friar has been here? Money that could have been going to good causes.'

'That's nothing to do with Estienne.'

'Maybe. Maybe not. But it's odd, isn't it, that it seems to have started with his arrival in the town. I wonder what your pothiker friend's wife thinks about it.'

'Rosabel? She doesn't blame Estienne for the fire.'

'Only because you've convinced her not to. Have you spoken to him yet about what he was doing at the abbey?'

'He says he was invited. By a monk.'

He chuckled. 'I suppose you think that was me.'

'Was it?'

He shook his head sadly. 'I don't need to play games, Walter. Given enough rope the friar will hang himself without my help. We must just hope he does so before too much more damage is done.'

He pushed himself off the post and started to walk away.

Angrily, I called after him: 'Prior Henry has his own ideas about who was responsible for the quicklime attack.'

He stopped. 'Oh? Who?'

'Saint Edmund.'

I knew as soon as I said it it was a mistake. But I couldn't stop myself. Arnold has a way of raising my shackles. He just laughed.

'Why not?' I said, irritated. 'It's a perfectly reasonable explanation. The holy saint must be very displeased with what has been going on in his house lately - all this constant bickering. It should surprise no-one that he would wish to make his presence felt and to try to restore his own authority.'

Arnold shook his head sadly. 'Walter, even you can't be that naive.'

'You said you wanted the abbey's authority restored. Are you saying the prior is wrong?'

'I don't have to. No-one is going to believe this. They'll see it for what it is: a desperate attempt to divert attention from the real culprit. I wouldn't be surprised if it wasn't you put the idea in Henry's head.'

'It was entirely his own idea as a matter of fact.'

'Really? Not Edmund's then?' he smiled.

'That's not what I meant.'

He shook his head. 'The tide is turning, Walter. Soon we will see this man for what he really is.' He nodded to the group of children who'd been singing. 'Even the street urchins know it. If I were you I'd get him to leave while he still can.'

'Is that a threat?'

He shook his head. 'A prediction.'

Arnold continued back in to the abbey grounds.

Damn! Me and my big mouth. I shouldn't have mentioned Henry and his harebrained scheme. By evening he will have had second thoughts and by tomorrow he'd have forgotten all about it. But now I'd let the cat out of the bag. Come compline it will be all over the abbey. And won't Arnold be making hay with it.

I carried on across town to Onethumb and Rosabel's house.

'God bless all in this house,' I intoned and made the sign of the cross.

'You can save your blessings brother, there's no-one here but me,' Rosabel said drying her hands.

174

'Onethumb's at his work and the children are next door with their grandparents.'

'That's all right. It's you I wanted to speak to. How are you? Got your voice back I hear.'

'No thanks to you. I could have died in that hut. And by the way, whose going to pay for a new one?'

'I didn't set the old one alight.'

'No, but if you hadn't badgered me into joining those silly Clare women I wouldn't have been targeted.'

'You don't know that the fire had anything to do with that.'

'Father told me about the brace on the hut door. Someone must have locked me in.'

I frowned. 'You saw no-one lingering nearby?'

'Like who?'

'I don't know. Estienne mentioned a stranger – in a robe.'

'A monk, you mean? No, I didn't see a monk. And it hardly matters anymore. I'm finished with it all. So if that's all you came for you can go - some of us have suppers to prepare.'

'Actually there was one other thing,' I said sitting down on a stool.

'What?'

'I want you to go back.'

Her eyes widened to saucers. 'Go back? Are you mad?'

'Don't you want to know who it was tried to harm you?'

'Oh, you mean get him to try to kill me again. And next time possibly succeed.'

'He won't try again.'

'And if he does?'

'I'll put flowers on your grave,' I grinned.

'Anyway, how can I go back? Estienne knows I wasn't a genuine convert. If he didn't before he will now. He'll never let me in again.'

'I think he will. I'll tell him you're keeping watch for me. And besides,' I grinned. 'He's an eternal optimist. He thinks he can save the Devil. Compared with you that's small beer. Oh come on Rosa, you know you want to.'

She pulled a face. 'Why do you want me to go back?'

'I think there is going to be more trouble and I can't be there myself. I need someone who will be able to give me fair warning. Someone I can trust.'

'I'll think about it.'

'Do, but don't take too long.' I got up to leave. 'By the way,' I added sheepishly. 'I wanted to apologize. I never had the chance before.'

'For what?'

'For my behaviour in the marketplace. For my …' I tried to think of a suitable euphemism: 'My indiscretion.'

She shrugged nonchalantly. 'It doesn't matter.'

'Nevertheless, I was wrong. I have admitted fault to my confessor and he has duly punished me. I am to recite a thousand Hail Marys and an equal number of Paternosters, if you want to know.' I smiled awkwardly. 'You, er, haven't mentioned any of this to Onethumb, have you?'

'Nothing to mention. I've had small boys make a better fist of seduction than you did. You say the price you paid was a thousand Hail Marys?' She shook her head sadly. 'You were done.'

Chapter Sixteen
REACTIONS AND RECRIMINATIONS

Onethumb stormed into my laboratorium without bothering to knock. No surprises there, I'd been expecting him. Even before he was fully in the room he was haranguing me with a whole battery of gestures: stamping his feet, waving his arms about like a demented windmill, letting me know in no uncertain terms what he thought of my sending Rosabel back to the Poor Clares.

'I can understand your anger, my friend,' I replied equably, 'but what could I do? She insisted on going. If I'd refused she'd have gone anyway, you know what she's like.'

Onethumb signed that he didn't believe a word of it and that he'd forbidden Rosabel absolutely to go.

'Oh well, that'll work,' I scoffed. 'Telling Rosabel *not* to do something is a sure way to get her to do it.'

Onethumb started flapping his arms about again even more incoherently than before. I frowned and tutted and told him to calm down before he had a heart-attack.

Rufus, who had been watching all this, now chimed in:

'I know a story about a wife who always did the opposite of what her husband wanted. If he wanted a cold dinner she would give him a hot one. If he wanted to sit in the sun she would choose the shade. If he said up she said down. Whatever her husband said, she always said the opposite. Then one day she fell in the river.'

Onethumb and I both looked at him.

'Well go on then,' I said. 'She fell in the river - what happened to her?'

'Her husband jumped in to try to save her. But instead of swimming downstream after her he swam upstream.'

'And?' I prompted.

He shrugged. 'She drowned.'

'Well that was pretty stupid,' I said. 'Why didn't he swim downstream?'

'He said that since his wife always did the opposite of what was expected of her he naturally assumed she would float upstream.'

I was dumbfounded. It was the longest speech I'd ever heard Rufus make. Onethumb just stared at the boy. Speechless himself – or should that be *sign*-less? - he spun on his heel and stormed out slamming the door after him.

'Was that true?' I asked Rufus once the rafters had stopped vibrating.

'No. But Onethumb was angry. I thought it might calm him down.'

'It certainly had an effect. But tell me, how did you know what he was saying? It took me years to learn his sign language.'

'I've watched him when he brings our supplies. His signing technique is really quite simple. It didn't take me long to learn the rudiments.'

'First shawms and now sign-language. You know Rufus, you are a constant source of amazement to me.'

'Is that good or bad?'

'I'm not sure.'

He nodded. 'Will Onethumb remain angry with you for long?'

'Hm? Oh, Onethumb isn't angry. Don't take any notice of all that bluster. He's just a little upset that I didn't consult him first before asking – I mean, *allowing* - Rosabel to go back to Estienne, that's all. He'll come round soon, you'll see.'

I glanced nervously at the door and bit my thumbnail.

With Rosabel back with the Poor Clares keeping an eye on things for me I could hope for a brief respite – at least until the next crisis. The way things had been going that shouldn't be long in coming. In the meantime we still had Percival to bury, the one fatal casualty of the quicklime attack.

This was simultaneously both a sad and a joyous occasion. Sad, because we would no longer see Percival's cheerful countenance in Chapter or at mealtimes; and joyous, because we knew he had at last achieved his life's ambition of arriving at Saint Peter's gate in the sure and certain hope of passing through to the other side. God speed that it should be a quick and painless passage - Amen.

Actually, I say "cheerful countenance" but if I'm honest Percival was a miserable old stoat. I know we shouldn't speak ill of the dead but in Percival's case it's difficult to do anything else. In his younger days he was always the first to offer his arm whenever a brother needed disciplining for some misdemeanour

– me more often than not. He positively relished wielding the birch and kept a private collection handy next to his cot in the dormitory. He had a particularly effective technique honed after years of practice to achieve maximum pain with minimum effort. I for one was not sorry when arthritis eventually prevented him from gripping anything heavier than a lettuce leaf. He certainly suffered later in life with his hands; they were so crippled I often wondered how he managed to wipe his arse. In old age he had so many ailments, real or imagined, that he was always coming to me for cures. He became such a frequent patient, in fact, that I ended up prescribing tincture of opium for all his disorders whatever their cause which he seemed quite happy about.

Having said all that I wouldn't have wished the manner of his death on anyone. Enduring a burning, choking suffocation with every breath must be a terrible way to die. However, I took comfort from the thought that Percival was probably too befuddled by opiates to have known much about it. In any event his suffering was now over and we were to commit his body to the good Suffolk earth - meaning the monks' graveyard just beyond the east end of the abbey church.

These interments are normally low-key affairs. Abbots get buried with pomp inside the convent walls with their graves clearly marked for future veneration. Samson, for instance, lies beneath the floor of the chapterhouse with a fine piece of granite marking the spot, while Baldwin, perhaps our greatest abbot, has a magnificent tomb behind the choir altar of the abbey church. We ordinary monks receive no such memorial. In fact we receive none at all, not even a coffin, just a linen shroud into which we are sewn and then dropped into an anonymous hole in the ground which is then refilled with nothing on the surface to say we'd even existed. No doubt I will end up in such when it is my turn to go, hopefully some time in the distant future.

Nevertheless Percival's conventual brothers were all there to launch him into the hereafter - whatever we thought of him in the here and now. A few did shed a tear of regret, among them Kevin I noticed, much to my surprise. In life Percival was another who like Arnold chided Kevin for his mannerisms never missing an opportunity to persecute him. I should have thought Kevin of all people would be relieved to see the back of him. But then, Kevin weeps easily.

That done, we returned to the abbey to our daily chores. A moment to pause and reflect perhaps? If only. That new crisis I was warning about earlier was just a blink of a watery eye away.

Chapter Seventeen
EDMUND GIVES HIS ANSWER

'Prior Henry's done *what?*'

'Collapsed. He's frothing at the mouth and burbling – like this.'

The man - one of Henry's servants - started jerking his limbs violently and making gurgling noises in his throat.

My blood ran cold. Was this what Henry had been afraid of? Was Edmund punishing him for his impertinence just as he had Sweyn Forkbeard, Abbot Leofstan and all the other doubters who had violated the holy martyr's sanctity? Henry never doubted Edmund's powers. He respected the efficacy of the saint's thunderbolts. But he'd also been confident his purpose would be looked upon favourably by the saint and was going to pray for his blessing. Was this Edmund's reply?

Quelling the tendency for my voice to quake, I turned back to the two servants:

'Where is the prior now?'

'On the floor of his office.'

'What? You mean you just left him there?'

'We were too afraid to touch him,' protested one.

'In case Edmund did the same to us,' agreed the other.

Furious as I was, I suppose I couldn't altogether blame them. Everyone knew the Sweyn story - for those who didn't there was a painting hanging on the wall behind Edmund's shrine. It had been done by one of our more artistic monks and was very realistic if a bit graphic. It showed the old Danish tyrant at the moment of desecrating the shrine turning purple in the face and clutching at his throat, his eyes protruding from their sockets and his tongue gagging just before he dropped dead. Above him hovered an angel pointing inexorably in the direction Sweyn was about to go: down to Hell, and little horned devils already pulling on his arms and legs. But I couldn't think of that now. I had to think of Henry.

'I must go to him,' I said reaching for my medical satchel.

'Are you sure, master?'

'What would you have me do, leave him to die alone? And you two will come with me.'

The two men exchanged glances. 'Who us, master?'

'Yes you, master. We may need to move him to the infirmary. And just be grateful I don't have you dismissed for abandoning your master in his hour of need.'

'Do you want me to come too?' asked Rufus.

'No. You stay here while I -'

But before I could finish my sentence the two servants were already out the door and running. They evidently valued their lives more than their jobs. But I couldn't just leave the prior lying on the floor of his office. And I wouldn't be able to pick him up on my own. It was a good thing Rufus was less fazed by such notions than Henry's servants.

I sighed heavily. 'All right. You'd better come.'

The sight that greeted us in the prior's office made my heart sink. I'm used to seeing patients in various stages of distress and discomfort of course, but usually family members or friends have at least placed them on a bed. Henry was simply lying on the floor where he'd fallen. Several of my brother monks were crowding round the doorway looking in but not one of them dared venture inside - they too had seen the painting on the chancel wall. I pushed through them and slammed the door shutting out their prurient gaze.

My first thought was the same as the two servants, that Henry had been the victim of a sudden attack of apoplexy. He was lying on his back with white froth coming out of his mouth and his breathing was laboured. But at least that meant he was still alive - just.

'It's all right Henry, I'm here,' I said to try to reassure him. 'You're in safe hands now. Let's get you up.'

Between us Rufus and I managed to get him onto his day-bed. It was then I noticed a wine goblet lying on the floor beside the desk that looked as though it had been dropped and the contents spilled onto the floor. I picked it up and examined it. Some of the wine was still in the bottom. I sniffed it but could detect no odour. That didn't mean anything of course. In light of this I changed my diagnosis from apoplexy to poisoning.

'Henry, have you taken anything?' I asked him, but he was too befuddled to reply.

Whether he really had been poisoned or not I had to assume he had and to act accordingly. The key to any poisoning is to get it out of his body as quickly as possible before it became fatal. I just hoped we weren't already too late.

'Quickly,' I said to Rufus. 'Turn him on his side.'

I then stuck two fingers down his throat to make him gag. Henry vomited and a small quantity of foul-smelling bile came out of his mouth. But it wasn't enough. We needed get more out. He then started shaking and his entire body went into spasms. I was afraid he would choke on his vomit. I stuck my fingers down his throat again but even less stuff came out than the first time. Now I was panicking and did something I don't normally do – I froze. I just didn't know what to do for the best.

And this is where Rufus really showed his worth. Without a word he calmly got up and went to my satchel where he retrieved a bottle. I didn't recognize the bottle and certainly hadn't put it there. It appeared to contain some fine black powder which Rufus began pouring down Henry's throat.

'What are you doing?' I said stopping his hand. 'You'll kill him!'

'No, I will save him.'

Something about the way he said it made me hesitate. I watched nervously while he poured more of the black powder into Henry's mouth followed by some water. Henry cough and gasped.

What had he done? He was choking for sure!

But then Henry coughed again and back up came the powder as a thick black gunge. Rufus repeated the procedure several times until no more gunge came up. Henry groaned but he seemed better.

I looked questioningly at my assistant.

'Charcoal,' Rufus explained. 'The powder soaks up the contents of the stomach. Mixed with a little emetic it clears the stomach of all its contents.'

I was impressed. 'Where did you learn to do that? You've obviously done it before.'

He shook his head. 'No. I only heard about it.'

'Then how did you know it would work?'

'I didn't.'

I gasped. 'And yet you tried it anyway?'

Rufus shrugged. 'He is still alive.'

He then calmly put the bottle back in my satchel while I continued to tremble at the thought of what might have happened. But I had to admit Henry had calmed down and was breathing more easily.

Rufus found a blanket and placed it over our patient while I went back to examining the wine goblet more closely. In the bottom were the dregs of whatever it was Henry had been drinking. I sniffed it but it simply smelt like sour wine. If it had been me I would have thrown it away, but with Henry's loss of taste and smell I don't suppose he'd noticed. I picked the goblet up careful not to spill the dregs, wrapped it in a cloth and put it into my satchel just as I heard the door open.

'Will he live?'

I looked up to see Arnold standing in the doorframe. Crowding behind him were the other brothers too timid to venture inside.

'God willing,' I replied.

'God – and Saint Edmund?'

I pouted. 'Perhaps.'

'You don't sound as sure anymore that the saint was involved.'

'I'm sure Prior Henry will be able to tell us once he recovers,' I replied irritably.

186

'*If* he recovers.'

'Why should he not?'

'Edmund does not forgive easily. Remember Abbot Leofstan. As I recall the story the good abbot did survive his brush with the saint – but he never fully regained his power of speech.'

'I'm not sure Edmund had anything to do with it this time. I suspect a human hand.'

'As do I,' agreed Arnold, 'which is why I have called a special meeting of the Chapter - to discuss just that possibility.'

'*You* are convening a meeting?'

'We could ask Prior Henry – but I doubt he'd be very responsive just now. And as I'm next in seniority the decision falls to me.'

I couldn't argue with that. After the abbot and the prior the sacristan was indeed the third most senior member of the abbey. With the absence of one and the other incapacitated, Arnold was in command.

'That's your privilege, of course,' I conceded. 'When do you wish to hold it?'

'Now.'

He certainly wasn't wasting any time. Before Henry was in a position to overrule him, no doubt.

'You'll permit me to conduct the prior to the infirmary first?'

Arnold's lip curled. 'Of course. We wouldn't want to start without our esteemed physician.'

So saying, he turned and walked out.

I looked down at the stricken prior on his cot. His eyes were closed but his colour was better and he was sleeping quietly.

'Come on Henry,' I muttered. 'Don't die on me now. I need you. Estienne needs you. We *all* need

187

you.' I frowned and turned to Rufus: 'Go and get a trolley.'

'Which trolley, master?'

'Oh, any trolley Rufus – do I have to spell out everything for you in detail?'

He thought about it. 'Yes.'

I shook my head at the boy. So useful a few minutes ago, so utterly hopeless now. He really was an enigma.

'Just find a trolley, Rufus. The funeral bier will do. It's in the workshop being repaired - and let's just pray he doesn't need it for real.'

'Are you not going to the chapterhouse?'

'Yes, but I have an errand to run first.'

I needed to find out exactly what was in the wine goblet, assuming that was the cause of Henry's ailing, and before the Chapter meeting. I had no way of analysing it myself, but I knew someone who did.

I took Henry's cup together with its residue, dried now to a crust, to my brother Joseph's shop in Heathenmans Street. As an apothecary he is used to analysing substances and has the facilities for doing so. Behind his shop there is an unprepossessing shed that you'd think was just a wood-store but contains treasures that make my laboratorium look like a child's play-pen by comparison. Bottles and packages from all over the world line the walls, apparatus that defy description. I've no idea what any of it is for and hesitate to touch in case I break something.

After I'd explained where the cup had come from and my suspicions about it I handed it over to his expertise. Joseph took the cup with great solemnity and studied it carefully then sniffed the contents just as I had done. Then he added a little of what he called "evaporative water" – ordinary water as far as I could see but he said not, that boiling and collecting the condensed form somehow purified it. I took his word for it.

Having thus reconstituted the residue he sniffed it again. Then – and this is where I became nervous – he dipped the tip of his little finger in the substance and touched it to the edge of his tongue. I expected at any moment he would collapse on the floor and begin frothing at the mouth as Henry had done. But no. He merely nodded his head and proceeded to the next stage of the analysis.

This involved carefully decanting the liquid into another vessel and then testing it with candle flames and coloured crystals and a cornucopia of other substances. There was a lot of smoke and fizzing. I marvelled at his skill. There is nothing more thrilling than to watch a genius at work. Thinking myself something of a natural philosopher, I frowned and nodded sagely at each stage of the process as though I knew exactly what he was doing (I didn't). What was the nature of the exotic substance in the cup? I wondered. The ground-up bezoar of a mountain goat perhaps? Some coral snake fang secreted between the toes of a mermaid? The desiccated droppings of the flightless ju-ju bird?

Eventually he pronounced his conclusion:

'Fly agaric.'

I frowned. 'Fly where?'

'It's a toadstool. It grows on woodlands and heaths. It has a distinctive bright red cap with white spots. It's very common. Even you must have seen one or two poking up at the roadside in the autumn.'

189

'Yes, I am familiar with woodlands, thank you,' I said petulantly. 'I own one – or I used to. Is that all it is, then? A mushroom?'

'Not just any mushroom, Walter. A particularly pretty one. One of my favourites.'

'I'm delighted you like it. At what point did you realise?'

'As soon as I smelt it. I recognized the odour.'

'It has no odour.'

'To the undiscerning nose, perhaps.'

I frowned. 'What was all that nonsense with powders and coloured smoke?'

'Oh, I do that to impress the clients. And don't look at me like that. I have a business to run. If I told them they could get most of my ingredients from their own middens I'd never sell anything.'

I shook my head. 'Is this fly agaric poisonous?'

'Most assuredly – if given in sufficient doses. But you'd need about fifteen specimens to kill a man. There's not enough here to kill a fly. That's why it's called *fly* agaric, by the way. Because mixed with milk it's used to keep flies away.'

'I'll remember to tell the abbey chef.'

'Oh, I'm sure he already knows. In some countries it's also used as an hallucinogenic for religious purposes.'

'Primitive twaddle.'

'I said it won't easily kill a man but even small doses would make him ill. I'm not surprised the prior was as sick as you say.'

'Then it had to be deliberate. Something like that doesn't happen by accident and he certainly didn't poison himself.' I shook my head. 'I can't think why anyone would want to harm Prior Henry. He's so inoffensive.'

'Fortunately your quick-thinking action with the charcoal would have evacuated most of it from his system.'

'That wasn't me. That was my assistant, Rufus.'

'Really? How interesting.'

'What I need to know is will there be any lasting effects?'

'I shouldn't think so. The prior will have a bad stomach for a few days, but after that he should be fine.'

'Just long enough for Arnold to achieve his goal,' I groaned.

'Ah yes, your bothersome sacristan. He suspects this new friar might be responsible for most of the trouble that's been taking place recently – this too, no doubt.'

'You're very well informed – but then of course you always are. You're right, Arnold has a hatred of friars and this one in particular which is why Estienne would have even less reason that most to want to harm Henry. He's one of his few supporters.'

'What do you know about him?'

'Not much. He's French – or Burgundian at least. At any rate he's a very good preacher, and an accomplished musician. He plays a shawm. But of course you'd know all about that, too.'

His face went blank. 'Why would I know about that?'

'Because it's an Arabic invention and you're half Arabic.'

'I was born in Suffolk.'

'Yes, but your parents are from the Outremer.'

'I see,' he nodded. 'You think Arabs inherit all their skills in the womb. Maybe I should disappear up a rope, or fly off on a magic carpet, perhaps?'

'Don't be tetchy, Joseph. All I meant was that you may have heard about or even studied shawms – more so than I would.'

'As a matter of fact I have.'

'There you are then.'

'The shawm, as you rightly say, is an Arab instrument brought back to Europe by Christian armies returning from the Outremer – after they'd finished murdering my countrymen, that is.'

'As did yours mine,' I countered. 'And I thought you said you were English?'

He waved that away. 'It's become a popular instrument in Mediterranean countries. So I suppose war does have some uses.'

'Indeed it does. If my father hadn't gone to care for our troops and your father the same for his, you and I might never have met.'

'And I might be a fully qualified doctor with my own practice in a sunny courtyard in Damascus instead of a struggling shop-keeper here in dull, damp Bury St Edmunds.'

'Something to be thankful for then,' I grinned.

Having been born and grown up together we'd had this argument a thousand times before. It always ended the same way – with me winning.

He handed me back Henry's wine cup by now washed and dried.

'By the way, I hear you've been upsetting my staff.'

'Your staff?'

'Onethumb.'

'Oh, that was nothing.'

'I hope you're right. He was very angry this morning and it didn't take me long to coax the reason out of him. He even invented some new signs specially for you. Your ears beneath that thick pate of yours should have been burning.'

'We're fine. You've no need to worry. Onethumb is like my own son. He knows I wouldn't do anything to disturb our relationship.'

'I'm glad to hear it. Just don't take him for granted, that's all I ask.'

'I won't.'

'And now, you'd better get back to the abbey. Your Nemesis awaits.'

Chapter Eighteen
CHAPTER AND WORSE

My Nemesis. He meant Arnold of course – not so much my Nemesis as Estienne's. We would have to see. I arrived back just as the summoning bell was beginning to toll. I quickly returned Henry's cup to his office and made my way over to the chapterhouse.

The chapterhouse at Saint Edmundsbury is not normally the most rowdy of venues. Frankly, there are times when I've known graveyards with more life in them. Chapter is not a time for robust debate but rather one of quiet deliberation and reflection. Once the initial prayers have been intoned and a chapter from the Rule read out, monks - and we older monks in particular - can normally settle down for an hour in which to catch up on lost sleep while those with particular axes to grind can hold forth on whatever topic takes their fancy. The trick is to nod off in a way that gives the impression of concentrated contemplation – until one starts to snore, that is, and then one relies on one's friends to poke one in the ribs pretty smartly.

That said, there have been occasions when Chapter has livened up a bit – like the series of fractious meetings over the choice of our present abbot that took place a decade ago. In mitigation, that time we were not on our own. Half the baronage of England were crammed into the chapterhouse along with sixty monks and even on a couple of occasions the king himself. Then tempers did get very heated indeed with monks and peers very nearly coming to blows. Such moments are rare and for that reason memorable. This was looking like becoming another. I still think of it even today as "the Arnold Chapter". And from the look of things he was going to make the most of it…

'Ah. Brother Physician. Nice of you to join us.'

'Sorry to have kept you waiting, Brother Sacrist,' I said taking my seat. 'I was otherwise engaged.'

'Of course,' he nodded. 'The prior. I take it he's been safely transferred to the infirmary?'

'Indeed.'

'How is he?'

'Near death's door.'

At this a groan of consternation went up from the assembled brotherhood, so I added quickly:

'But I am pleased to report that following the timely intervention of myself and my assistant, Brother Rufus, he is likely to make a full recovery.'

'For which we must give thanks to Almighty God,' said Arnold.

Murmurs of "Amen" to this.

'However,' he went on, 'in light of Prior Henry's - hopefully temporary – incapacity, it has fallen to me to conduct Chapter business.'

My hand immediately shot up.

Arnold sighed. 'You wish to add something further, brother?'

'Only to ask if this is really necessary. This isn't the usual hour for Chapter. Shouldn't we wait until tomorrow by which time the prior may be well enough to resume his responsibilities?'

Some nods of agreement to this.

'In normal circumstances I'd agree with you. But these are not normal circumstances. Recent events have given some urgency to the situation. We don't know how long the prior will be away. We need to decide on our response as soon as possible.'

'Response to what?'

'I'm sure I don't need to remind Chapter of the events of recent days. That is what we are here to discuss. And there is a lot to get through. So, if there are no more objections we will get on.'

Some uncomfortable shifting on seats and shaking of heads but no objections. Arnold had the floor. But it quickly became apparent that we were to be treated not so much to a discussion as a sermon – and one I imagine Arnold had been writing, literally or figuratively, for months:

'My brothers. This century, the thirteenth after the Passion of Our Lord, has been a difficult one, as we all know. We have suffered war, insurrection, famine. Abbots, popes, even kings have come and gone. The people have suffered terrible hardships. But through it all this abbey and its community have endured. And why is that? It is because we have kept to the true path, the path laid down by Saint Benedict our founding father. Throughout all these tribulations this abbey has been a beacon of stability, a light shining in the darkness.'

Lots more murmurings and nods of approval.

'However my brothers, today that light is under threat. Others seek to dim its strength and even supplant it with their own. This has not gone unnoticed least of all by the king-martyr himself whose presence in the abbey's shrine has long safeguarded and protected us. And although with his children Edmund is a gentle shepherd, with transgressors he is a lion. He has been very patient with us but his patience is not inexhaustible and those who defy him will in the end feel the strength of his wrath.'

'Who is it disturbs our peace?' came a voice.

'The friar!' replied another.

Groans and nods of agreement.

'Indeed,' said Arnold solemnly. 'The friar.'

At this point I was about to intervene again but Kevin got there before me:

'I must protest!'

'Oh,' said Arnold with a slight curl of his lip. 'Brother Kevin wishes to protest.'

Some snorting and giggling at this but Kevin would not to be put off:

'There is no evidence that Frère Estienne was involved in any of these recent events as you call them.'

'Is there not? Well, let's see. We'll start with the widow Mab. All right, her death may have been from natural causes. But isn't it strange that it should have occurred so soon after an altercation with the friar? And the friar was close by when she suffered her fatal collapse even if he wasn't directly involved. His malign influence could be felt even at a distance.'

'But you've just admitted she died naturally,' objected Kevin. 'How can that be taken as evidence?'

'Taken on its own it doesn't,' agreed Arnold. 'But when combined with others doubts begin to mount up, the scales begin to tilt.'

Kevin started again to object but he was shouted down:

'Sit down!'

Blushing, Kevin did so.

'So let us continue,' said Arnold. 'Next there was the fire that nearly killed the tanner's daughter. A totally innocent victim whose only crime was to be too close to the friar.'

Innocent? Rosabel? He clearly didn't know her very well.

'Then of course we have the attack on this very place in which we now sit. I don't have to remind brothers of that terrible morning which culminated in the death of our dear brother Percival. Once again, who was there but the friar? The scales tilt a little further. And now finally we have this attack on Prior Henry.'

Kevin looked round confused. 'Prior Henry? But he's just ill, surely? A bad bottle of wine I was told.' He looked across at me for confirmation.

I grimaced in pain. Oh Kevin. When will you learn to shut up? Arnold had laid a huge bear trap and you've fallen right into it:

'Yes,' Arnold smiled. 'Let's hear from our esteemed Brother Physician. He will confirm, I am sure, having just had the substance analysed, that Prior Henry was in fact poisoned.'

Poisoned! The word sped around the chapterhouse like a cat with its tail alight. No wonder Arnold wanted to wait until I arrived before starting the meeting. I couldn't deny it. Joseph had proved the substance in the cup was poison. But how did Arnold know? The answer of course is that he didn't. He'd simply had me followed to Joseph's shop and guessed the rest.

I felt I had to speak up: 'There's no indication of who might have done it, if indeed it was deliberate.

It might even have been an accident. At the moment Prior Henry can neither confirm nor deny.'

Arnold snorted. 'Oh really, Walter.'

'Why would Estienne wish to poison the prior?' I stumbled on angrily. 'No-one has been more generous towards him.'

'It's in the nature of the beast. As I keep trying to tell you, these people have no scruples. They wish to supplant us - not just in this abbey but in all abbeys and priories everywhere. Prior Henry has been generous towards this man – that's the sort of person he is. But I would suggest even he has belatedly come to realise his error and is trying to redress the issue and has made himself the friar's enemy as a result.'

'How on earth do you come to that conclusion?'

'Quite simply. This coming shrine-opening ceremony. It is Henry's own design, is it not? He is reaffirming the ascendancy of the holy saint and martyr – and thereby the abbey. That is what it's all about. That is what the friar wishes to deny and why he poisoned the prior.'

A lot more nodding at this. I would have liked to argue the point further but the trouble was there was a crumb of truth in what Arnold was saying. Henry was trying to arouse interest in Edmund with the shrine-opening ceremony but his reasons were more complicated than Arnold would have us believe. As for poisoning Henry, Estienne would have had to be here to do it and only Henry would be able to confirm that. But logic has no place where emotion is concerned. And the emotion I was sensing was anger. Oh Henry, where are you when we need you the most?

'If your assessment of Estienne is true then why haven't you been targeted?' I said to Arnold. 'No-one has been more vocal in his opposition than you.'

'Maybe I will be. Maybe I'm next on his list. Mark my word, this latest outrage will not be the last. Which is why we must act now before it is too late.'

'Act in what way?'

'I propose we take a vote on whether to take back the house so generously donated to the friar.'

'We've already voted on that,' I objected.

'That was before the recent attacks. The situation is now completely different. We cannot permit this Judas to continue to enjoy our hospitality unchallenged. He is a cuckoo in our nest. I propose we eject him before he ejects us. On a show of hands, then – those in favour of rescinding the donation?'

Dozens of hands went up.

'Those against?'

Mine and Kevin's were the only two.

'I declare the motion carried,' said Arnold.

There the meeting abruptly ended.

Outside, Kevin quickly caught me up.

'Can he do that, Walter? Just take a vote like that?'

'He already has.'

Kevin cringed. 'What will happen now?'

I shrugged. 'Estienne will be asked to surrender the house and probably be hounded out of the town entirely. It's what Arnold's been wanting all along. He's won.'

'But the vote's not binding, is it? It would have to be confirmed by either Prior Henry or Abbot Hugh?'

'If Arnold moves fast enough it may be done before they can stop it.'

Kevin frowned. 'This is all Arnold's doing. It wouldn't surprise me if he didn't poison Henry just so he could have that vote.'

I laughed. 'Even Arnold isn't that ruthless.'

Tears of frustration welled up in Kevin's eyes. 'But he can't make Estienne leave. Not yet. He just *can't!*'

'Try not to distress yourself, old friend,' I said placing a comforting hand on his shoulder. 'All is not lost yet. I have every confidence Henry will recover quickly and put things back where they were.'

'By then it may be too late.'

He went scurrying off. I had never seen Kevin quite so agitated before. He clearly didn't want Estienne to go - partly I imagined because Arnold did. Such is the pettiness of abbey politics.

Chapter Nineteen
WITH MURDER IN MIND

I flatter myself I know when I'm beating my head against a wall. I've done it enough times to recognize the symptoms: a throbbing pain over the eyes; an inability to focus properly; that dizzying sensation that I am about to fall flat on my face. I'd lost the argument with Arnold, there was no point in pursuing it - at least for the moment. A more productive approach would be to try to find out who really was behind these terrible events. Whoever it was their aim clearly was to implicate Estienne, someone who really didn't like him very much. But who?

Not Arnold. For all his misguided bluster his purpose was an honourable one. He really believed that he was defending the City of God on Earth and that newcomers like the grey friars were undermining the citadel walls. Maybe that sounds a little apocalyptic but it's how he saw it.

So if not Arnold then who? One of the other monks? There was the mysterious man in a monk's robe who'd purportedly left a note inviting Estienne to meet the day of the quicklime attack. And then there was that other monk seen stealing the sack from the lime kiln. Was it even the same man? It's not easy for a monk to leave the abbey grounds unnoticed – as Rufus discovered to his cost. And just because he wore a monk's robe didn't mean he was actually a monk, of course; anyone can put on a robe.

Someone in the town, then? Estienne had made enemies of the husbands of those nuns – even Onethumb. But why involve the abbey? Why not simply attack Estienne directly?

I'd have to give the matter some more thought, but for the moment I had other concerns. I was still the abbey's chief medical officer and Prior Henry was my patient. I therefore went to the infirmary to see how he was faring.

As its name suggests, the infirmary is a place reserved for the sick and the elderly. In Bury it is a self-contained building located in a quiet corner of the precinct well away from the general bustle of the abbey, a place of rest and comfort. It consists of a pillared hall lined with beds down both sides and its own chapel at the far end. The complex also has its own refectory, even its own cloister. The philosophy is to treat the whole person, body, mind and spirit, all of which need to be in balance if the patient is to return to good health.

I say it is for the sick but they're not the only ones accommodated here. Every few weeks a group of monks is selected for bleeding – something that is thought to be beneficial to general health. A quantity of blood is taken usually from the arm after which the monk is permitted to remain in the infirmary for a few days to recover. This is not as unpleasant a ritual as it may sound. In fact it is a time of welcome relief from the mundane rigours of normal abbey life. Many of the usual abbey rules are relaxed in the hall. The beds are more comfortable than in the monks' dormitory; it is warm - the hall being heated by a fire; and the food is better than normal abbey fare. Brothers are even permitted a little conversation. My old friend Jocelin used to comment that at such times monks would gossip and tell each other secrets of the heart they might otherwise not reveal.

However, these indulgences are still regarded as a breach of the Rule and after their return to the abbey monks are required to seek absolution and to cover their heads as a sign of penitence.

As prior, Henry's bed was placed at the far end of the hall nearest the chapel in order to be closest to the source of spiritual healing - understandable given his status, but it meant I had to pass all the other beds on my way to his. Henry wasn't the only patient in the infirmary just then. There were still those recovering from the effects of the quicklime attack. They all knew of my sympathy with Estienne and were watching with hostile eyes as I passed - those still able to see, that is. Henry's eyes, when I got to him, were closed in sleep.

'How is he?' I whispered to Thomas.

'Thirsty mostly. I've tried him on a little small beer but he kept bringing it back up. So I gave him some boiled water which he did manage to keep down. No sustenance - obviously. He still cannot speak and he's very drowsy.'

'His colour is better though.'

'Should we bleed him do you think?'

I took his pulse. It was thin and rapid – a sure sign of internal turmoil. The internal workings of the body is still something of a mystery. I know that the pulse and the heart are connected in some way though I'm not sure how. When blood is withdrawn the pulse becomes thinner and more rapid and the heart-beat weaker in sympathy. My general approach is that the less that is done the less that can be undone. In other words, if you don't know what you're doing leave well alone.

'Maybe not for the moment. Let's see how he is in the morning.'

'Then how about a prayer to Saint Raphael?' Thomas suggested. 'The patron saint of healing.'

That couldn't do any harm. We both bowed our heads for a moment of silent prayer.

'Mind you,' frowned Thomas. 'As an archangel, Raphael was never in human form so perhaps he may not fully appreciate human suffering. Saint Gereon of Cologne, on the other hand, was very much human and the patron saint of aching heads having had his own amputated. Another prayer to him do you think?'

We bowed our heads again.

'And perhaps one more to Saint Gertrude of Nivelles,' I suggested when we'd finished.

Thomas looked up with interest. 'Gertrude of Nivelles? I've never heard of her in connection with healing. What is her speciality?'

'Rats,' I said nodding towards the quicklime victims. 'We don't want a repeat of the last episode.'

'Oh – quite,' said Thomas.

But before we could address the blessèd lady the infirmary door opened and another apparition appeared: Rosabel, still in her Poor Clare robes, marched straight down between the line of beds towards us followed by Rufus to much noisy objection from the other patients.

Thomas held up his hands. 'I'm sorry sister, but women aren't permitted in here. And you,' he scowled at Rufus, 'should know better than to bring her.'

'She did not know where to find you,' Rufus explained.

'It's all right, Thomas,' I said. 'I know this woman. What is it Rosabel? What's happened?'

Rosabel looked nervously from me to Thomas and back again. 'I think you'd better come, Walter.'

'Where?'

'The friar's house.'

Rufus never runs anywhere but he can surely stroll pretty quickly. The three of us went out under Anselm's arch and straight up Churchgate Street at a forced march. I am no longer a young man and had to skip to keep up with him. As we approached the top of the hill I had to stop him to catch my breath.

'Goodness me, Rufus, slow down,' I said putting a hand on his shoulder and puffing. 'Before I faint from exhaustion.'

It was then that I heard it. It was the sort of noise that comes each Shrovetide when the annual football match between the abbey and the town kicks off: the barely-suppressed excitement of a hundred determined male voices. Some kind of raucous event was under way but I couldn't quite tell what or where it was. It sounded like a ball being kicked repeatedly. We rounded the corner to find the street blocked by a crowd of men and I was shocked to see that half of them were monks from the abbey. But it wasn't the thud of boot on pigskin I heard but another sound, the unmistakable thwack of cane on flesh.

206

Fearing the worst, I pushed my way through the crowd and was appalled by the scene I found there. A circle of men had formed in the street: one half were monks from the abbey, the other were men from the neighbourhood. I recognized many of them as being the husbands of the women who had joined Estienne's Poor Clares. In the middle was erected a post and tied to it, stripped to the waist, was Estienne, his back bloodied and torn as he was being beaten by Rafe, Annie Spiketongue's husband. The punishment must have been going for some time for he was hanging by his wrists and barely able to stand.

'Quickly,' I said to Rufus. 'Fetch the sergeant from the sheriff's office. And for goodness sake, boy, this time *run!*'

He disappeared into the crowd. I then took a breath and stepped into the middle of the open space between Rafe and Estienne.

'What's the meaning of this outrage?' I demanded.

Rafe stopped for a moment, his hand still twitching the cane at his side. 'Step aside brother if you don't want to get hurt. He's only getting what he deserves.'

'By whose authority?'

'These men here,' he said pointing his cane towards the townsmen. 'And these.' He indicated the monks.

I looked from one side to the other. Angry faces stared back at me. Many of them I recognized including, I was ashamed to see, Onethumb who at least had the decency to avoid my eye.

Monks and townsmen they may be, but this was no human thing. It was a mob - a mindless, anonymous creature capable of behaving in a group as they wouldn't contemplate doing individually. I'd seen one like it before during Abbot Samson's time when fifty-seven Jews were massacred outside the gates of the abbey. Amid the religious hysteria of that time Jews all over the country were being attacked, and these in Bury were desperately seeking our protection which, to our shame, we denied them. We kept the gates locked against them and buried our heads inside our cowls while outside the townsfolk murdered indiscriminately. Their killers were ordinary decent folk I knew and saw every day yet together they acted like a pack of wild dogs. Afterwards they couldn't believe themselves what they had done but by then of course it was too late. Fifty-seven innocent men, women and children lay dead outside our gates. This time it was only one man but my fear was that something similar might happen again.

'He's stolen our wives,' said Rafe.

'He's done nothing of the sort,' I retorted. 'They chose to join him.'

'He has twisted their minds,' insisted another man who I recognized as Edric, a local tailor. Normally he was such a quiet, unassuming family man and as honest as the day was long. Others in the crowd I also knew, all looking angry.

I faced him and his companions. 'You men know this is wrong. And you monks have no business even being here. If you have a grievance, let the sheriff resolve it.'

'We don't need the sheriff,' said Rafe flicking his cane again. 'Now stand aside, brother, please!'

We were at the brink. At any moment it could tip over into the abyss. Where the hell was Rufus?

At last I heard the sound of marching feet as soldiers strode into the middle of the arena and formed a cordon around the stricken Estienne. They immediately started pushing the crowd back. One of the monks was knocked over in the confusion but fortunately the sergeant saw him and helped him to his feet. But it was only a brief respite.

'I will take the boy into custody,' he announced in a voice loud enough for everyone to hear.

I turned to him in horror. 'But you can't! He's done nothing wrong.'

'*Protective* custody, brother,' said the sergeant under his breath. 'You see what the mood is here. If I leave him they will tear him to shreds.'

He was right of course. But by now the crowd was pressing in again. The soldiers were being corralled into an ever-tighter circle around the stricken Estienne, and they were losing control. In a few moments the mob will have taken Estienne. Then, just as all seemed loss:

'Hold!'

I turned to see who had spoken. To my amazement and relief it was Prior Henry. He was standing unsteadily with one hand resting on a stick the other on the shoulders of Brother Thomas. Thank God! Like a ministering angel he had arrived just in the nick of time.

The monks nearest him instantly fell on their knees kissing his hand: 'Heaven be praised brother, we thought you were dead!'

'Well clearly I'm not.' He turned to the sergeant: 'Sergeant, what's going on here?'

'As you see, brother.'

Henry took in the image of Estienne, naked and bloodied and still hanging from the gibbet. Then he glared at his own men:

'Cowards!' he bellowed snatching back his hand. 'You bring shame on Edmund's house! What are you doing in this dreadful place? Return to the abbey at once, prostrate yourselves before the high altar and beg the holy martyr's forgiveness! Mine you will not receive.'

'But brother -' one or two of them began.

Henry held up his hand: 'No! I will hear no excuses. I will deal with you all later. Go now before I faint with grief!'

Slowly the monks began to disperse.

But that was only half the crowd. The other half – the townsmen – were still there. But into the gap left by the monks more angels now streamed: their wives still dressed in their nuns' robes. They immediately started attacking their husbands, beating them with their fists and kicking them back to their homes. And suddenly it was over. The mob had become men again. I for one was relieved.

Henry was clearly exhausted by his efforts and Thomas was having difficulty holding him up. I signalled to Rufus to go to him while I went to help Estienne.

The boy looked half dead, blood oozing from his welts. Taking his weight in my arms I looked about for help and caught Onethumb's eye.

Rosabel saw it. 'Well?' she demanded. 'Go on!'

After a moment's hesitation Onethumb came over. He held Estienne up while I cut him down.

'Welcome back,' I said.

*

On Henry's instructions we took Estienne to the abbey infirmary - to the very bed, in fact, he had himself just vacated. Despite his weakness Henry insisted on returning to his office. He wanted it known that he was back and in control.

'Besides,' he said trying to smile. 'If Estienne did try to poison me he won't be able to do it again while he's with us, will he?'

'You don't really think it was Estienne who poisoned you?'

'Someone did. Presumably the same person who's been doing all these other dreadful things. Someone who wishes to discredit the abbey.'

'Not the abbey. Estienne. It's been suggested Arnold wanted you out of the way while he dealt with him. And he very nearly managed it, too.'

'His Chapter,' Henry nodded. 'Yes, I heard about that. Well if it's any consolation I've already told Arnold I will reverse the vote depriving Estienne of his house.'

'And he accepted?'

'Under the circumstances he had no choice. Estienne can keep the house for as long as he wants, free of all encumbrances. I will also add a sizeable donation out of sacristy funds to do with as he wishes. There - does that make you feel any better?'

'It's a start. But it's not Arnold who's had his back sliced to shreds. What do you intend doing about the monks? They were happy to go along with it.'

'What would you have me do?'

'Have them whipped at the very least. Give them a taste of their own medicine.'

'Yes, I could do that. But on reflection I think I will do – nothing.'

'But Henry, they were about to lynch Estienne. If you hadn't arrived when you did they would have done.'

He frowned. 'They were sheep without a shepherd. I was ill. There was no-one to deny them.'

'Well Arnold certainly wasn't going to.'

'Arnold wasn't there either.'

'Ha! The cry of the coward throughout the ages: "I was elsewhere at the time". Where was our noble sacristan, then, while others were doing his dirty work for him?'

'Actually he was visiting me in the infirmary. When he heard what was going on he was as appalled as we were.'

'So he says. It was his words that incited the others to act as they did. There ought to be more than mere financial pain.'

Henry sighed. 'Walter, there is a time for punishment and a time for reconciliation. I'm sure nothing like this will happen again. And now that I'm back in harness I intend to make sure nothing like it does happen again. The sergeant I am sure will do the same in the town. No, I think you'll find the worst is over. We must try now to put this ghastly episode behind us and move on.' He raised a cautionary finger. 'The ceremony, Walter. That is the key. All will be well once we've had the ceremony. You'll see. And now, if you don't mind, I think I'd like to rest for a while.'

I found Arnold lurking outside the prior's office. For once it was him who wanted to speak to me rather than the other way round.

'I just wanted to say it wasn't my idea.'

'Conscience pricking you is it, Arnold?'

'I don't expect you to believe me, Walter, but I assure you I knew nothing about what happened in the town. Upon my oath. I don't hold with violence.'

'You mean you didn't think your constant campaigning against Estienne wouldn't have an effect? That's a little naive isn't it?'

'It isn't just me. You saw what was happening. Half the town is against him.'

'Once again you are overstating the case, Arnold. Most of the town are indifferent.'

He shook his head. 'You know, all this could have been avoided if he'd simply left when he was first asked.'

'I don't think he's going to be doing that now, do you?'

'In that case I hold to my earlier prediction. This will not be the end of the matter.'

Chapter Twenty
OLD WOUNDS

I went straight from Henry's office to the infirmary to look in on Estienne. Waiting outside - predictably - was Kevin. I inwardly groaned. Kevin was becoming a real nuisance. Weeping and wailing is all very well, but where was he when the mob was baying for Estienne's blood? Seeing him I hastened my pace.

'How is he?'

'I'm just about to find out.'

'May I join you?'

I hesitated to say yes unsure whether Estienne would really want visitors in his present condition, least of all an old fusspot like Kevin. But he had been Estienne's most vocal supporter - his only supporter apart from me - so I suppose he had some sort of claim.

'All right. But please remember what he's just been through. If he says he wants to be left in peace we must respect his wishes.'

'Oh most assuredly,' agreed Kevin nodding hard. 'Yes indeed.'

Thomas met us at the door. He had an anxious look on his face and we soon found out why. Most of the beds were occupied by victims of the quicklime attack and were none too pleased at having Estienne among them. With him occupying the same bed as Henry we had to run the gauntlet of their comments as we passed:

'What's he doing here?'

'He isn't even a monk.'

'You should throw him out.'

'Charity, brothers,' said Thomas hurrying past. 'Remember the parable of the Good Samaritan.'

Thanks to Thomas's skilful ministering Estienne looked better than he did when I last saw him. He was lying on his front with his back exposed. The welts from Rafe's caning had been cleaned up and didn't look quite so bad as before. There were one or two lacerations but I'd seen worse. Thomas had rubbed salt in the wounds which though painful is the surest way to prevent suppuration. I also couldn't help noticing that not all the welts were fresh. Some looked as though they had been there for some time. I was curious to know how he got them but this wasn't the time to open old wounds - literally or figuratively.

Kevin gasped when he saw him. 'Oh, my poor boy! What have they done to you?'

Estienne winced as he turned to face us. He was obviously in some pain.

'How are you feeling really?' I asked him.

'A bit sore but otherwise I'm all right, thank you brother.'

'It's an appalling state of affairs,' I said in a loud enough voice for the man in the next bed to hear. 'I can only apologize for my brother monks. We will of course be seeking redress against the perpetrators.'

'You don't need to apologize for us,' said the monk. 'He got what he deserved.'

'Brother, please,' frowned Thomas.

Kevin turned to the man. 'Brother Andrew isn't it? I thought I recognized the voice. One of my leading tenors in the choir. I've a feeling I may not be requiring your services from now on.'

'Suits me,' shrugged the man and turned to face the wall.

'You see how it is, my son,' I said quietly to Estienne. 'Perhaps now you might reconsider what I said about leaving?'

'Oh, but that would mean Arnold will have won.'

'You're not in competition with him,' I frowned irritably. 'Anyway, he's already scored one victory over you. Most of your Poor Clares have returned to their husbands.'

Estienne gave a wry smile. 'I guessed that much.'

'But that's not really what I came to tell you. I believe someone is orchestrating all this. The fire, the quicklime. Do you understand what I'm saying? Someone is deliberately trying to implicate you. I don't suppose you have any idea who it might be?'

'I cannot say.'

'Cannot or will not?'

'Cannot.'

'Whoever it is won't stop, you know? At this rate you'll end up dead. And it's not just you. These men here have suffered as well. If you know something don't you think you owe it to them to speak out?'

'Listen to what Brother Walter is saying,' echoed Kevin. 'You should say if you have any suspicions.'

But he just shook his head. 'I'm sorry. Not yet.'

'Oh yes,' I nodded. 'I was forgetting. Your mission. What's so important that it's worth risking your life for?'

'Something I have to do.'

216

'Whatever it is it's been overtaken by other matters. It's not just you any more.'

'I can't help that.'

I frowned. 'You're being very foolish, Estienne.'

'I think you should stop now,' said Thomas coming over. 'He needs to rest.'

Reluctantly we moved away. When we were out of earshot Kevin touched my elbow. 'Brother, may we speak?' He took me to one side. 'I think the boy is right.'

'About what?'

'I think perhaps we should respect his wishes. If he doesn't want to reveal who his tormentor is we should not press him.'

'You've changed your tune. A few minutes ago you were all for knowing.'

'I'm thinking of the boy. What if he's wrong? What if he accuses someone and it turns out not to be the case? It could go very badly for him.'

'You mean worse than it already has?'

'Have you any idea who it might be?'

'Not yet. But I'm working on it.'

'Arnold has to be a strong candidate, surely.'

I shook my head. 'I don't think so. It would be easier if it was. But he wasn't even at the whipping. He was with the prior at the time and Henry says he was at outraged as the rest of us when he heard.'

Kevin snorted. 'Outrage is easy to fake.'

'I believe it was genuine. Look, I know you've had your own difficulties with Arnold, Kevin, but believe me it's not him. It's someone else. Someone we haven't even thought of yet.'

Thomas joined us. 'I've given him a sleeping draught. His wounds are clean. It will take a few days for them to heal but after that he should be all right.'

'Thank you for taking care of him Thomas, I know you don't have to. If there is any extra cost, for food or anything else, let me know.'

Thomas shook his head, then lowered his voice. 'I don't know if you noticed brother, but those wounds on his back…'

'I thought you said they were healing?'

'They are – the latest ones. But there are others, older.'

'Yes, I noticed them. How much older do you think?'

'Hard to say. Some years. What's his history? Do we know?'

'I know very little about him. He's French from the Alsace region - that's all he's told me. Oh, and he knows Marseilles.'

'Maybe there then.'

'Maybe. Look, do me a favour, Thomas. Keep an eye on him for me. And keep your other patients away from him. I don't want any more unpleasantness.'

'Rest assured brother, while he's in my care no harm will come to him.'

I left the infirmary and went up to the sergeant's office. I got the impression he'd been expecting me.

'Are you going to arrest those men?' I demanded.

'For what?'

'I don't know. Abduction? Kidnap? Assault? At the very least they took the law into their own hands.'

'No-one has made a complaint.'

'*I* am making a complaint.'

218

'Then you arrest them - beginning with that friend of yours with the funny hand.'

Onethumb. I'd forgotten about him. Behind me I heard the clerks snigger. I flopped down on the chair opposite his desk.

'Look Robbie - may I call you Robbie?'

'If you wish. My name is Gilbert.'

More sniggering from behind. I shifted uncomfortably on my chair.

'I am fearful for the lad's safety.'

He shook his head. 'No need. The nunnery is no more. All the wives have returned to their homes. The men have nothing more to complain about - except maybe the food. From what I've heard they'll all be on cold pottage for the next month.'

'This isn't a joke Robbie – I mean Gilbert.'

'I'm not treating it as such. Don't worry, my clerks have taken note of who was involved and I've warned them against any repetition of what happened today. The prior has assured me your monks have been similarly warned. As far as I'm concerned the matter is closed.'

I frowned. 'What about everything else that's been going on recently? The fire. The attack on the chapterhouse. Prior Henry's poisoning. Have you made any progress on those?'

He sighed. 'Brother, if I investigated every fire that breaks out in Bury I'd never do anything else. What goes on inside the abbey precinct is the abbey's business. And the prior assures me his was a nasty dose of food poisoning from which he is now recovering.'

'All very convenient.'

'Meaning?'

'Someone is trying to harm Frère Estienne.'

219

'Who?'

'I don't know, but you've seen evidence of it yourself. That business about the widow Mab for one.'

'He's not complained to me. Until he does I don't see what more I can do.'

'By which time he may be dead.' I got up to leave. 'You know sergeant, you're not the man I thought you were.'

'That's more or less what those husbands said to me. I can't please them and I can't please you. It sounds to me as if I've struck the right balance.'

The clerks sniggered again.

On my way back to the laboratorium I caught sight of Udo apparently sunning himself outside the south door of the church instead of working on the statuary. As soon as he saw me he started back inside. God damn the man he knew I wanted his work finished soonest. Was this how he proposed to do it? I was just in the mood for a confrontation and followed him in.

'What were you doing just now?' I demanded. 'You know my orders. I want you out of here by Saint Edmund's Feast.'

'A call of nature, *fratello*. Unless-a you want me to piss on the chancel floor.'

'What? Oh, yes, I suppose so. But what about this scaffolding?' I said rapping my knuckles on an upright. 'I had hoped it would have been taken down by now. At this rate it will still be up at Christmas.'

'It might have been if I'd been allowed to get on with-a my work instead of having these constant interruptions.'

'What constant interruptions?'

'You for one.'

'I've only spoken to you you twice – and only briefly.'

'Twice too many.'

I frowned. 'Who else has disturbed you?'

'The choir school.'

'The choir school? How have they been stopping you?'

'Apparently they are performing for this tomb-opening ceremony.'

'Yes. I believe Brother Kevin has composed a special piece for the occasion. So?'

'So naturally they want to practise – in-a the church. Each time they do my man and I have to down tools because the hammering "distracts the boys".' He rolled his eyes to heaven. 'Lovely singing, of course. *Bellissimo!*' He kissed his fingertips. 'But each-a time it puts me a little more behind.'

'Brother Kevin has been distracted himself the past few days,' I said. 'I'll have a word with him.'

'Please do. And now if you'll excuse me brother, I have-a the statue to put up.'

He gave me a smug smile and went back up his ladder.

I decided not to tell Henry about the delay. He was trusting so much on the ceremony to put matters right, I didn't have the heart to disappoint him. Besides, these arty types are apt to exaggerate. I was sure with a little bit of effort and good will there would be enough time for Udo to finish positioning the Samson rebuses and get cleared away in time for Saint Edmund's feast day. That should ease matters a little. Surely nothing else could go wrong?

221

Chapter Twenty-one
AN UNEXPECTED
VISITOR

I was wrong. It could.

'What? Here? He's coming here? To the abbey? Here? Today?'

'Today or tomorrow. Outriders were spotted on the road this morning - the royal coat of arms was clearly visible on their livery. There's no doubt about it. The king is coming. Forgive me master, I must tell the prior.'

The servant ran off to spread the news.

With the prospect of King Henry's imminent arrival the already febrile atmosphere of the abbey turned to mild panic. Small wonder. Normally we need at least a month to prepare for a royal visitation. A king's cortège consists of hundreds of individuals from clerks to washer-women, cooks and wheelwrights, retainers of every shape and description. Then there are the barons with all their servants, the prelates with all theirs, lawyers, diplomats, judges - the entire government of England in fact followed in the king's wake. All this was about to descend on us.

The last legitimate king of England to visit us, as opposed to that would-be phony king, Louis of

France, was the present king's father, King John, a decade earlier. On that occasion he only stayed a couple of nights before moving on to Windsor and thence to Runnymede Meadow where he approved the Baron's Charter, latterly known as *Magna Carta*. There must have been five hundred people in his retinue that time not including camp-followers. The wagon-train alone took a day to pass by. All these people needed accommodation, all needed to be fed. Like a plague of locusts they fell upon us devouring everything in sight. That time it took the town and abbey a year to recover. I shivered at the thought of it happening again.

Nevertheless we did our best to be ready for the onslaught. All soldiers' leave was cancelled, the abattoirs primed for slaughter, the townsfolk ordered to hang their brightest fabrics out the windows and be ready to cheer while aldermen and their wives donned their best finery and waited nervously outside the town's south gate along with the prior and half our complement of monks.

It was all for nothing. There was no royal visitation. An entourage of sorts did arrive but it was not at all what we were expecting. In the middle of an escort of half-a-dozen royal-coated soldiers was not King Henry astride his white charger - but Abbot Hugh sitting upon a donkey. The mistake was understandable, although the servant who first broke the news lost a month's pay for getting it so wrong. It turned out that Hugh had "borrowed" some of the king's men for his "dash" to Bury. And the reason? Apparently he had heard increasingly alarming reports coming out of the town and decided he had to return in order to sort matters out in person. This he proposed to do in the chapterhouse the following day.

Every monk was required to attend - even those in the infirmary whether recuperated or not. They shuffled in looking like the dead rising from their graves on Judgement Day. And indeed some kind of reckoning was coming our way judging by the expression on Abbot Hugh's face.

He waited until we had all settled in our seats around the walls of the chapterhouse before beginning his address. He began quietly:

'War in France. Insurrection in the north. A new papal nuncio arriving at any moment from Rome. Have I not enough to worry about? I did at least think I might be able to leave my own abbey in safe hands. Yet what do I hear? Talk of Greek fire. Of brother fighting brother. The prior poisoned.' He shook his head in disbelief. 'I'm absent for five minutes and this is what I come back to.'

That was a little disingenuous. Since his confirmation as abbot a decade earlier Hugh had rarely spent longer than a month at any one time in the abbey. Indeed, no-one had seen him since Easter and that was for just the last crucial three days of the holiday. The truth is Abbot Hugh was a man with political ambitions beyond the parochial. Unlike his predecessor, Samson, Hugh preferred the national stage to our little local one. But you had to admire his perspicacity - he kept himself abreast of the goings-on at the abbey thus proving that his spy network was as good as anybody's in Bury.

'Not *Greek* fire, Father Abbot,' Prior Henry interjected meekly. 'It was lime. That is, er, quicklime ... yes.'

Hugh glowered at him. 'Amusing little ditties have been made up - did you know that? They're being recited all over the council by servant boys. Saint Edmund's has become a laughing stock.' He banged his hand down on the chair-arm making us all jump. 'I will not have it!'

By "council" of course he meant that group of advisers closest to the king. It consisted of all the leading barons and senior clerics of the day including the abbot of Bury. Hugh's standing among his peers on the council rested on the reputation of the abbey, which I suspect is what was really behind his presence here today.

'What progress have you made in identifying the perpetrators of these outrages?' he demanded.

Here Arnold half-rose from his seat. 'We have a suspect in mind, Father Abbot.'

Hugh nodded. 'This friar. What's his name again?'

'Er, Frère Estienne de Saverne, Father Abbot.'

'How certain are you it's him?'

'We are confident the matter will be resolved soon,' said Arnold.

'I hope so. But that's not all that's been going on in my absence, is it? I hear the tomb of the blessèd king-martyr is to be opened.' Here he turned his gaze directly on Henry. 'When was I to be informed of this most sacred event? When it was all over, I suppose.'

Henry squirmed in his seat. 'We did not wish to trouble your reverence with our trifling matters at such a difficult time.'

'The opening of the most sacred shrine in Suffolk - possibly, in all England - is no trifling matter. You, Brother Prior, have proposed yourself to oversee this ceremony, I believe.'

Henry could only nod and give a sickly smile.

'Well it won't happen.'

'Oh, but Father Abbot,' protested Henry, a note of panic in his voice. 'It's all arranged. Invitations have been sent out. We cannot cancel now.'

Hugh shook his head. 'I don't intend to cancel. On the contrary. Now that I'm here, I propose to do it myself.'

Gasps went around the chapterhouse, a few half-hearted hand-claps of approval that quickly petered out.

I could see Henry's shoulders sag, though whether from losing the key position in the ceremony or at the prospect of having the abbot here for longer than he was expecting I couldn't be sure.

'But Father Abbot,' he started to protest. 'The war in France. Trouble up north. Should you not be getting back to Winchester to advise the king?'

'The king can cope without me for a few days,' he sniffed. 'It's less than a week to Saint Edmund's feast day, is it not?'

'The twentieth,' acknowledged Henry.

Hugh nodded. 'Then we will proceed with the ceremony as arranged - but with me officiating in place of the prior. As for the rest, I want to hear no more talk of fires or poisons or rats. Hopefully by the time I leave order will have returned to the abbey and the reputation of this house restored to where it should be. Thank you for your forbearance, brothers. This Chapter is at an end.'

He made a perfunctory sign of the Cross then held out his hand for the brothers to brush our lips against as we filed out.

When it came to my turn to kiss the abbatial ring he whispered for me to remain when the others had gone.

What now?

I hovered while the last of the congregation left feeling their suspicious glances on me as they passed. Abbot Hugh and I had known each other for years, of course, since long before he became abbot. We'd had our moments in the past. Indeed, I'd accompanied him when he was finally confirmed as abbot by the late king on the banks of the Thames at Runnymede immediately after the sealing of the Great Charter. The king had called me for a private audience then – on a private matter, nothing to do with Hugh. But I'm not sure he has entirely trusted me since. I supposed I was about to find out.

'This friar,' he began when we were alone. 'What's his name again?'

'Frère Estienne, Father Abbot.'

'I'm told you are friendly with him.'

'Friendly, father?'

'Don't be coy, Walter. You've been defending him – yes?'

'I thought someone needed to.'

'And that is because you believe he's innocent?'

'I think someone's been deliberately trying to make it appear as though he is responsible.'

'Oh? Who?'

'I don't know yet.'

'You don't seem to know much.'

'Neither do his detractors.'

'Meaning Sacristan Arnold.' He nodded. 'Good man, Arnold. Efficient. Loyal. But if there's the slightest doubt about this friar's guilt I would advise caution. The pope himself is keen on these people,

227

and the way things are at the moment Honorius is the last person the king wishes to alienate. We have few enough friends in Europe as it is. I'll have a word with Arnold later.'

'If you could, Father Abbot, it would be most useful.'

He grunted. 'In the meantime I want you to carry on ferreting - you're good at that. And if you can keep the friar's name out of it it won't go unnoticed.'

'I will do my best, Father Abbot,' I bowed graciously. 'Will that be all, Father Abbot?'

'No. You're also in charge of the tomb-opening ceremony, I believe?'

'I wouldn't say "in charge", father.'

'Oh? What would you say?'

I shrugged. 'Brother Prior knew of my involvement when the tomb was last opened in Abbot Samson's day and thought my modest recollections might be of use.'

'Eleven ninety-eight,' said Hugh stroking his beard thoughtfully. 'Four years before I took the cowl. That's always been a great sadness to me. I should have liked to have been here to see it. I envy you. It must have been a wonderful thing to behold.'

I thought of Edmund's corpse wrapped head to toe in miles of bandaging looking like the victim of a terrible fire.

'It was a truly exceptional experience, father.'

'And one which I intend to repeat. Henry should have consulted me first of course but what's done is done, we are where we are. So tomorrow I want to see the tomb, re-acquaint myself with the layout of that part of the abbey and with the ceremony programme – I take it there is one?'

228

'I believe Brother Prior has given the matter some thought.'

He nodded. 'And since you're such an expert you can accompany me. Act as my guide. Show me what's being arranged. Something extraordinary I hope.'

'I don't think you'll be disappointed, father.'

'I hope not. I want to put on a good show. Something that will be remembered for a generation to come and enhance the stature of the abbey.'

'And its abbot, Father Abbot.'

He glared at me. 'Not *me*, Walter. My office.'

'That is what I meant, father.'

Well, that went better than I was expecting. With Abbot Hugh on our side things might be looking up. Mind you, if it did turn out Estienne was responsible for all the outrages I was sure his support would evaporate pretty quickly. What it wouldn't do, of course, was help find who really is responsible. But I now had the abbot's blessing to carry on with my investigation. Outside I saw Arnold waiting to go in to see the abbot. He was looking pleased with himself, too. That would change once he'd spoken to Hugh. I'd love to have been a fly on the wall.

I decided to pay another visit to Estienne to give him the good news - he could do with some after all he'd been through. But when I got to the infirmary I found his bed empty.

'What do you mean he left? When did he leave?'

Thomas shrugged. 'Presumably while we were all in Chapter. Like everybody else I was required to attend.'

'I asked you to keep an eye on him for me.'

'I'm not his gaoler, Walter. I couldn't compel him to stay. He's not even a member of the abbey. He was free to come and go as he pleased.'

I nodded. 'You're right of course Thomas, forgive me I wasn't thinking. It was good of you to even take him in. As you say, he's not one of our people. Any idea where he went? Back to his house presumably.'

Thomas shook his head. 'I don't think so. Or if he did, he didn't stay there very long.'

'How do you know?'

'Because when I discovered he was gone I sent one of my servants after him with some clean dressings for his wounds. But when he got to the friar's house he found it deserted.'

'Did this servant try to find out where he went?'

'No. He came back and reported to me. But there was nothing I could do. Estienne discharged himself. He was no longer my responsibility. I had to leave it there.'

He might but I couldn't. I had to go and check for myself. But when I got to the house it was as Thomas had said, the place was empty. You'd hardly know anyone had ever been there. It looked as though Estienne had finally taken my advice and gone on to pastures new. After all he said about fulfilling his "mission", I wondered why. Did he take fright at the prospect of having to deal with Abbot Hugh? Or had he simply had enough and taken the opportunity to slip away while we were all in the chapterhouse? I was disappointed that he didn't feel he could at least say goodbye. But maybe it was for the best.

Thus ended the brief episode of Bury's first friar. It was a bit of an anticlimax really. Though he caused a great deal of angst while he was here there was little to show for it once he'd gone. I wondered if I'd ever see him again. Somehow I had the feeling I would.

Part Three

Chapter Twenty-two
A CHANGE OF HEART

Tuesday the eighteenth of November. A new day, a fresh beginning. I could put the unfortunate events of the recent past behind me and devote all my attention to the opening of Saint Edmund's tomb. I have to admit I was beginning to feel quite excited about it. Abbot Hugh said it should be a momentous event and he was right. It certainly wasn't something to be taken lightly. Edmund was one of the most venerated saints in the entire English hagiography, if not Christendom's. Only the opening of Becket's tomb in Canterbury or Saint Peter's in Rome would be more significant.

The ceremony was scheduled to take place on the three-hundred-and-fifty-fifth anniversary of the saint's death in two days time. The purpose, you will remember, was threefold:

Firstly, to prove that the body of the blessèd king-martyr was still in the coffin, for those who had the temerity still to doubt it. The rumour that the body was purloined by the French Dauphin had to be quashed once and for all. To do this it was essential that the body should not only be in the tomb but that it should be seen to be there. He was too important to leave any uncertainty lingering for without Edmund none of it – the abbey, the town or any of us - would be here. It was likewise in the interests of the French to say the body wasn't there, which made it all the more vital to prove them wrong.

Secondly, assuming the saint is in the tomb, it is necessary from time to time to attend to his physical needs. At the very least his hair would need cutting and his nails trimmed. I sense your scepticism at this suggestion. Strike such thoughts from your mind and remember that a saint – any saint, but particularly one of such high esteem as Edmund - is utterly untainted by sin and his body is as incorrupt and as fresh as the day it was first interred. (I know I once referred to the saint's body as "a sack of dried up old bones", but I was young and foolish at the time and have come to regret it since). It therefore follows that things like hair and nails must perforce continue to grow and that occasionally they require attention - and not a moment too soon for the last time this was done was twenty-seven years ago and by now the poor man's needs must be urgent. (Even if his nails and hair didn't need attention on this occasion it would be prudent to pretend that they did as this would be further evidence that the body in the tomb is indeed Edmund's and not some interloper planted there by the perfidious French).

The final and perhaps most important reason the tomb was being opened now was to reaffirm the abbey as the primary form of Christian worship in Bury and any other form (for example, friars of whatever shade or hue) came a poor second. With Estienne gone this particular aspect was no longer quite so urgent but it was nevertheless a useful one. Abbot Hugh would doubtless add that the ceremony would restore the abbey's reputation so badly damaged by recent events - and thereby his own standing as its head.

Everyone knows the story of Saint Edmund's martyrdom: how this last great Christian king of East Anglia was murdered by the heathen Danes and how his severed head, guarded between the paws of a wolf, was discovered in woodland by crying out "Here! Here! Here!". (Some cynics have suggested the wolf had another purpose in mind for the severed head, but we need not dwell on them). The rest of the body having been recovered, it was taken first to London for safe-keeping from the still-marauding Danes and then, some years later once the threat had receded, it was returned to Bury, or *Beodericsworth* as Bury was then known, and incarcerated in the abbey church where it has remained ever since.

That was in the year 1010. Rarely since then has the tomb been opened: once by Sweyn Forkbeard, the father of King Nut in 1014, and then again by Abbot Leofstan in 1060. Both had harboured doubts about the saint's holiness which Edmund rewarded by partially paralysing Leofstan and striking the heathen Sweyn dead on the spot. These two miracles together secured Edmund as England's premier and most robust saint.

Since then, however, few have set eyes on the sacred body. The most recent opening had been in 1198. I was present on that occasion having been invited by Abbot Samson to witness the translation of the body to a new shrine, the old one having been destroyed by fire. The ceremony was conducted in the middle of the night and witnessed by only a few chosen monks so as not to expose too many to Edmund's wrath. You see, with saints one can never be sure how they will react to having their peace

235

disturbed. The reason it had become necessary that time was due to the negligence of the shrine wardens whose duty it was to care for the saint and who had fallen asleep on the job. A stray candle had toppled over and set fire to the coffin which they didn't notice until the flames had taken hold. Some, including my friend Jocelin of Brackland, wondered if the fire had actually been deliberately caused by the saint himself angry at having been taken for granted for so long. Luckily nothing untoward happened on that occasion, but we all knew of the efficacy of Edmund's thunderbolts. For those who did not there was the painting depicting the destruction of Sweyn Forkbeard hung on the wall above the shrine as a reminder. If that did not strike terror in the hearts of the most determined doubters nothing would.

On this occasion, however, Prior Henry wanted as much public scrutiny as possible for the reasons I have given, to which end several local dignitaries and churchmen were invited to be witnesses – though not, I might add, Bishop Pandulf of Norwich. No doubt Henry recalled that when the body was translated from King Nut's roundel to the newly-built apsidal east end the then bishop of East Anglia, Herbert, tried to muscle in on the proceedings and take the glory for himself. Henry didn't want the same thing happening again. The whole point of the exercise was to affirm the abbey's authority not dispute it. However, the coffin had lain undisturbed for over a quarter of a century and nobody knew what we were going to find when Henry opened it which is why he asked me, as one of the few surviving witnesses of the last opening, to recall what I could of it.

I have to say I can't remember the exact sequence of events leading up to the opening - it was more than a quarter century ago. But as far as I remember the coffin had been removed from the old shrine first and left on one side *pro tem* while the new one was being prepared to receive it. Then a day or so later, having fasted and prepared ourselves mentally and spiritually, we braced to raise the coffin lid.

My old friend, Jocelin of Brackland, in his own Chronicle describes better than I what happened next. The sixteen nails holding down the lid were removed with some difficulty and then everyone other than Abbot Samson, Sacrist Hugh and myself, were ordered to stand well back as the lid was lifted. What we found inside was a silk shroud covering the body which was itself wrapped head to toe in linen. I recall Abbot Samson pausing at this point fearful of touching the sacred flesh. No doubt remembering what happened to Abbot Leofstan when he got to this stage, he uttered a prayer to the saint begging to be excused his impertinence and assuring him of his devotion. He then went on to examine the body with trembling hands, touching the eyes and face and nose which he noted was rather prominent, and then over the rest of the body including the saint's fingers and toes each individually wrapped. All seemed to be in good order. No thunderbolts. No shaking of foundations. No tearing of the temple curtain. So far so good.

Having made it thus far unscathed Samson thought it safe to invite other witnesses to share in the wondrous moment. Half a dozen monks were ushered forward to gaze upon the sacred body. There were also a few unofficial witnesses – monks and some of the vestry servants - who, having got wind that something was up, had secreted themselves in the vault above the body and had a birds-eye view of all that went on below.

There's not much more to add. Having satisfied himself that all was well with the body Samson re-wrapped it in fresh linen cloth and placed a new document commemorating the night's events inside the coffin which was then re-sealed, the panels carefully replaced to the outside and the whole nailed down using the same sixteen nails. The job having been completed with no mishaps, we all heaved a huge sigh of relief.

All of this I related to Abbot Hugh as we made out way along the nave of the abbey church towards the chancel at the far end of which stood the shrine. I did notice while I was talking that the abbot had grown uncharacteristically quiet which I put down to the awesomeness of the moment. It was only later I discovered the real reason.

A little before I met up with the abbot that morning I'd received an urgent summons from Prior Henry. I thought he was going get me to try to persuade the abbot to allow him to perform the opening ceremony, but I was wrong. It seemed he wasn't at all perturbed that the abbot had decided to take his place - on the contrary, it was something of a relief. He was still convinced his poisoning had been at the instigation of the saint as punishment for merely thinking about opening the tomb. If true, what would he do when it came to the actual ceremony itself? He was therefore quite relieved that Hugh had taken over from him so that any saintly anger might be directed at him rather than at Henry. No, what concerned Henry was that the abbot's inspection this morning should go off without a hitch, to which end he had suddenly awoken in the night with a disturbing thought:

'The painting, Walter,' he whispered.

I shook my head. 'Painting, Brother Prior?'

'Of Sweyn. The one hanging on the wall behind the shrine.'

Ah! He was talking about the painting I mentioned earlier. I suspected Henry was worried that if the abbot saw it he might take fright and change his mind about leading the ceremony.

'But surely he already knows about the painting. He must have seen a thousand times.'

'Not for a while. I'm hoping he's forgotten about it. I don't want him reminded of it now.'

I understood and assured him I'd remove it before the abbot saw it. And that's what I'd intended. But when I went to do so I saw the painting was already gone. Someone else must have had the foresight to remove it. All well and good. In any event I didn't mention Sweyn or Abbot Leofstan to Hugh in my introductory discourse so maybe Henry was right and the abbot had forgotten about them. But now as we approached the shrine I noticed Hugh dropping back a little seeming reluctant to get too close.

Suddenly, a few yards away, he stopped dead in his tracks.

'What day did you say the ceremony is to take place?'

'The twentieth, father. The day after tomorrow.'

He then slapped his forehead as one who has just been reminded of something of vital importance.

'I've just remembered. I have to be in Salisbury on the twentieth.'

'Salisbury, Father Abbot?'

'The new cathedral. The one replacing Old Sarum. It's being consecrated on the twentieth. The king will be there. The archbishop, the justiciar – everybody will be there. I must go.'

So saying, he spun on his heel and started striding back the way we had come.

'But you'll never make it to Salisbury in two days, father,' I called after him. 'It'll take at least a week. You'll have missed the consecration.'

But he wasn't listening. 'You have my permission to continue with the ceremony,' he called back over his shoulder. 'Don't worry. I have every confidence it will be a success.'

I scurried out after him but he was already half way to the abbot's palace.

But then I too stopped in my tracks. Arnold was standing a few feet away and looking very pleased with himself. It took me a moment to realise why. Beneath his scapular he was concealing something bulky which he now brought out to show me. It was the painting of Sweyn's apoplexy, of course. Not only had he been the one to remove it but he must already have shown it to the abbot and told him the story in every gory detail. No wonder Abbot Hugh was looking so distracted.

Poor Henry. It looked as though he was going to have to run the gauntlet of Edmund's displeasure after all.

Chapter Twenty-three
DEATH ON THE NAIL

And so we come at last to the actual ceremony itself. Following Abbot Hugh's hasty retreat, it was going ahead as originally scheduled, with Prior Henry as *maître des cérémonies*. For those of you who haven't yet availed yourselves of the joy of visiting the shrine of Saint Edmund, I will endeavour to describe it for you:

The tomb is located directly behind the high altar in the semi-circular apse that comprises the extreme eastern end of the abbey church. The shrine is vast, the size of a small house, plated in gold and silver, bespangled with gems of every description and standing proud on a plinth of polished green Italian marble. The whole is surmounted by a golden lid and topped by three gold crosses with a 3lb candle at each corner kept permanently lit. Spaces beneath the shrine were left for pilgrims to kneel in prayer and shuffle as close to the body as possible - and even hiding the occasional fugitive seeking sanctuary; but that's another story.

As I said, Henry was determined to make the occasion a celebration. A lavish feast was therefore planned for after the ceremony for all the guests to be held in the monks' refectory. In addition an enormous tent was erected outside in the Great Court for a hundred of the town's poor. And it didn't end there. I've already mentioned the music being composed specially for the occasion by Brother Kevin. This was to be continued afterwards with dancing and games for the children of the town as a sort of birthday (death-day?) party in honour of the saint. Originally it too was meant to be held out in the open air, but this being England in November the weather could not be trusted so it was decided to hold it inside the nave of the church instead. This, as you will see, turned out to be a fatal mistake.

But that's for later. To return to the main event: several dozen souls - lords and their ladies, monks, priests, aldermen, masters of the guilds and their wives - in short, all the great and the good of Bury, were crammed into the limited space between the altar and the shrine, a space even more depleted by Udo's scaffolding that was still infuriatingly in situ despite my repeated requests, and Udo's repeated assurances, that it wouldn't be. The work to position Samson's sculptures still had not been completed, it seemed. (No doubt he was looking down from his place beside the throne of God and chuckling to himself that he was still a significant presence in the abbey, albeit only in the form of Barnack stone). Despite all extraneous paraphernalia having been removed – mainly the two giant copper cauldrons for receipt of the offerings of pilgrims - space was still so limited that only about half the abbey's sixty-something monks could be accommodated.

Positioned around the shrine were the chief participants in the ceremony: Prior Henry, dressed in his finest robes, at the head end; Arnold as next in seniority to his right hand and Robert the cellarer to

242

his left. The rest of the obedientiaries, including me, were stationed a few feet away so as not to obscure the view of the guests. Determined to have his "odour of sanctity", Henry had had the floor garlanded with lilies – where he got them from in November I will never know. Behind us in the choir we could hear Kevin's singers start an antiphon, preparatory to the main proceedings.

So it began: Having circumambulated the tomb twice accompanied by two acolytes and drenching it and everyone else with holy water, Henry bowed at each corner to the accompaniment of another acolyte jingling a hand-bell. Prayers were offered up to Edmund – a special one composed by Brother Raymond from the scriptorium. It was all going very well. The music had stopped and I noticed even Kevin come into the apse no doubt anxious as everyone else not to miss the shrine-opening. All that was left now was to lift the coffin lid and expose the contents.

The moment had arrived. I was extremely nervous. What would we find inside? Henry took up his position again. At his slightly hesitant signal two monks placed their hands under the edge of the lid and lifted.

Nothing happened. The lid did not move.

I held my breath. What was this? Edmund holding on to the lid refusing to allow us to remove it? But no. A nail – probably one of those sixteen mentioned by Jocelin in his chronicle - had caught the edge of the coffin and held it fast. We all waited while a pair of pincers was found and the offending nail removed.

They tried again, this time with more success: off came the lid which was carefully laid to one side.

Just as Samson had done twenty-seven years earlier Henry now ordered everyone to stand well back - just in case. His eyes widened to saucers as he gazed into the coffin and for one dreadful moment I thought that the rumours about the Dauphin's robbers were true after all and that the coffin was indeed empty. But no again. We could all see the outline of a body lying inside wrapped in bandages just as I remembered it, the saint's famously distinctive nose showing proudly above the side of the coffin. We all breathed a sigh of relief.

A finger crooked in my direction. I stepped forward.

'Well Walter?' Henry whispered. 'Is this the body of the king-martyr or not?'

I looked at the mummified thing masked beneath yards of linen. It could have been Edmund. It probably was him. On the other hand it could just as easily have been my mother's molecatcher who had sported a similarly prominent nasal appendage. But this wasn't really the moment for semantics.

'As far as I can tell,' I whispered back.

Henry nodded. As he put his hands inside the coffin his face took on an expression of ecstasy mixed with that of a condemned man who knew he was about to die: a sort of pained resignation. It was then as I was returning to my place that I happened to look up - and saw the angel descending.

There was no time to think. I gave Henry a tremendous shove sideways and myself dived out of the way. A moment later the stone carving crashed to the ground breaking into several pieces. There were screams as bodies fell in all directions. The ground shook and bits of masonry flew everywhere - I felt a sharp pain as a piece sliced my cheek.

Then – stillness. For a moment nobody moved. We were all in shock. My mind raced to memories of Abbot Leofstan and Sweyn Forkbeard. Henry had dreaded how Edmund might react to the ceremony. Was this his response?

As the dust started to settle I looked frantically across at Henry but the statue - one of the angels being replaced by Samson's rebuses - seemed to have missed him by inches and for a moment I thought disaster had been averted. I was wrong. A few feet away beneath the broken masonry and lying absolutely still was another body: Arnold, his head smashed and his blood and brains spattered across the tiles and up the marble base of the shrine. There was no doubt about it: even from this distance I could see he was dead. From my supine position I peered up to the top of the scaffolding from whence had come the angel and as the air cleared I could just make out one pair of eyes staring back down at me out of the gloom:

Estienne's.

Chapter Twenty-four
OF MURDEROUS INTENT

Dazed as I was, this was no time to be lying on my back contemplating the vicissitudes of life. With the dust still filling the air I got to my feet, shook myself and went over to examine Arnold. But there was nothing I or anyone else could do for him. His head had been completely crushed by the angel statue. I said a brief prayer over his body and looked around to see if anyone living needed my attention. Apart from a few cuts from bits of flying masonry it didn't appear anyone else was badly injured. The carving had miraculously – or perhaps not so miraculously – fallen exclusively on Arnold. Cellarer Robert, who had been closest to him when the statue fell, was shaken but unharmed. Of those around the coffin that left only Prior Henry. He had been quickly bundled out of the church by half a dozen monks and over to the prior's house where I found him still dressed in his robes seated in his day room and surrounded by hand-wringing brothers all talking in excited whispers.

Other than his face and tonsure being covered in bits of masonry and dust he seemed to have escaped unscathed. But he was clearly in a state of shock and the brothers flapping around him were only making matters worse. So as his physician I ordered them all out except for myself and Henry's chaplain, Brother Ignatius.

'He seems all right,' said Ignatius. 'No bones broken. He was wearing so many robes I doubt anything much could have penetrated. What about you? You were closer than most of us. There's blood on your face.'

I put up may hand and felt a small cut on my cheek where the fragment of masonry caught me.

'It's nothing. I'm fine.'

'Here, drink this. It'll clear your throat.' He offered me a cup of wine and then another to Henry who took it with a shaking hand and looked up at me with a hunted look:

'It has come to pass, Walter,' he whispered.

'What's come to pass, Henry?'

'The prophesy. Just as I feared.'

'The prior believes it was the saint who threw down the angel,' said Ignatius, *sotto voce*.

I snorted. 'That's nonsense!'

'No Walter, it is not nonsense,' Henry insisted. 'Don't you see? Edmund has struck. He has given his answer. I am being punished for my arrogance just as Abbot Leofstan was for his and Sweyn Forkbeard before him. That statue was meant for me.'

'Really? Then all I can say is he's a rotten shot. He missed you by a good yard.'

He looked at me sternly. 'Do not mock, Walter. It is only by the Grace of God that I was not crushed.'

I sighed. 'What makes you so sure you were the target?'

'An angel, Walter. An *angel* - think of that! What more proof do you want?'

'Henry, there are angels all over the roof of the apse. They've been up there so long it's a wonder more haven't fallen on the shrine before now.'

He gripped my arm. 'The shrine! Dear God I'd forgotten about that. Was it damaged? Please tell me it wasn't.'

'Do not fear, Brother Prior,' Ignatius reassured him. 'The shrine was left untouched.'

'Thank God!' said Henry crossing himself.

'Not that it would have mattered if it hadn't been,' I said. 'It would need one of the rocks at Stonehenge to fall on it to make any impression on that colossus. Besides, that's not how the sheriff's sergeant sees it. He thinks it was a deliberate act by a living hand rather than a heavenly one. He's arrested Estienne.'

Henry looked stunned. 'What? Why?'

'Because he was up there on the scaffold when the angel fell.'

'But I thought he'd already left Bury.'

'We all did. It seems we were wrong. Or maybe he came back specially. You invited him, remember?'

'I don't understand,' frowned Henry. 'Why would Estienne wish to do me harm?'

'Not you, Henry. Arnold.'

'Ah yes, poor Arnold, I was forgetting. How is he? Was he badly injured? I didn't see.'

The chaplain and I exchanged glances.

'Brother Arnold is dead, Brother Prior,' said Ignatius gently.

Henry groaned. 'This is all my fault.'

'I don't think so, Henry,' I said. 'Arnold was the intended target. And unlike Edmund, Estienne's aim was spot on.'

'But why?'

'I should have thought that was obvious. To pay him back for what he's done to him.'

Henry frowned shaking his head. 'No, this is not right, not right at all. Where is the boy now?'

'In the town gaol I imagine.'

'You must get him out.'

'Oh? How?'

'You must go to the sergeant and explain that it wasn't Estienne's fault. He was merely acting as Edmund's instrument.'

'His *instrument?*'

'Yes of course. Edmund was just using him for his own purposes. He induced Estienne to act on his behalf just as he induced him to release the rats.'

'I think you're getting a little confused now, Henry.'

'No I'm not. I've never been so clear on anything in my life. Edmund waited until the coffin was opened – until the very *instant* it was opened - before causing the statue to fall. The timing was deliberate. He wanted to leave no-one in any doubt who was responsible.'

'Then why did he hit Arnold and not you?'

'That was your fault.'

My jaw nearly hit the floor. '*My* fault?'

'Yes of course. If you hadn't interfered the statue would have hit me.'

'Henry, I saved your life.'

'And in the process destroyed Arnold's. But I don't blame you for that. You acted in good faith. Nor do I blame Frère Estienne. Unlike you he had no choice. He was merely acting as Edmund's surrogate. Yes, that's right. That's what happened,' he said drumming his fingers on his chin. 'You must go and explain all this to the sergeant.'

'I will not. He'll think I'm mad.'

He glared at me. 'Are you doubting the power of the saint *again*?'

'I'm questioning whether Edmund would use a proxy to achieve his goal. He was quite capable of punishing Leofstan and Sweyn by himself. I'm sure he could have done the same to you if he'd so wished. He didn't need an "instrument" or a "surrogate" to do it for him before. Why should he bother this time?'

But Henry was determined. 'He had his own reasons for doing so. We ordinary mortals cannot discern the wisdom of the saints.' He set his jaw. 'Well if you won't tell him, I will have to.'

He stood up, still in his full regalia of cope, stole, alb and chasuble and clutching his staff, if still a little wobbly on his feet. Bits of masonry fell off him onto the floor.

I took his arm to steady him. 'Henry, you're in no fit state. And you can't go dressed like that. The sergeant will definitely think we're all mad.'

'Then you'll do it?'

I sighed. 'What makes you think he'd even listen to me?'

'You know him. He respects you.'

'Hardly, after our last encounter.'

'Walter, do this for me. I cannot compound one error with another. The boy is innocent. I am the guilty one. I alone must atone for my sins.'

'Henry, don't you think you're taking this a little far?'

He looked at me sternly. 'Half the chancel ceiling lying smashed on the floor. One of our dearest brothers killed. How far should I take it? And besides, there's something else. Something I haven't told anyone.' He gripped my arm and lowered his voice. 'I saw him, Walter. He came to me as a vision, just like you said. It really happened. Not in a dream. In daylight when I was in the infirmary.'

'Who came to you Henry?' I sighed.

'Edmund,' he mouthed silently.

'That was the fly agaric. You were hallucinating.'

He shook his head vehemently. 'No Walter. Edmund came to warn me and I heeded him not. I dare not ignore him again. And neither must you.'

There was no arguing with him while he was in this frame of mind. I left him with Brother Ignatius.

Outside I found Kevin hovering again. Was I to have no peace? Like the rest of us he had masonry dust on his robe but otherwise looked uninjured.

'Walter! Is it true? Has Arnold been killed?'

'I'm afraid so.'

He gasped and covered his mouth with his hands. 'Oh dear lord! And the boy?'

'Arrested.'

He gasped again. 'But it was an accident surely?'

'I honestly don't know, Kevin. But if it's any consolation Prior Henry doesn't think Estienne was to blame.'

'But he was in the loft - alone.'

'He was indeed. At least, I think so.'

'You *think* so?'

I grimaced. 'It's complicated.'

I didn't want to get into another discussion about saints and miracles.

'Look Kevin, much as I appreciate your concern I really haven't time to discuss it now.' I started towards the abbey gate.

'Why? Where are you going?'

'To see Estienne - if they'll let me.'

'May I come too? Oh *please* Walter. To offer comfort at this dreadful time. The poor boy, all alone and without a friend in the world. He must be terrified.'

By then I'd lost the will to resist. All I could do was shrug my shoulders.

'Why not?'

All the way up to the sergeant's office I debated with myself whether to mention Henry's theory about the saint to him or not. Did I believe it? Not for a moment. And if I was to convince the sergeant of it I would have to believe it or at least seem to. If he was convinced it would mean Estienne's immediate release. If not he might just throw me in gaol for wasting his time. He'd been among the invited guests along with his wife. I didn't think he'd be in much of a mood for leniency.

I might have discussed it with Kevin except having a sensible conversation with him was impossible at the moment. He kept up a running commentary the whole way, mostly insisting on Estienne's innocence because he was such a nice young man – another argument that would cut little ice with the sergeant. In the end I decided to hold fire on Henry's madcap theories at least until I could assess the sergeant's frame of mind. It was fortunate, however, that he'd been on hand to apprehend Estienne or the boy might have been torn apart by the guards. Not that Estienne put up any resistance. He'd just stood and allowed himself to be taken. It was almost as though he'd wanted to be caught.

When we finally made it into the sergeant's office it was obvious straight away that he was less than happy. He had a number of little cuts on his hands and face from flying masonry. Kevin was no help either blundering straight in and proclaiming Estienne's innocence before I could even get a word out:

'It was an accident, sergeant. There's no question about it. I insist you release the boy immediately.'

'And you are?'

'I am the abbey novice master - a senior official of the abbey. I request – no, I *demand* that you release him at once.'

'What my colleague means,' I said smiling obsequiously and trying to push Kevin aside, 'is that we shouldn't be too hasty to judgement.'

The sergeant looked as though he was getting ready to deliver a well-directed rebuke, so I got in quickly:

'Er, how is your wife by the way? Not injured I trust. I'd be happy to examine her if you so desired – free of charge, of course.'

'She's fine. Thank you.'

'Good. Excellent. But I'm available - should the need arises. Which I'm sure it won't,' I grinned. 'Er, do you know what happened yet perchance?'

The sergeant glared at me. 'What do you think happened? A life-size statue of an angel fell forty feet from the gallery on to Sacristan Arnold killing him instantly and injuring twenty others in the process.'

'Deliberate do you think?'

'Not something that could have happened accidentally, I shouldn't have thought. And since Frère Estienne was the only person up there at the time...'

'A simple accident,' insisted Kevin. 'It's obvious.'

'Not to me.'

'You're quite sure Arnold was the target?' I asked.

'Given their history I'd say it was a safe bet, wouldn't you?'

'Oh,' I grimaced. 'You heard about that.'

'I should think the whole town heard about it.'

'Has he confessed?'

'He hasn't denied.'

'That's not the same thing at all,' frowned Kevin and shaking his head furiously. 'Not at all. Silence is not admission, not by any means.'

'So what happens now?' I asked quickly.

'If he's guilty he'll hang. And the way I'm feeling at the moment,' he said picking another shard of masonry from his tunic and flicking it at Kevin, 'I'd put the rope around his neck myself.'

'Oh, but there'll be trial, surely?' said Kevin. '*Please* say there'll be a trial.'

The sergeant shook his head. 'There will not.'

'What? That's outrageous!'

'It's the law.'

'How can it be the law? Surely everyone's entitled to a fair trial?'

'Not in this case. He was the only one present when the incident occurred. And he's confessed.' The sergeant was plainly growing irritated with Kevin.

'I thought you said just now he hadn't confessed?' I said.

'As good as. Now, if you don't mind...' He indicated the door.

I could see there was no way Estienne was going to be released at the moment. I needed to find out what actually happened up in the shrine loft, and there was only one person who could answer that.

'Can I see him first? As his spiritual confessor. You wouldn't deny a condemned man the means to make his peace with God?'

'Oh yes sergeant, *please* let us see him!' begged Kevin. 'For the sake of his immortal soul.'

The sergeant pursed his lips. I could see he was in two minds whether to let us or not. Finally he sighed.

'Leave your knives here.'

When the door to Estienne's cell was opened Kevin went rushing in ahead of me and took Estienne's hand in his own:

'My dear boy, are you all right? Why did you kill him? I know you and Arnold had your differences, but even so. To hurl a statue down on him like that. What made you do it?'

My eyebrows went up. So much for insisting it was an accident.

Estienne delicately extricated himself from Kevin's grasp. 'I'm fine, brother. Thank you for your concern.'

'Are you sure you're all right?' I asked him. 'You're very pale. That gash looks nasty.'

There was blood on the side of his head presumably where the guards had knocked him down.

'A slight bump that's all.'

My relief that he was all right quickly gave way to anger:

'What in God's name were you doing up there on the scaffolding?'

He shrugged. 'I was invited.'

'I know, by Prior Henry. But he didn't mean the loft. He meant down on the ground with the rest of the guests.'

'I think I understand,' said Kevin sagely. 'You didn't think you'd be welcome among the other guests - am I right?'

'Something like that.'

'I thought that's what you'd do.'

'Then what happened up there?' I asked him. 'Was there a statue loose? Did you lean on it too hard?'

He shrugged.

The boy was as infuriatingly evasive as ever. But this was no time for playing childish games.

'Estienne, I don't think you realise the seriousness of the situation. Brother Arnold is dead, his head crushed to pulp. If you won't explain yourself the sergeant will have no option but to assume you killed him deliberately. If that's not what happened then you must say so now.'

'I cannot tell you any more than I have.'

'Do you understand what I'm saying? No-one is going to speak up in your defence. You've made too many enemies.'

He shrugged again.

God in heaven, what was wrong with the boy? Did he *want* to be executed? If I'd had any hair on my pate I'd have been pulling it out by now. I tried another tack:

'You think you're being courageous by not answering? I don't. I think it's cowardice. If you won't speak then you lie by omission and I cannot absolve that which you do not confess freely and sincerely. You will go to your maker unshriven. Is that what you want?'

'I do not wish to confess. I do not want absolution.'

I was wasting my time. More importantly, I was wasting his and he had precious little left.

'Then on your own head be it.' Exasperated, I got up to leave. 'Come on Kevin. We're clearly not wanted here.'

'Oh!' said Kevin tearfully.

'Will you do something for me, brother?' Estienne asked.

'Certainly not. If you won't help yourself why should I?'

He lowered his eyes and nodded. 'Quite right. I don't deserve it.'

My heart went out to him. This may well be his dying wish.

'What do you want? No, don't tell me – your shawm.'

He smiled. 'I feel naked without it.'

'I doubt whether the sergeant will allow it. But I'll try.'

All the way back to the abbey Kevin was still insisting Estienne was innocent when he wasn't blubbing incoherently. I didn't know myself what to think but there was obviously more going on than he was saying. Yes, Arnold had been his nemesis but I thought he'd shrugged it off and decided to move on. Coming back to Bury specifically to kill Arnold and to do so in such a public and dramatic way just seemed so bizarre. Apart from anything else he wouldn't have known what Udo had been doing in the loft above the shrine or anything about loose angels, and he would surely have had to know. And then to simply wait around afterwards to be arrested? No, it was wrong. It was all wrong.

Kevin and I parted company at the abbey gate. As I turned towards my laboratorium I noticed one of the monks I recognized from the infirmary a few days earlier hovering nearby - Brother Andrew, the monk who Kevin had chided. Not that you could miss him. He still had a white patch over one of his eyes.

'It may be nothing,' he said, 'but I thought you'd want to know. My bed was next to his, you see?'

'His? You mean Frère Estienne?'

'Yes, the friar. We chatted a little. In those circumstances people open up. They say things they might otherwise not say.'

That was what Jocelin had meant about monks gossiping in the infirmary. It seemed even Estienne wasn't immune to such seduction.

'What did he say?'

'Not much. Only that perhaps you should look closer to home for your answers.'

'Closer to home? What does that mean?'

'I don't know. I have no love for the friar. Like Arnold, I think these people are dangerous. And he did this to me,' he said touching his eye-patch. 'But he seemed sincere. And he was genuinely distressed about something.'

'You don't know what?'

He just shook his head.

'Did he say anything else?'

'No, that was all.'

But that wasn't all for I knew something that perhaps no-one else did. I couldn't be certain but when I was lying on my back in the apse looking up at the loft I thought I saw something. It was dark up there and there was a lot of dust in the air so maybe it was just wishful thinking on my part. But if I was right then Estienne wasn't alone in the loft. Someone else was up there with him.

Chapter Twenty-five
THE WHISPERS GROW LOUDER

Despite what I told Estienne I wasn't quite ready to give up on him just yet. But there was now a new urgency to the situation. The sergeant was quite right in what he told Kevin. Under the law anyone caught red-handed in the act of committing a crime could expect swift justice without recourse to a trial, and no-one could have been more red-handed than Estienne. He didn't even try to deny it. As far as the sergeant was concerned it was case proven. I could have told him about the shadowy figure I'd seen up in the loft with Estienne but he would only have accused me of trying to save Estienne from the noose – which of course I was – and that might make matters worse. Besides, I couldn't be entirely certain Estienne would corroborate my observation. For some reason he seemed determined to be found guilty. And if he didn't I would lose what little credibility I had left with the sergeant. No, if I was going to save him I was going to have to find another way, and there was little time in which to do it. But where to begin?

Udo, our temperamental sculptor, was the obvious place to start. I found him skulking round the back of the church trying not to draw attention to himself. As soon as he saw me he he started backing away:

'I have-a nothing to say to you, brother. Those statues were firmly fixed when I left them. There is-a no way you can blame me for that monk's death.'

'I'm sure the statues were perfectly fine,' I reassured him. 'No-one's seeking to blame you. That's not what I've come about.'

That relaxed him a little. 'What is it then-a you want?'

'Just to ask - in the days leading up to the shrine-opening, did anyone visit the site?'

'Lots of people visited the site, brother. You for one.'

'Apart from me. I'm thinking specifically about anyone who might have wanted to come up onto the scaffolding.'

'You mean like that friar?' He shook his head. 'No. I would have remembered. Anyway, I do not allow people up there while I am-a working.'

'And when you're not working?'

'When was I not working? - you saw to that. And when I was not my apprentice, Eric, was. He would not have let anyone up either. He knows-a my rules.'

'You're sure about that? What about at night?'

He shook his head. 'Not even then. Eric and I slept on site. My art is-a far too valuable.' He lowered his voice. 'Believe it or not, brother, there are-a thieves even among the righteous. Can you believe?' He tutted and shook his head in despair.

'Deliveries of raw materials, then? Someone must have brought the stone up to you.'

'Pah!' he snorted. 'When-a did you last see an English workman carrying stone up a ladder?'

'Blunted tools?'

'We sharpened them ourselves.' He gave a smug smile. 'I am sorry brother, but there is-a no way anyone could have come onto the scaffold without one of us seeing them.'

This was turning into a game of hunt the thimble. There had to be something.

'All right then food. Presumably you ate occasionally?'

'We had the regular abbey meals – if you can call them that.' He pulled a face. 'Disgusting.'

'Where did you eat? Not in the refectory with the monks?'

'No. We eat on site.'

'So someone must have brought it to you - yes?'

He nodded grudgingly. '*Sì*, sometimes a monk, sometimes a servant. I know what you are going to ask, but we always came down-a to eat.'

'Every meal? You're telling me no-one ever brought food up to you, not once in all those weeks? Please think carefully before you answer, Udo. A man's life may rest on it.'

He gave me a coy look. 'Maybe once towards the end. We were busy - you in particular were always pushing us to finish. But it was only the one meal.'

'Who?' I asked. 'Who are we talking about? Who brought you that meal?'

'One of the monks. Do not ask which one, you all look-a the same in your black habits.'

'But it was a monk, not an abbey servant – you're certain about that?'

He nodded reluctantly. 'I am pretty sure it was a monk.'

From there I went to the kitchens.

At the abbey we don't have regular kitchen staff. Monks take it in turn to cook and serve in the refectory on a sort of rotary system. I've even been known to lend a hand myself on occasion although I can usually find some pressing medical emergency to take me away from the abbey when my turn comes. I rarely get criticized for doing this. Knowing my culinary skills – or lack of them - my brother monks are happy to see my turn usurped by someone who can do more than boil an egg. Strictly speaking this is against the Rule which stipulates that every monk must share in all abbey tasks however menial even if, as in my case, this means most of the food is inedible and ends up either with the pigs or in the almonry for distribution to the poor.

Now I wanted to know who had been on duty in the days leading up to the shrine-opening ceremony. Brother Gildas, the current *chef du jour*, showed me the latest roster:

I frowned. 'Are you sure this is right?'

Gildas looked over my shoulder. 'Yes, that's the roster for last week.'

'But this says Brother Sidney was on serving duty. He was badly burned in the quicklime attack. I'm sure last week I saw him in the infirmary.'

'Ah, yes,' nodded Gildas. 'That's right, he was. Brother Martin took his place.'

I was disappointed. 'You're certain it was Martin?'

'Oh yes. I never forget Brother Martin. He's a terrible cook. Bags of enthusiasm but no sense of timing. Burns everything. Do you know he even burns soup?' He chuckled.

'Last week the food was fine. So someone must have taken Martin's place.' I raised questioning eyebrows.

Gildas cringed. 'If I tell you, you must promise to keep it to yourself. I don't want to get Martin into trouble.'

'You won't.' I crossed my heart.

He whispered the name in my ear.

I frowned incredulity.

He nodded. 'I know. I was as surprised as you.'

I tried to make sense of what I'd just learned. If Udo was right then I knew how the murder was committed. If Gildas was right then I also knew the killer's identity. But the two didn't match. It simply wasn't possible.

Maybe Gildas got it wrong. Or Udo. Maybe one or other got the weeks muddled up - it's easily done. I needed more evidence before I started throwing wild accusations about. The trouble was I was running out of options - and more importantly time. For all I knew Estienne might already be swinging from the scaffold. No, I was sure if the sentence had been carried out I'd have heard. And despite the summary nature of the process there were still certain formalities that had to be gone through first. Those supercilious clerks in the sergeant's office would have to scribble away to formulate the correct documentation to justify an execution - we weren't a completely barbarous nation yet.

I went to see the prior to see if he could have a word with the sergeant and persuade him to delay matters for a while - or better still, make a plea for clemency. In the Church we don't execute people anymore even for murder - at least, not members of the clergy. But we were back to the same old problem: Estienne may be a religious but he was not a member of our community and whatever the pope may say, friars had not yet been fully recognized as a legitimate branch of the clergy in England.

'Estienne may not be a monk but Arnold certainly was,' I told him. 'Doesn't that make a difference?'

Henry shook his head. 'It might if he'd been the murderer. Arnold was the victim.'

'What if I could prove the real murderer was a monk of the abbey?'

Henry was shocked. 'Can you?'

I was sorely tempted to say yes but all I could do was shake my head.

'Then I'm afraid we are in the hands of the civil authorities.'

When I got back to the laboratorium Rufus wasn't there. He came in a few minutes later.

'Where have you been again?'

'In the church, praying.'

'Very commendable. For anyone in particular?'

'For Arnold. For Estienne. For the prior. For you -'

'Yes, all right Rufus, you don't have to give me a list. I get the idea – you prayed for everyone. Very good.'

Almost immediately there was a knock at the door. The last thing I wanted right now were visitors so I let Rufus answer it. In a moment he was back.

'It's the gatekeeper.'

I frowned. 'What does he want?'

'You.'

'Can't you deal with it?'

'I don't know. Can I?'

'Well don't ask me, go and find out.'

He did but was soon back again.

'He wants you.'

Infuriating boy. I went to the door.

'Yes, what it is?'

'A message for you, brother.'

'From?'

'Your brother, Joseph. He came earlier but you were out.'

'Couldn't you have given it to my assistant?'

'He said I was to give it to you, personally.'

I sighed. 'What's the message?'

'Nothing much. He wanted me to write it down but I didn't have a quill. Besides,' he lowered his voice confidentially. 'Between you and me, brother, I can't read nor write.'

'You don't say.'

'Hm,' he nodded. 'I do. But I told him to tell it me anyway. He didn't think I'd remember it, but I did. With letters, see, I stumble, but with numbers I soar,' he grinned and whistled as his hand flew like a bird.

'What numbers?'

He cleared his throat. 'Eight, seven, one, three.'

I frowned. 'What?'

'Eight, seven, one, three.'

'Yes, I got that. What are they for?'

'Fucked if I know. Just said to give them to you: Eight, seven, one, three.'

'Well now you have. Thank you.'

'My pleasure, brother. Always keen to help the monks.'

With that he turned on his heel and went back to his gate.

I closed the door.

'Eight, seven, one, three.'

'Master?'

'Nothing Rufus. It's just something the gatekeeper said. Carry on with what you were doing.'

Eight, seven, one, three.

What was I supposed to make of that? Joseph must have thought I'd know or he wouldn't have been so cryptic. And they must be important or he wouldn't have gone to the trouble of bringing them to me in person. Perhaps I should go to the shop and ask him. But the thought of trudging back up to town again… I shook my head.

Eight, seven, one, three.

Perhaps if I wrote them down they would make more sense. I found a scrap of parchment and some charcoal and wrote:

EIGHT
SEVEN
ONE
THREE

and stared at them. No, nothing. I tried writing them as numerals:

8 7 1 3

Still nothing.

'Rufus – does this mean anything to you?'

I showed him the parchment. He glanced at it briefly. Then he did something unprecedented. He took the piece of charcoal from my hand and added two dashes so that it now read 8-7-1 3.

'Why did you do that?'

'It makes more sense that way.'

'I don't see how. It looks the same to me.'

But then it clicked. Of course! I slapped my forehead. Clever old Joseph. And clever Rufus, too, for spotting it. But why didn't Joseph explain it to Rufus? It was almost as though he didn't want the boy to know.

I looked at the back of Rufus's head. Like me he was tonsured but unlike me he still wore the un-dyed robe of a novice. Like grey friar's robe.

Slowly the hairs on the back of my neck began to tingle. I stood up and went over to him.

'Rufus, do you remember the conversation we had that time I was in Chapter? Perhaps you've forgotten the occasion. It was just after the quicklime attack and I came back here to find all the rat cages empty.'

'I can remember it precisely.'

Yes, I imagine he could probably repeat the conversation word for word.

'Repeat it for me now.'

'All of it?'

'Exactly as you remember it.'

It was uncanny, like he was reading it from hand-written notes he'd made at the time as a clerk might in a court of law:

'You said, "Dear God, how could this have happened?" I replied, "I cannot say, master." You then said, "But you were here the whole time".'

'That's right,' I interrupted him. 'I asked you if anyone had come in to the laboratorium.'

Rufus shook his head. 'No. You asked, "Did you *see* anyone come in?" I replied, "I saw no-one".'

Yes, that must have been literally what was said. I thought for a moment.

'What if I had asked instead, "Did anyone come in?" What would your answer have been then?'

'I would have answered, "Yes, someone came in".'

'And you didn't see them because…?'

'I shut my eyes.'

The tingling in my neck now spread quickly down the length of my spine.

'Did this person you didn't see also open the cages and let all the rats escape?'

'He did.'

'But you didn't try to stop him?'

'I did not.'

'Who was it, Rufus? Who let the rats escape?'

'I cannot say.'

'You must.'

'I cannot.'

'I'm telling you you can.'

'Are you ordering me?'

'I am.'

His face, never expressive, started to twitch as though he were being pulled in two different directions at once and he didn't know which way to go. He held his breath. Finally he shook his head.

'I'm sorry,' and breathed again.

'All right Rufus, never mind. I think you've already answered it.'

'Will that be all?'

'For now, yes.'

He started to walk away.

'No – wait. Take off your robe.'

'My robe?'

'Yes, your robe, take it off.'

He did so.

'Now lift up your shirt.'

'I am wearing nothing underneath.'

'I'm aware of that.'

'But abbey rules concerning nudity -'

'Don't argue with me Rufus, just do it.'

He lifted his shirt.

'Now turn around.'

It was as I thought. Yes, it was all coming together. But I still needed to do one thing more in order to be certain. I took my scrap of parchment with the numbers on it and went over to the abbey records room. It took me a while but I finally found what I was looking for: the last piece of the puzzle. Clever of Joseph to have worked it out.

But now I had, too, and I knew for certain who was responsible for killing Arnold and for all the other terrible things that had been happening. And most importantly, why.

Chapter Twenty-six
AN EXCEPTIONAL
TALENT FOR MURDER

Constant interruptions - that's what Udo said. At the time it meant nothing to me. What it actually meant, of course, was that I wasn't the only one doing the interrupting. Someone else also wanted to check on the progress of work on the Samson memorial. My reason was because I was anxious that the work be finished and the scaffolding removed in time for the shrine-opening ceremony. But why would anyone else wish to know? The answer was for the exact opposite reason: to delay the work for as long as possible thus ensuring that the scaffolding would still be there during the ceremony and consequently no-one else would be up in the vault loft at the crucial moment – no witnesses, that is.

'Witnesses to what?'

'Why, to your murder of Brother Arnold of course.'

'My what?' Kevin looked at me in astonishment. But then he laughed. 'Oh, I see. This is one of your famous jokes.'

I shook my head. 'No joke, Kevin. You murdered Arnold and now you're trying to murder Estienne.'

He stopped laughing and looked at me with incredulity. 'What are you talking about?'

'It's quite simple. You were the one constantly interrupting Udo's work by repeated unnecessary rehearsals in the abbey choir - Udo confirmed as much. Each time he and his man had to down tools until you'd finished. That way you managed to put him back by at least a week.'

'For what purpose?'

'I just told you. To make sure the scaffolding was in place during the shrine-opening ceremony. I couldn't figure out the reason why at first. But then I remembered the last time the shrine was opened and some of my brother monks secreted themselves in the loft space above the shrine in order to see what was going on down below. With the scaffolding there this time no-one would be up there to see you kill Arnold – no witnesses. It was also you who got yourself on to the kitchen roster so you could bring food up to Udo and at the same time check on which statues were loose - Gildas confirmed that. He was quite surprised when you volunteered, by the way. You never have before. But then he didn't know the reason.'

'Walter, you're losing your mind. It was Estienne toppled the angel that killed Arnold, everyone knows that. You saw him yourself. In any case, how could it have been me? If you remember I was standing next to you on the chancel floor when the statue fell - unless of course you think I can be in two places at once.'

'Yes, that bothered me for a while, why you were so keen for me to see you. Then I understood. You were establishing an alibi for yourself for when the statue fell.'

271

'But if I was on the chancel floor how could I have toppled the statue?'

'Oh, I don't mean you personally pushed the statue off the parapet. But you were responsible.'

'How?'

'By inducing someone else to do it for you. It was Henry gave me that idea by the way, so I can't take the credit for it. He thought it was Saint Edmund. But I think it was you.'

'Really? And who exactly have I been inducing?'

'Rufus.'

He drew back in astonishment. 'You mean your assistant? I hardly know the boy.'

'Of course you know him. He's your son.'

At this Kevin reeled. 'I'm not listening to this,' and he started to walk away.

'Eight, seven, one, three.'

He slowed and stopped. 'Now what are you blathering about?'

'I wasn't sure myself at first. I thought the numbers sounded familiar but couldn't quite place them. It was Rufus who put me right. He recognized them straight away - well, he would, wouldn't he? Eight, seven, one, three: the eighth day of the seventh month of the thirteenth year - the day you and he joined the abbey together. It's all in the abbey records - I've checked. You both joined on the same day.'

'A coincidence.'

'I don't think so. You arrived together and you registered together - father and son.'

He turned and gave a wry smile. 'Aren't you missing something? I'm sure I don't need to point out to you that in order to father children a man has to be

272

capable of performing with the ladies. I, famously, prefer boys.'

'No you don't. You're not that way inclined at all. It's just an act you put on to conceal the fact that you're Rufus's father.'

'And why would I wish to do that?'

I shrugged. 'You tell me. Perhaps you were ashamed of him – he is a bit odd. Perhaps you feared the abbey might agree, think it was a case of like father like son and reject you both. I don't know. Whatever the reason, you wanted your association with him kept quiet.'

'I told you, I don't know the boy. I've hardly ever spoken to him.'

'Well you see that's another lie. You were his novice master for ten years. Technically you still are which is why he still wears the white cloak of the novice school – the cloak, incidentally, that the limester's daughter remembered when you got him to steal a sack of quicklime for you, the one used on the chapterhouse.'

'Oh, I'm responsible for that as well, am I?'

'Indeed you are. Arnold wasn't the only one absent from the chapterhouse that day. You flounced out under the guise of having been insulted by Arnold only so that you could throw the quicklime in through the chapterhouse window. You also released my rats – Rufus told me it was you, by the way, once I'd finally asked the right questions. You also sent the note to Estienne inviting him to meet you at the abbey grounds, and you probably set the fire that nearly choked my best friend's wife to death as well as poisoning Prior Henry. You did all that in order to foment hostility towards Estienne.'

He contrived to look astounded. 'To what possible purpose?'

'Ah, well now, that's the key question, isn't it? It took me a while to work it out and I'm not entirely sure I've got the story quite right yet, but I'll give it a shot - you can correct me where I go wrong. Let's start by going back a few years - to the year before you and Rufus arrived here in fact, the year 1212. You remember it, I'm sure. It was a time of great religious turmoil. Jerusalem was in the hands of the infidel; heresies were springing up all over Europe. The Church was under attack from all sides. There was a yearning to spread the Gospel and recover the Holy Land for Christ. Where armies had failed it was thought the innocence of children might succeed. Their intention was to march to Jerusalem and convert the Muslims to Christianity. Insane when you think about it now but at the time it seemed plausible. Children from all over Europe flocked to the rendezvous point near Vendôme in France - among them your twelve-year-old son, Rufus. That was where he met Estienne for the first time. How am I doing so far?'

Kevin didn't reply, so I continued:

'Estienne, as we have seen, is a highly gifted speaker and was probably a charismatic preacher even in those days. He would have easily overawed a young impressionable boy like Rufus. When enough children had gathered they set off for the Holy Land in high spirits singing psalms and praising God. But they never got there. Hardly any wonder really - thousands of children walking half way across the world dependant entirely on handouts for their survival? It was doomed to failure. They went south towards the Mediterranean expecting the waters to part for them so they could walk to Jerusalem. When that didn't happen many of the children were sold into slavery or died of starvation or worse. Rufus and Estienne both made it as far as Marseilles but something happened to them there, something terrible - they both have the same scars on their backs to prove it, I've seen them. Rufus did eventually manage to get back to England but by then he was a changed person. Damaged beyond repair and for that you blame Estienne - am I right?'

'Go on.'

'From here I admit I'm a little vague, but I'm guessing some time after his return Rufus's mother must have died - from a broken-heart possibly? No doubt you blame Estienne for that, too. So, widowed and with a son to care for, you decided to abandon the world and become a monk. You had to take Rufus with you of course, he could hardly have survived on his own. But you didn't want the abbey authorities to know, so you put on this act to hide the fact that you are Rufus's father. Or maybe you're just naturally flamboyant. Some men are.'

'This is all very interesting,' said Kevin. 'But how does Arnold fit into it?'

'I'm coming to that. Arnold, as we know, was not the most tolerant of people. He despised what he saw as your unnatural ways and humiliated you mercilessly. It must have been galling suffering all those years and knowing the truth but never being able to admit it. But you put up with it for Rufus's sake. Then out of the blue Estienne arrives in Bury. That must have been a shock. No wonder you were so tongue-tied when you first met – not, as everyone assumed, because you were attracted to him. Quite the reverse. You were appalled. Suddenly here were your two greatest tormentors in Bury at the same time. It must have seemed as though the king-martyr himself was mocking you. But then Prior Henry announced he was going to open the shrine and suddenly you saw a way of wreaking revenge on both of them. You would kill Arnold and have Estienne hanged for it. How deliciously ironic. It was just an idea at first but the more you thought about it the more irresistible it became. It wouldn't be difficult to drum up opposition to Estienne – there was already plenty there. You just had to play on existing prejudices with Arnold his chief persecutor.'

'And how was I to achieve this fantasy?'

'Exactly the way you did. You fostered Arnold's natural suspicion of Estienne by those silly tricks with quicklime and rats. You did the same to the townsfolk by setting fire to Rosabel's goose hut. All designed to generate ill-feeling towards the lad.'

Kevin feigned innocence. 'But Walter, I was Estienne's greatest supporter, you of all people know that. I even came to give him comfort when he was in the infirmary and when he was in gaol.'

'No you didn't. You came to gloat. You couldn't resist it. You knew Estienne couldn't tell me the truth without incriminating Rufus, and that was something he would never do.'

'And Percival? How exactly did he fit into this diabolical scheme of mine?'

'He didn't. You never meant to harm Percival, although I don't suppose you were too sorry when you did. Another jeerer getting his just deserts.'

Kevin shook his head. 'I'm sorry Walter, but as a theory it lacks credibility. You say Rufus killed Arnold. Why? What reason did he have? If what you're saying is true it should have been Estienne he wanted to kill, not Arnold. Yet by all accounts they got on well together. Rufus even mended that damned flute of his.'

'Shawm. And yes, that must have infuriated you. To your mind Rufus should have hated Estienne for what he did to him all those years ago. But you know as well as I that Rufus is incapable of hating anyone. No, Rufus killed Arnold for one reason only: because you told him to.'

Kevin snorted. 'Now you really are insane. No-one commits murder on the mere say-so of another.'

'Rufus would if it was you told him. That's something else I've learnt about the boy since he's been my assistant. You and I have something in common. We are probably the only two people in the world he would obey without question - me because I am his master and you because you're his father.'

'Rubbish!'

'It was a clever plan, but it nearly went wrong.'

'Oh? How?'

'By poisoning Henry. That was a mistake. I realise the idea was to foment further ill-feeling towards Estienne but you very nearly got him banished altogether. No wonder you were in tears. You needed both Arnold and Estienne together for the final part of your plan to work.'

'Which was?'

'Rufus's invitation to Estienne to join him on the scaffolding above the shrine. Estienne accepted, probably hoping for the reconciliation he had always sought. Except Rufus was simply doing your bidding once again. You told Estienne in the gaol that you knew he would go up into the loft. I should have picked up on that at the time but I wasn't thinking of you then. Once they were up there alone together all

Rufus needed to do was to push the angel off the scaffold at the crucial moment and then step back out of sight leaving Estienne to take the blame. I know Rufus was there, by the way. I saw him.'

'Then why don't you tell the sergeant?'

'Because Estienne would deny it, as you know perfectly well. He won't implicate Rufus.'

Kevin gave a wry smile. 'It's an amazing story, Walter, I have to congratulate you. Unfortunately you can't prove a word of it. And nobody would believe you. It's too fantastical. And as you say, Estienne will simply deny it. He thinks he's done enough wrong to Rufus already. No-one will suspect Rufus of killing Arnold. They certainly won't suspect me. A dozen people saw me beside the shrine when the statue fell. As far as anybody knows Estienne was the only person up in the loft at the right moment so only he could have thrown the angel down. And now Estienne's in gaol awaiting the hangman's noose. I will of course continue to protest his innocence to the end and weep copious tears at his funeral. No doubt Arnold's friends will sneer about that, too. Let them. Inside I will be laughing.'

He was right of course, I couldn't prove it. It was all conjecture. But I had hoped that by confronting him in this way I might be able to shame him into admitting what he had done. I could see now it was a vain hope. And without his confession Estienne will surely hang. In frustration I blurted out:

'You're right, no-one will believe it. It is, as you say, too fantastical. So maybe I've got it wrong and Arnold was right. Maybe you really are the simpering effeminate fool you pretend to be. Is someone like that capable of hatching such an ingenious plot? I doubt it. It would take a man - a real man. And you, Kevin, are simply not man enough.'

When he turned back his eyes were on fire. 'And what about you? The great Walter de Ixworth. You're as bad as all the rest with your pretend liberal ways. I've always known what you really think of me, making out to be my friend and all the while laughing behind my back. Don't think I'm surprised because I'm not. Not man enough, am I? I'll show you who's not man enough. I did it. Everything you said. I let your precious rats out. I drenched the brothers in quicklime. I started the fire in that stupid whore bitch's house – oh yes, I've seen you slavering over her, don't think I haven't. I even poisoned Prior Henry and I had Rufus kill Arnold exactly as you said - stupid boy would do anything I told him. It was me. It was all me.'

'Then admit it. Be the man you say you are and own up to what you have done. You won't hang and neither will Rufus, I promise. You're both fully members of the Benedictine Order. As such you're under Prior Henry's jurisdiction and he won't permit it. You've already taken out your revenge on one man. Let that be enough. Oh Kevin, you're not an evil man. You have given so much joy with your wonderful talents. I can see you've been badly treated and for that I am sorry. But do the right thing now. Show you are above these other wretches. Set Estienne free and receive the absolution of the Church and the salvation of your soul.'

He looked at me hard. 'I could, couldn't I? I could go to the sergeant right now and have Estienne set free. It would take just a word from me. So easy.'

'Oh yes, brother,' I begged. 'So very easy. And so right.'

But his mouth curled into an ugly sneer. 'Never! He'll hang and no-one will ever know the truth.'

My shoulders drooped. 'God will know.'

'Then let God be my judge.'

We were interrupted by the two keepers of the shrine who came running out of the church followed by a pack of women. They were pale and breathless and looked terrified.

'What is it?' I asked. 'What's happened?'

'It's the friar,' one of them panted. 'He's escaped.'

My stomach lurched. I glanced quickly at Kevin. 'Good. I hope he gets away.'

'No, you don't understand,' said the other man. 'He's taken the children.'

Here all the women started talking at once. It took me a moment to understand what they were babbling about. But then I realised. It was the town children who had come into the church for the ceremony. These women were their mothers.

I turned back to the two shrine wardens who were cowering behind me: 'What do you mean he's taken the children? Where has he taken them?'

'Down into the catacombs.'

I frowned. 'What catacombs? The abbey doesn't have any catacombs.'

The two men looked at each other. 'We must tell him,' said one.

'We can't,' said the other. 'We are sworn to secrecy.'

'Come on one of you, speak or I'll let these women tear you apart.'

'Beneath the abbey church there are tunnels,' explained the first man. 'Under the foundations of the old church from ancient times, before the abbey was built. Only the keepers of the shrine are supposed to know about them. They are – *were* – the means to evacuate the saint's body should the Danes return.'

'What are you talking about? There haven't been any Danes in Bury for over two hundred years.'

'That's why they were forgotten.'

I shook my head. 'Where are these catacombs?'

'Through King Knut's doorway - that's what they call the entrance in the crypt. But no-one is supposed to know where it is.'

'Well someone does. Estienne for one.'

'There's something else,' said one of the men.

'What?'

'Your boy went with him.'

Now Kevin perked up. 'Boy? What boy? You mean Rufus?'

The men nodded. 'He followed the friar into the tunnel.'

Kevin went pale. If I ever doubted Rufus was his son before I did so no longer.

'Show us.'

They led us into the church and along the north aisle to the north transept and from there down the stairs that led to the crypt below. The women followed us - I couldn't have stopped them if I'd wanted to. It was dark down there lit only by torches. But there was no sign of any other entrance or exit. The children, Estienne and Rufus had all vanished. Finding them seemed an impossible task. If Estienne had led the children into these tunnels they would surely be lost for ever.

Then I heard a sound above the babbling of the women.

'Sshh!' I said. 'Quiet everyone! Stand still and listen.'

We all cocked our ears. Somewhere as though a long way off came the sound of Estienne's shawm. It was getting fainter as though moving away.

I turned to the two shrine keepers. 'Where's this doorway?'

They showed me. I held up the torch. At first I saw nothing but then I saw the shadow of a false wall. Behind was a door. It was the entrance to the tunnel all right.

Kevin started to go in. 'I must go to him.'

But before he could we heard a rumbling sound like distant thunder. Then a great rush of air and dust billowed from the entrance.

'The tunnel!' gasped one of the keepers. 'It's collapsing!'

Some of the women screamed and others tried to push past us to get into the tunnel but I pushed them back.

'No, it's too dangerous. We are too late.'

There was more rumbling from the tunnel and more dust filling the crypt. It became impossible to breathe. It was obviously useless to remain.

'Quickly!' I said. 'We must follow the line.'

I didn't really know myself what I meant but once outside the church it was obvious. All along the courtyard we could see it, a long thin depression appearing as the tunnel rapidly collapsed beneath our feet. It was moving so fast we could hardly keep up. Under the courtyard it went and out into the street. Passers-by jumped back in amazement as the ground disappeared before them as though some giant subterranean creature were burrowing through the earth.

Outside I felt familiar eyes on me and searched the crowd of anxious-looking parents. Onethumb and Rosabel stared back at me with terrified eyes. That could only mean one thing: Little Rosa and Hal were among the children abducted by Estienne and were in the underground tunnel. Panic as well as fear now gripped me. I knew we had to get them out.

We followed the line as it progressed up the hill. A cart trundling past lost its back wheels while two horses shied and nearly threw their riders. Then half way across the square the tunnel suddenly stopped. There was another terrifying rumble and a wide circular depression formed in the ground. Some of the mothers screamed fearful that their children were being buried alive.

'No, look!' yelled one of the shrine wardens. 'There they are!'

Sure enough, up the hill at the top of the Mustowe was a marvellous sight indeed. Dozens of children were emerging one by one from a hole in the ground, coughing, covered in dust and looking dazed. I looked hard. Yes, among them were Hal and Little Rosa and were immediately scooped up by Onethumb and Rosabel.

'Dear God thank you!' I muttered under my breath.

I waited until all the children were out and safely in their parents' arms. Miraculously, none seemed to be missing. But of Estienne and Rufus there was no sign.

Epilogue

The older I get the more I find myself reflecting on past events, but whenever I do so it is the embarrassing moments that stand out. Something will stir a memory and I will cringe over what I did or didn't do, or at some offence I gave. Having reached the ripe old age of sixty-one there seem to be more of these moments than any other - so many in fact that I sometimes think my entire life has been one continuous embarrassment. But I cannot go about with my hands permanently covering my face in shame.

Maybe if I'd done things a little differently the tragedy that I have been unfolding might never have happened. If I'd been a little more assertive with Arnold, say, or if I'd simply given in and allowed him to drive the lad out of town at the very beginning. Either way he might still be alive today. And not just Arnold but Rufus and Estienne too, and Brother Percival. It is a thought that will trouble me to the end of my days.

What actually happened in the catacombs will probably never be known for certain. One of the older girls, Liana, told us what she knew which wasn't much. It seems the children had been seated in the nave of the church awaiting the shrine-opening ceremony when they heard the crash of the angel falling, though they didn't know it was that at the time. In the confusion that followed the monk in charge of them told them to remain in their seats while he went off to investigate. So they waited. And they waited. But the monk didn't return. Meanwhile there was a lot of activity with many people coming and going. The children seemed to have been forgotten.

In the end they got bored with waiting and decided to leave which was when Estienne made his appearance. Although he wasn't a monk they knew him having seen him often enough around the town. So when he started playing his shawm and invited them to follow him around the nave they were happy to do so - they thought it was all part of the celebration. Then he began to lead them dancing down into the crypt.

It was then that the other man appeared, the monk with red hair. At first they thought he was part of the celebration too, but when he began arguing with Estienne they realised he wasn't. He seemed to be trying to get the children away from Estienne but Estienne was having none of it. They didn't know this new man and didn't like him - he seemed strange. So when Estienne told them to hide in the tunnel until he'd gone they didn't hesitate to obey. But the other monk followed too and was soon remonstrating with Estienne again this time inside the tunnel.

By now the children were becoming frightened. It was dark and cold in the tunnel and they didn't like it very much. They wanted to leave but they couldn't tell which way to go to get out. They'd also lost sight of Estienne and the red-haired monk although they could hear them still arguing in the darkness somewhere behind them. Then there came a crash and rumbling noise and the ground began to shake. The little ones started whimpering saying they wanted their mothers. Meanwhile the rumbling noise got louder and dust started filling the air making it difficult to breathe. Some of the children were crying openly now, very frightened indeed. Liana tried to calm their fears but even she began to fear they were never going to get out.

But then they saw a glimmer of light ahead of them in the distance and decided to make for that. The tunnel seemed to be going uphill and got narrower as it went. Some of the children wanted to go back but Liana managed to persuade them to carry on. And it was a good thing they did. As they drew nearer the source of the light they could see it was an opening and the light was daylight. Crawling through the opening they were amazed to find themselves at the top end of the Mustowe far from the abbey. Liana was the last to leave just as the tunnel finally collapsed behind them.

As soon as they were out their parents saw them and came running over. Now everyone was crying and hugging, children and parents alike more in relief than anything. But all the children managed to get out safely, Liana was sure of that, although she never saw what happened to Estienne or the red-haired monk.

*

Why did Estienne do it? I suppose the obvious answer is as an act of revenge on the townsfolk for the appalling way they had treated him. In any event, I don't believe he really intended to harm the children. He just wanted to give the townsfolk a fright. The fact that someone – and it can only have been Estienne - opened up the tunnel exit at the top of the Mustowe that enabled the children to escape proves it. But would Rufus have realised this? Probably not. All he would have seen was children being led into danger. Somewhere in that damaged mind of his he retained a memory of that other group of children also led by Estienne with disastrous consequences and he knew he had to prevent it.

So what caused the tunnel to collapse? That surely wasn't part of Estienne's plan. You have to remember the catacombs hadn't been used for three hundred years. In that time many thousands of carts, horses and people must have trundled over the top - it's a wonder it hadn't collapsed before. My guess is something got accidentally dislodged in the fight – a wooden prop perhaps - and the whole rotten structure came crashing down burying Estienne and Rufus together in one final violent embrace. But that's just my theory.

There's not much to see above ground anymore. The road was levelled off so you'd never know the catacombs had even existed and no doubt in time they will be forgotten entirely. But if you pass along the road today you might just detect a slight depression where the line of the tunnel once ran. Prior Henry had the entrance in the crypt walled up and its location lost for ever. A traveller's inn was later built over the Mustowe exit and named *The Angel* in memory of the event that initiated the catastrophe. I believe they make a good living from patrons willing to pay for the privilege of viewing it – another sort of pilgrimage. I do occasionally see Kevin kneeling in the road above the spot where it is presumed Rufus and Estienne lie buried. My brother monks assume that he is grieving for the loss of Estienne. They, of course, know nothing of his connection with Rufus. He could put them right but not without admitting his crimes which he can never do for that would mean incarceration within the abbey walls. So he will have to put up with their sneers and smirks - one more indignity he has brought upon himself and will have to bear in silence. And that, in case you are wondering, is why I never told anyone of Kevin's confession to me. Not for reasons of priest-penitent confidentiality but because not knowing if your child is alive or dead seems punishment enough to me. He asked for God's judgement. Maybe this is it.

Elsewhere life slowly returned to normal. Udo finally completed the Samson rebus memorial and dismantled the scaffolding – and not a moment too soon. Prior Henry got over his trauma over the shrine-opening ceremony although I believe with every twinge, rheum and sore throat he still wonders if this is the expected retribution from the saint. (I've even caught him on occasion testing the tips of his fingers to see if he's losing sensation). In the weeks that followed a whole raft of letters arrived from Abbot Hugh in Winchester demanding to know what had been occurring in "his" abbey. Prior Henry solemnly read out each one in Chapter along with his reply. But gradually Hugh's interest, and the letters, dried up as more important concerns took his attention.

I did eventually summon the energy to walk the quarter mile to Heathenmans Street and ask Joseph how he managed to come up with the date of Rufus's and Kevin's admission to the abbey. And do you know what he said? I told him. Apparently when I was considering Rufus as my next assistant Onethumb had asked his age and I'd looked it up. It completely slipped my mind – another sign of increasing age. He'd also worked out the connection between Estienne and Rufus – that business about the charcoal cure for Henry's poisoning gave the clue. He'd learnt the trick from Estienne. Of course he had. It was an Arab cure which they both had learned in Marseilles. Obvious when you think about it, only I was too stupid to have realised.

A few weeks later I was on my way to visit a patient in the town when I saw a familiar figure hobbling towards me. It was Rafe, the husband of Annie Spiketongue. He was walking with a limp and had a cut over one eye.

'What happened to your foot?'

'A disagreement over Annie's mother. Annie wanted her to come and live with us. I put my foot down.'

'That foot?'

He nodded.

I stifled a laugh.

'And the eye?'

'Last night's supper. At least she's back,' he smiled cheerfully. 'My Annie.'

'No more cucking stools?'

He just shrugged and hobbled off.

We are still awaiting our first batch of Franciscans. Under the circumstances it was thought best to hold off for a while and let things settle down a bit before accepting any more. In any event I gather Fratello Agnellus had never even heard of Estienne. He wasn't a member of the Order of Friars Minor in London or anywhere else. His true origin remains an enigma.

So why did he come? Out of guilt for what happened all those years before with Rufus, perhaps? Was that what he meant by his "mission", to find some form of reconciliation with Rufus? He tried several times to connect with Rufus but never quite managed it - not because Rufus didn't want to be reconciled but because he never saw the need for it. Rufus was beyond all that. Oh, and I am once again without an assistant.

A final thought: it is only assumed Estienne and Rufus died in that tunnel. Without digging up half the town we are never likely to know for certain and neither the prior nor the sergeant will permit it. They just want to put the entire unhappy episode behind them – let the dead bury the dead. But given Estienne's escapological skills it wouldn't surprise me if he did manage to get away. And in this respect I would add just one last thing: some time later I heard a strange story about an incident in a town in northern Germany involving a piper, a tunnel, some rats and some children. The town in question is called Hamelin which is near Hanover I believe. When I heard the tale I have to admit to feeling a slight shiver of *déjà vu*. But it's probably just a story.

HISTORICAL NOTE

FRANCISCANS

Friars (from the French, *frère* meaning "brother") began life in Italy in the early 1200's. At the time there was a desire in Europe to return to ideas of simplicity and poverty as exemplified by the life and ministry of Jesus Christ. Francis of Assisi wasn't the first to promote such ideas but he was the first to win approval from the pope.

Franciscan rule forbade ownership of property and required members of the order to beg for food while preaching. They travelled and preached in the streets and boarded in church properties. A female follower of Francis, Clare of Assisi, founded the Poor Clares in 1212 which became the women's branch of the movement.

A small group of Franciscans first arrived in Canterbury in 1224 led by Agnellus of Pisa and became known as the grey friars in order to differentiate them from the Dominicans who were the black friars. From Canterbury they soon moved to London and from there to most of the principal towns of England including Bury St Edmunds.

In Bury they were regarded with suspicion and for a long time were refused permission by the abbey to locate within the *banleuca* – the boundary of the town as defined by their founding charter of 945. They only finally made it inside the town in 1257 as a result of a papal bull and even then their oratory and buildings were burned by the abbey's supporters in an attempt to drive them out. Friars were never popular in Bury.

THE CHILDREN'S CRUSADE

Before literacy there was oral tradition, tales handed down by word of mouth over generations. The problem with this way of remembering is that each time the story is retold it changes slightly so that eventually it bears little resemblance to the original – rather like the children's game known as Chinese Whispers or Telephone. King Arthur and the Round Table is perhaps one of these, Robin Hood and his Merry Men another. Like all such legends they have a kernel of truth at the heart of them.

The Pied Piper of Hamelin is another such story, a strange conflate of rats and children disappearing down holes in the ground and led by an enigmatic figure dressed in colourful clothes and playing a piped instrument. How this story originated is unknown but it may have grown out of that extraordinary movement eight hundred years ago that came to be known as the Children's Crusade.

It seems that around the year 1212 several thousand children gathered somewhere in central France led by two boys, one French and one German, with the intention of marching to the Holy Land in order to convert Muslims to Christianity. Their idea was to walk across Europe and live by begging from the people they encountered on the way. The children never made it to the Holy Land. Many died on the way or simply gave up and went home while others were sold into slavery.

HENRY RUSHBROKE

Not much is known about Prior Henry Rushbroke except that he succeeded Prior Herbert who died suddenly of unknown causes on 10th September 1220. Henry went on to become the abbey's thirteenth abbot in 1235 dying in 1248. His tomb still containing his skeleton lies in the floor of the ruined chapterhouse of Bury abbey alongside Abbot Samson and three other abbots.

FLY AGARIC

This is a mushroom that grows wild throughout the northern hemisphere. It has a bright red cap covered in white dots. It is mildly poisonous and is noted for its hallucinogenic properties and used in some cultures for religious purposes. Incidentally, if rubbed over the body it can give the sensation of flying which is sometimes thought to be the origin of the notion of witches flying on broomsticks.

SHAWMS

The shawm is a double-reeded woodwind instrument that originated in the eastern Mediterranean and was probably brought to Europe by returning Crusaders. In modern times it has been succeeded by other members of the double-reed family – oboe, bassoon and *cor anglais*. The body is conical in shape, usually made from a single piece of turned wood and terminates in a flared bell rather like a trumpet. It was played like a clarinet (which has one reed) or a recorder (which has none). Its sound is loud and nasally and for that reason was regarded as an outdoor instrument.

SWW September 2018

UNHOLY INNOCENCE

May 1199. Richard the Lionheart is dead and his brother John has just been crowned King of England.

John travels to St Edmund's abbey in Suffolk to give thanks for his accession. His visit coincides with the murder of a twelve-year-old boy whose mutilated body bears the marks of ritual sacrifice and martyrdom. This isn't the first time such a thing has happened. Eighteen years earlier another child was murdered in the town in similar circumstances.

Abbot Samson needs to find out if this is indeed another martyrdom or just an ordinary murder and appoints the abbey's physician, Master Walter, to investigate. Walter discovers a web of intrigue and corruption involving some of the highest in the land but unbeknown to him his own past holds a secret which will put his life in danger before the final terrible solution is revealed.

ABBOT'S PASSION

Easter 1201. Following a treaty between King John and King Philip of France, England is at last at peace. Alas the same cannot be said for Saint Edmund's Abbey. The pope's new legate has arrived determined to stir up controversy. For Abbot Samson this brings the possibility of a new ally against an old enemy. But his intrigues lead to disaster with Brother Walter being placed in mortal danger and a full-scale battle in the nearby village of Lakenheath.

In the middle of all this the legate's clerk is murdered and a London merchant is wrongly accused. In desperation the man is granted sanctuary at the abbey's shrine, but it is only a brief respite. The whole weight of the judiciary and the church are against him.

Amid rape, religious bigotry and trial by combat Walter has to find the real murderer before a terrible injustice is done and the wrong man is hanged.

WALTER'S GHOST

Summer 1206. Before it was renamed, Bury St Edmunds was known as Bedricksworth after the ancient family who lived there. Now the last surviving member of the Bedrick clan, Arnulf Bedrick, wants an heir to carry on the family name. Marrying for a fifth time, this is his last chance to achieve it. But Arnulf has a secret.

Now jump forward seven hundred years to New Year's Day 1903. The antiquarian and celebrated writer of ghost stories, M. R. James, is excavating the graves of five medieval abbots of Bury. But in one of the graves he discovers something that shouldn't be there.

How are the two events connected? What is the secret found buried in the abbot's grave? Over it all hovers the ghost of Brother Walter who drives the investigation on to solve not only a seven hundred year old murder mystery but also another in the twentieth century in the way only Walter can.

MONK'S CURSE

December 1211. After thirty years as abbot of Saint Edmund's, Samson is dying. Before he takes his last breath, however, he calls Brother Walter to his bedside in order to recite the tale of the Green Children of Woolpit. This is a well-known local legend about two children who were found wandering in a Suffolk field half a century earlier.

Samson also reveals he has recently been visited by a mysterious woman who claims a murder is about to take place. But Walter cannot find out who the woman is or anyone else who has seen her. Did she really exist or was she, like the green children, just another product of a dying man's imagination?

Walter is reluctant to get involved but as he starts to investigate he realises there is more to both tales than first appears and eventually unmasks a tale of abuse and corruption going to the very heart of government.

Can Walter finally solve the mystery of the Green Children of Woolpit and prevent a murder being committed, or is he already too late?

BLOOD MOON

November 1214. King John has returned to England having lost his empire to King Philip of France. Humiliated and desperate for support, he again travels to Bury St Edmunds where Abbot Samson has died and a battle is raging among the monks over who will be his successor.

In the midst of this there arrives in the town a seemingly inconsequential young couple and their maid. The wife is heavily pregnant and gives birth in the night to a baby daughter.

But then the maid is mysteriously murdered and it is soon apparent that the family is not all that it appears. With rebellion looming, abbey physician Walter of Ixworth is drawn once again into investigating a murder and a conspiracy that threatens to engulf the country in civil war and ultimately leads to the final nemesis that is Runnymede and Magna Carta.

NINE NUNS

Summer 1219. A group of nuns from England set out to travel to the south of France in order to found a new convent. Against his better judgement Walter agrees to accompany them to ensure they arrive safely at their destination.

But they never get there. Instead, one by one the nuns disappear in mysterious circumstances.

What happened to them? Were they murdered? If so where are the bodies? Or is the ship on which they travelled simply cursed as some believe?

Vanishing nuns, shipwrecks, pirates, murder. Walter becomes embroiled in matters he does not understand that will place his own life in peril not once but several times before the end of the adventure.

DEVIL'S ACRE

January 1242. Brother Walter is dying. He is an old man but the prospect of death does not disturb him - indeed, he welcomes it to meet with old friends and see God in the face. But before he finally joins the Heavenly host he is determined to solve one last mystery that has been plaguing him for decades.

But there are dark forces afoot that want to frustrate his efforts and are prepared to go to any lengths to keep secret events that even now could disturb the government of England - even murder.

In his mind Walter returns to those far off times when Abbot Samson took him on a bizarre journey away from the comforting familiarity of Bury Abbey and into the wilds of barbaric Norfolk where the abbot's power is limited and be met by a far greater one in the guise of the Warenne family of Castle Acre - or as some still choose to call it, the *Devil's Acre*.

THE SILENT AND THE DEAD

Winifred Jonah seemed like an ordinary Norfolk housewife, jolly, plump and harmless. Yet her bland exterior concealed a sinister secret. At fourteen she had already murdered her aunt and uncle and forty years later it was her husband's turn to die. Even so she might have made it to her own grave without further incident if she hadn't met Colin Brearney. He thought she was going to be a pushover, but he had no idea who he was taking on. The day Colin knocked at her door was the beginning of a nightmare that could only end in blood, silence and death...

Printed in the USA
CPSIA information can be obtained
at www.ICGtesting.com
LVHW091218100624
782798LV00002B/182

9 781727 476125